Butterfly

ALSO BY ASHLEY ANTOINETTE

Luxe

Luxe Two: A LaLa Land Addiction

Moth to a Flame

Guilty Gucci

Love Burn

The Prada Plan series 1–5

The Ethic series 1–6

Butterfly

ASHLEY ANTOINETTE

ST. MARTIN'S
GRIFFIN
New York

This is a work of fiction. All of the characters, organizations, and events portrayed in this novel are either products of the author's imagination or are used fictitiously.

First published in the United States by St. Martin's Griffin, an imprint of St. Martin's Publishing Group

www.stmartins.com

Designed by Omar Chapa

The Library of Congress Cataloging-in-Publication Data is available upon request.

ISBN 978-1-250-13636-7 (trade paperback)
ISBN 978-1-250-13637-4 (ebook)

Our books may be purchased in bulk for promotional, educational, or business use. Please contact your local bookseller or the Macmillan Corporate and Premium Sales Department at 1-800-221-7945, extension 5442, or by email at MacmillanSpecialMarkets@macmillan.com.

First Edition: January 2020

10 9 8 7 6 5 4 3 2 1

I dedicate my art to Quaye Jovan Coleman. You are my son and my sun. All my intentions and love revolve around you.

Acknowledgments

Ash Army, I cannot even form the words to express how dear you are to me, so I will simply say thank you. From the depths of my heart I appreciate each and every one of you for indulging in my art.

Letter to the Fans

Ash Army! We have been through the most beautiful series together. Through ups and downs, heartbreaks and triumphs, you guys stuck with me through it all. I'm so grateful for every tear you cried and every heart I wrecked while penning Ethic's story. I loved the connection I felt to you guys. I know you thought it was over, but there is still so much to tell. While my dearest Ethic and Alani have sailed off into the sunset, Morgan is still trying to piece her life back together. She's a young girl who has been betrayed by love. She's been lied to. She's been hurt. She's broken, and now it's time for me to try to put her pieces back together, to fix the wings on this beautiful butterfly so she can do what Messiah always wanted her to do. "Live, Shorty." Thank you so much for the years of support, for all the Twizzlers, the gifts, the letters, the retweets, the reposts, the word-of-mouth promotion, and for the love. I am so undeserving of all of you, but no one has ever appreciated their fans more. I *love* Ash Army. You guys give me purpose. On sleepless nights when I'm haunted by these characters, I remember that you guys are waiting for me to spin another tale, and when it feels like I just don't have anything left, I'm motivated to push a little more. Thank you for being the gasoline to my fire. You guys ready to start another journey with me? A new but familiar one? There are some people in these pages who really missed you. Y'all know the drill. Grab your favorite drink. Put the kids to bed. Tell that significant other I need you for a little while. I hope you enjoy this new series. I hope it makes your hearts content, because it certainly made mine smile. For those of you who haven't read *Ethic* yet, feel free to dive. You won't be disappointed. For those who know, hold on tight. Y'all know how I get down. It's going to hurt before it feels better.

-xoxo-
Ashley Antoinette

Playlist

"Foolin' Around" by Changing Faces

"Rocket" by Beyoncé

"Lazy Love" by Ne-Yo

"Happy" by Pharrell Williams

"No, No, No" by Destiny's Child

"My First Night with You" by Mya

"I Miss You" by Beyoncé

"Hours" by Eric Bellinger

"Part II (On the Run)" by Jay-Z
ft. Beyoncé

"Secret" by Ann Marie ft. YK Osiris

"Girls Need Love" by Summer Walker

"Feenin'" by Jodeci

"Shame" by Summer Walker

"I'm There" by Summer Walker

"CPR" by Summer Walker

"Love You from a Distance" by
Bridget Kelly ft. Ro James

"Flexin'" by TXS

"Catchin' Feelings" by TXS

"Needy" by Ariana Grande

"Handle It" by Ann Marie

"Pull Up" by Ann Marie

"Belong" by Asiahn

"Kool Kid" by Layton Greene

"Naked" by Marques Houston

"One of Them Days" by Kiana Ledé

"A.D.I.D.A.S." by Ro James

"Butterflies" by Queen Naija

"Ribbon in the Sky" by Stevie Wonder

"How's It Goin' Down" by DMX

"City Girls" by Twerk ft. Cardi B

"While We're Young" by Jhené Aiko

"Knuck If You Buck" by Crime Mob

"Drip" by Asiahn

"I Do!!" by Cardi B ft. SZA

"Hold Me" by Janine

Butterfly

Prologue

Once upon a time, in a place called Ethic Land, there lived a princess named Morgan Atkins. She was beautiful, but she felt invisible because she couldn't use her voice. Born deaf, she always felt like she was different. Like she was unworthy of love and attention. When her family fell into peril at the hands of a man named Mizan, she was raised by Ethic. He was a king, and he loved her like she were his own, but even still, Morgan never quite felt like she belonged. It wasn't until she met a young man named Messiah, Ethic's young protégé, that she felt special. When Morgan began a secret affair with Messiah, she thought she had found true love, but her prince turned out to be a fraud. He was the brother of Mizan and was plotting revenge on behalf of his family. When Ethic found out, he banished Messiah from the kingdom, and Morgan was left heartbroken and pregnant. Unable to bear life without her love, she tried to kill herself, but God had a plan that didn't allow Morgan to give up just yet. She waited for Messiah, day in and out, but he never returned. Not because he didn't want to—his love for her was true—but because he was sick, and he didn't want her to watch him die. He had already caused enough pain with his deceit. He didn't want to harm her more, so he chose to die alone. By the time she found out about his condition, it was too late and Messiah was no more. Morgan gave birth to twins, the only evidence she had left of the love she had once shared with an incredible man. She wished she'd had more time. If only . . . she'd had more time . . . she wouldn't be settling . . . she wouldn't be thousands of miles away from her family, away from her friends. She wouldn't be running from ghosts of her past. If only Messiah had lived to love another day . . . things would have turned out much differently. He would have turned Princess Morgan into a queen.

1

"Morgan, sweetheart, you look magnificent! Such a pretty girl."

Morgan turned from the mirror and gave a faint smile as Christiana Fredrick entered the room. The mother of her boyfriend. The endearing, empowering, supportive mother of that man she slept next to every night. After two years of dating Bash Fredrick, Morgan would think that Christiana would know how much she hated to be called *pretty*. By now, Morgan hoped to have made more of an impression besides the initial one . . . that she was stunning, but it never failed. Each time she walked into a room, Christiana pointed out her beauty. Every single time, Morgan cringed on the inside. She hated being called *pretty*. It's all anyone ever saw in her. The outside, the beauty, the exquisiteness that God had blessed her with. Where most would love the attention, Morgan Atkins had grown to hate it. Being pretty was a curse. There was only one person who had ever gone deeper to see past it. One man . . . Her heart dipped in torment at the thought of him, so she tried not to think of him at all.

"Thank you," Morgan said, her tone so soft it was almost

muted. She turned back to the mirror and pressed flat hands against her blush-colored dress. Chanel. Gifted to her from the company itself because the Fredrick family were longtime friends of the head designer there. The handbag and shoes, also gifts. The dress Yara wore, also a gift. Tom Ford for Messari. Another gift.

"Where are my babies?" Christiana asked as she came behind Morgan and placed both hands on her shoulders.

Their eyes met in the mirror.

"Napping. No way will I be able to get Yara to behave if she doesn't get a nap before the performance," Morgan said, laughing.

"Terrible twos. Something every mother must survive," Christiana said. She reached for the hairbrush that sat on Morgan's vanity. She picked it up and brushed Morgan's hair gently. "Let's pull this up, okay? You're promoting a children's charity. We're going for class. A bun, to the back, would be perfect."

Morgan didn't respond as Christiana styled her hair because she knew her protests wouldn't matter. Her voice was muted just like before, when she was walking around unable to hear. People didn't understand her, so she had stopped trying to be heard. Morgan was just along for the ride.

Splitting her time between London and the States, she had developed a bond with Christiana. She had doubled up on classes with the help of her family and Bash's mother. It took an entire village to keep Morgan in school. Morgan should have been pleased with every aspect of her life, but there was an unbearable grief that crippled her. Something was missing. Messiah was missing, and knowing he had spent his last days alone, thinking that she hated him, thinking he was unworthy of her forgiveness, would haunt Morgan for the rest of her life. She couldn't live after that. After his death . . . after her loss. Living was impossible. She didn't know how to love anymore. She tolerated. She coasted . . . with Bash. Morgan was settling. Christiana removed the brooch on her white Chanel suit jacket and walked around Morgan. She pinned it near Morgan's collar.

"There. Now you're perfect. I'm going to go wake those babies. Hurry now. We have to get the pictures for the Christmas card before we leave for your event."

Christiana's heels echoed against the marble floor until she was out of the room.

Morgan pulled in a deep breath and stared at herself once more. "Perfect," she muttered.

She carried herself down the stairs of the beautiful home. It was royal, and just like an Atkins girl, she had chosen the prince . . . or close enough to it, in Bash's case. A true descendant of royalty. One of the only black royal families in England, in fact. It put a spotlight on them. It put pressure on her to be prim, to be proper, to love on Bash in public in a way more intimate than she ever expressed in private. His entire family accepted her. They loved her children. Bash was helping her raise them. She was grateful for him, but somehow, even with him doting over her every need, Morgan had never felt so alone.

"Ma-ma, my ma-ma." Messari's voice was like jumper cables to a dying car battery; it made her come alive, kept her chugging along. Her babies gave her life because they were pieces of the love of her life. She had never gotten the chance to tell him that he was the love of her life. Mini versions of Messiah. They had ended on such bad terms, and she felt the burden of that as she navigated her way through life. She wished the twins looked more like him so that she could stare into his face every day until she left this earth, but they were her spitting image.

"Hi, Mama's big boy," she signed. "I love you."

"I love you more," Messari signed back. At two years old, he was just forming words. They were barely coherent, but his sign language was fluent. Morgan worked every day with the twins, teaching them to sign.

He reached for her, and Morgan relieved him from Christiana's arms.

"It's their thing. Their secret language," Christiana said to the photographer, standing off to the side, as if an explanation were needed.

"My daughter's deaf, actually," Morgan corrected. "Messari is bilingual. Yara signs. Where is she, by the way?"

"She's right here."

Morgan turned to find Bash and his father walking into the room. Yara was resting peacefully on Bash's shoulder. The sight of them made Morgan smile. Bash was beautiful with her children. One would never be able to tell that he wasn't their biological father. No one knew, in fact, except her family and his. Everyone else thought of them as one big, happy family. Morgan was the undergraduate that Bash had fallen in love with and gotten pregnant, and although Morgan was young, they were very much in love. That was the story Christiana had spun when she had begun introducing Morgan around the family's elite social circle. She had been accepted instantly. Bash approached Morgan and leaned down to kiss her lips.

"You okay? My mama driving you crazy yet?" Bash asked.

Morgan smiled and shook her head. "I'm fine."

He kissed her lips again.

"Hey, Ssari man. You ready to take a big-boy picture with the fellas?" Bash asked.

Messari nodded and lunged for Bash. Bash laughed, catching the toddler with ease without ever disturbing Yara.

"Here, I'll take her," Morgan said. "She needs to wake up anyway."

Morgan placed a palm on Yara's diapered bottom and

shook her gently. Yara lifted irritated eyes at her mother, then turned her head the other way on Bash's shoulder.

"A daddy's girl," David said.

Morgan snapped eyes of discontent at Bash's father. It always cut her when anyone referred to Bash as the twins' father. She never corrected them, but it hurt all the same. Morgan walked around Bash's shoulder and signed to Yara.

"Come on, Mama's strong girl," she said.

"She's so pretty," Christiana admired. "She's perfection."

"Don't call her that," Morgan said. "She's strong, she's smart. She'll know she's pretty. She needs to hear the other things more."

"No one ever complained about being called *pretty*, Morgan," she said dismissively.

Morgan dropped it as she pulled Yara from Bash's arms.

"Okay, let's get these photos," Christiana said, clapping her hands to corral everyone.

Morgan stood off with Yara in her arms as the men took pictures. Messari was the highlight of the trio, bringing laughter and light to the shots. The ladies were next, and Yara's resting bitch face was inherited, Morgan was sure of it, directly from her sister, Raven Atkins. Morgan had never met a more temperamental baby than Yara Rae. The group family photo was next, then Morgan was out the door.

"I've got to get to the venue. We'll meet you guys there," Morgan called out as she and Bash hurried off the estate with the babies in their arms.

"Thank you for doing that," Bash said, kissing the side of Morgan's head. "She insisted you and the twins be a part of it this year."

Morgan nodded. "Of course. I appreciate how she includes us. She doesn't have to."

"She does," Bash corrected. "She does have to. You're the most important part of my life, Mo. I want to be clear about that."

They strapped the twins into car seats and then climbed into the front of Bash's Range Rover. It was time to make an appearance among London's elite, and Morgan plastered on a smile, hoping that her happiness looked believable.

2

The Royal Opera House was beautiful, and just pulling up in front of the building made her nervous. There was a grandness about it, a historic aura that filled the air as soon as Morgan placed her eyes on it. She felt out of place, and she hadn't even stepped foot inside yet.

"I feel like we should have started this small. It's such a huge venue," she whispered. She was intimidated. The task in front of her seemed daunting.

"It's fine. Everything will be fine."

Morgan placed doubtful eyes on the red carpet outside her window.

"You performed with Stiletto Gang in front of hundreds of people. This is no different," he said, reaching for her hand and giving it a reassuring squeeze.

The valet opened the door, and Morgan got out. She reached into the back seat for Messari as Bash retrieved Yara. They took the red carpet, holding hands and smiling for the flashing cameras of London's finest publications.

"Mo Money, are we going to see you back onstage with the Stiletto Gang anytime soon? Old performance videos have been surfacing online, and it's rumored you might be joining them onstage soon."

Morgan looked at the young black woman in front of her, and her mouth fell open.

Aria had taken Stiletto Gang to new heights, dancing background for some of the largest artists in the world, and she had been begging Mo to come back.

"Umm, I don't . . . I'm not . . ."

"Morgan is focused on her philanthropy right now. Giving back to the community and teaching the little ones to dance. The money from tonight will go directly toward the crisis in Flint, Michigan, her hometown, to help aid in the city's water crisis," Bash said.

He placed his free hand on the small of her back and ushered her down the red carpet until they were inside.

She found the parents of the other children waiting for her in the gallery. They were all dressed in blush-colored dresses, while the boys wore suits.

"Hi, everyone. Thank you so much. I'll take over from here. Parents have the first two rows reserved. We'll see you guys after the show," she said. "I've got them. You can sit and enjoy the show."

"You sure? This is a lot of little people," Bash said, his forehead wrinkling, showing his skepticism. Morgan had been corralling these little humans for the past three months. She had no qualms about handling things backstage; it was the grown people watching that made her nervous. The snobby elites of high London society.

She nodded and put Messari down. "I've got it."

She grabbed Yara and held her son's hand. "Okay, guys, come to Ms. Morgan," she called out. She bent down and placed

Yara beside her brother as the group of small kids gathered. Her babies were the youngest and smallest, causing the other kids to circle in behind them. "Are you guys ready to have some fun and show your mommies and daddies what you learned?"

"Yeah!" the kids erupted in unison, and Morgan laughed. The parents of these children might have been snobs, but these souls around her were pure. "Okay, let's do it. Hands in. On three, shout, 'Dance your heart out!'"

All the kids put their hands on top of Morgan's. Even little Yara and Messari. "One, two, three!"

"Dance your heart out!"

Morgan stood and held the twins' hands as the three of them led the others out onto the stage. Her stomach plummeted when she saw the packed house. Every seat in the opera house was taken. Christiana had done the job of filling the seats, and Morgan was floored at the amount of support.

"Hi, everyone. I'm Morgan Atkins, and I have some little people who would really like to sing and dance for you," she said. "Please put your hands together and welcome the very first MAM Academy dance recital."

Morgan ushered the children into place and placed Yara right in the middle. She couldn't hear the music, but she knew from experience that her baby girl could feel it. She would never exclude her.

"Eyes on me," she said as she hustled off the stage and stood directly in front of it.

Pharrell Williams's "Happy" played through the speakers, and the kids began dancing, singing, and most importantly, smiling. Baby Yara signed the words as the other kids danced around her. The crowd clapped along, and the sound of joyous laughter filled the theater as the children moved from that song to traditional Christmas songs. Morgan laughed and smiled the entire time. Pride swelled in her chest as she watched her twins. By the time the performance was over, the crowd was on their feet.

"Such a wonderful job!" Christiana was at her side before the kids were even off the stage. She ushered Morgan back up to the stage and took the microphone.

Morgan picked up her baby boy, and Bash pulled Yara from the stage. Morgan's gut turned with guilt. She was truly a daddy's girl, only Bash wasn't her father. The shame of that would never ease, but her children needed a father, and Bash wanted to fill the role. They needed him. He had been in their lives since before they were born. He had rubbed her stomach and felt them kick. He was just as much a part of their lives as any father should be. Blood couldn't make them any closer. She told herself that DNA didn't matter. Ethic had raised her as his own, and they weren't biologically connected. So it was okay for Bash to do the same, right? She forced herself to allow him free rein in his fatherhood role. Thoughts of what could have been haunted her. If she had just told their real father, Messiah Williams, the man she had pledged her soul to, that she was pregnant.

"We have already opened our hearts to these adorable faces. Now let's open our wallets, ladies and gentlemen. Let's make this a contributory and profitable night for Morgan's cause. I'm going to bring my son up here to say a few words," Christiana said. Bash's long legs trotted up the steps, and Yara bounced gleefully in his arms, pulling a smile out of Morgan. His black suit fit his ball player's frame well. The fabric wrapped perfectly over light skin, and the full, jet-black beard was an attempt to grunge up his look, but his kind eyes gave away his matching heart.

Bash took the microphone. "I'm extremely proud of you, Mo," he said, gazing at her like she were a dream . . . one he didn't want to awaken from. "And I love you. I love you and this family that we're building. I love the woman you're becoming. I just want to be a part of it . . . a part of you forever."

Morgan's heart plunged when she saw him lower to his knees. The crowd reacted in shock as he pulled out a black velvet box.

"Will you marry me?"

Tears filled her eyes as flashes of Messiah played in her mind. She covered her mouth with one hand, then pressed her forehead to her son's.

"No cry, Mama. No cry," he said, wiping her tears.

They appeared to be tears of joy. Women cried in this moment. They got emotional . . . it was normal. Only for Morgan, it wasn't. Morgan was crying tears of grief over the love she had lost, over promises she had made him. She had vowed to never take another man's last name . . . and then he had lied, and she had moved on, and then he had died, and although she was still walking and breathing, on the inside, she had died too. Bash was proposing to a ghost, to a shell of the person she used to be. She was rotten on the inside.

With hundreds of pairs of eyes on her, the most important pairs of eyes in all of London, people who had accepted her, people who had offered opportunities over the past two years, who had helped her acclimate to living abroad, who had offered resources and internships and job offers after she graduated . . . they all awaited her answer. She couldn't say no, but she couldn't say yes. Uttering the words from her lips would cause Messiah to rise from the dead just to kill Bash. Her chest was so tight that Morgan felt like she was having a heart attack. She nodded, and the worry on Bash's face dissipated, giving way to a gracious smile as he dropped his head and shook it in disbelief. He slid the ring on her finger, and it felt like it weighed a hundred pounds. It felt like a chain, like a noose. It was around her finger . . . why did it feel like it was choking her?

Why couldn't she breathe? He stood and rushed her, kissing her lips. Cameras flashed. They looked like a beautiful family, the four of them, onstage, preparing to start their lives together, but Morgan was filled with dread. Christiana relieved her of Messari, and Bash headed off the stage with Yara while Morgan took the microphone. She turned to the crowd, and she froze when she saw Aria standing at the back of the room with Isa at her side. Aria waved, and Morgan blew a kiss in return before wiping the tears from her face.

"Wow. That was unexpected," she said with a chuckle as the crowd joined in light laughter. "Thank you, everyone, for coming. I'll see you all at the reception. I can answer any questions you have at that time. Donations can be made there as well. Can we have one more round of applause for those beautiful babies? They're so brave. They really did a great job!"

The crowd clapped on cue, and Morgan walked off the stage, hurrying to meet Aria halfway down the aisle.

She threw her arms around her friend.

"He completely blindsided me," she whispered. "I'm falling apart."

"Okay," Aria said. "Not here, Mo. Hold on." Aria turned to Isa. "We're going to the ladies' room. I'll be right back."

Morgan rushed behind Aria, and when they were inside the restroom, Mo erupted. "Why would he do that? In front of all these people?"

"Bitch, first let me see the ring," Aria said.

Morgan hadn't even glanced at it, but the reminder caused her to hold out dainty fingers with the short manicure because Christiana insisted that it was proper length, and she gasped.

"Oh, he love you, love you!" Aria exclaimed. "Morgan, it's beautiful!"

"Who cares?" Morgan shouted, covering her face with her

hands. She felt her eyes burning. They prickled as tears over-whelmed her.

"Morgan, it's okay to be with him. You can't keep promises to a ghost," Aria whispered, frowning in sympathy.

"I didn't even get to say goodbye to him. I had so many questions. I was so fucking angry at him when he died. How could he die and leave this on me? I loved him, Aria, and I promised him."

"Morgan, I know you don't want to hear this, but you'll probably never love anyone the way you loved Messiah. He was your first love, and you two were so passionate. It was obsessive. It was almost dangerous. The way you loved one another . . . people don't love like that. I've never seen anything that intense, Mo. Nobody is going to make you feel that again. Be grateful that you felt it once in a lifetime, but don't stop yourself from being happy by trying to measure everything up to that feeling Messiah gave you. Bash has elevated you. Look at you. You're hosting a charity event in London. They've given you oppor-tunity, they're loving on the twins . . . he's a good guy. A little corny, but corny is good. Corny is safe. Corny . . ."

"Is boring," Morgan finished.

"He really loves you, Mo. I'm not saying marry him. I wouldn't push you toward that if it's not what you want, but I'm just saying ask yourself why you don't want to," Aria said.

Morgan pulled in a deep breath and nodded. "What would I do without you?"

Aria held up her hands and shrugged, then threw her arms around Mo.

"Oh, I missed you," Morgan groaned. "How are you here right now anyway? And with Isa?"

"And Meek," Aria added. "We wanted to surprise you."

Morgan twisted her lips in disbelief.

"Okay, Isa's been pushing up on it, and I told him he

needed to make a grand gesture. Bringing me to you was his grand gesture. A good one too, but he's still getting no play."

"Poor Isa. Still chasing it." Morgan snickered. "And Meek's here too?"

"You know Isa wasn't coming over here alone. He said he didn't want to listen to us girl talk for two days, so Meek had to come. Besides, your friends should be here for you. This is kind of a big deal," she said.

"Yeah, I guess," Morgan said with a shrug. "So, you and Isa?"

"Me and Isa nothing. Don't start. Nobody's checking for that boy. He's such a hoe. Bitches been blowing him up all day. My vagina will not be participating in any parts of Isa," Aria said.

Mo laughed and moved to the sink to fix her face before following Aria out.

"I swear you two are the only mu'fuckas on the planet that could have me waiting outside a fucking bathroom for twenty minutes," Isa griped when they emerged.

Morgan laughed and ran into his arms.

"What's good, sis?"

"Hey, Isa," she said, burying herself in his lanky frame. "It's really good to see you."

"You too, Mo," he said, kissing the top of her head. "You look real official out here. They treating you right all the way over here? Cuz I can break a nigga jaw real quick if you got any issues."

"No jaw breaking required," Morgan said, eyes beaming, joy filling her heart because his aggression was refreshing . . . it was her preference . . . that type of ride-or-die energy had been lacking from her life for years. "I'm fine."

"You good, G?"

Morgan followed Isa's eyes behind her, and her stomach

hollowed. Ahmeek walked out of the men's restroom, wiping his suit down in irritation. He was walking perfection, he always had been, but the past two years had done him well. He was a walking god in a black suit.

"Yeah, I'm good, bro. Fucking kids spilled cranberry juice all on my shit," he fussed. His brow pinched, causing wrinkles of disdain to fill his forehead, but when he lifted eyes to Mo, his brows lifted, stunned.

"Hi, Ahmeek," she said with a broad smile.

"If the goal was to stop niggas' hearts, Mo, goal fucking accomplished," Meek complimented, placing a hand to the left side of his chest, squinting with a smile.

Morgan shook her head, then looked at her feet, feeling her face flush red. "Thanks, Ahmeek. Come on. I can put you at a table in the back," Morgan said, leading the way to the reception.

She entered the room, and Bash's eyes gravitated to her. He was holding Messari and conversing with a group of people, but he stopped midsentence and excused himself as his eyes met Mo's.

He joined her. "Bash, you already know Aria. This is Isa and Ahmeek," Morgan said, introducing them.

Bash kissed Aria's cheek and extended a firm handshake to Isa. Isa let the hand linger and marked Bash with malicious eyes.

"Real smooth, man," Bash said, scoffing before moving on to Meek.

Morgan's brow crinkled as she stared at Meek. "Please, be nice." She mouthed the words, and after an awkward beat, Meek pulled a hand from his pants pocket to shake Bash's hand.

"Thank you," she mouthed.

She pulled Messari from Bash's arms.

"Hiiii, Messari," Aria cooed as she confiscated the toddler. "I missed your face!"

"Messari . . . ," Meek's voice held no accusations, but Morgan felt his stare penetrating her. She tightened her stomach to calm the queasiness building inside before rolling confident eyes up to him. It was both Meek's and Isa's first time seeing her twins. They both were staring at her like she was a target and they had hair triggers ready to fire.

"Yes, Messari and Yara. Bash, can you get Yara so they can meet her?"

"Yeah, of course," Bash said before kissing the side of her head and walking off.

"He doesn't know that I named our son after Messiah. Please don't make a big deal," she said.

"Say less," Isa stated. He was easy to appease, but she could feel Meek burning a hole through her.

Yara came running across the dance floor and clung to Morgan's leg. Morgan picked her up.

"This is Yara Rae Atkins," she said, picking up her daughter.

"They're beautiful, Mo," Meek finally said, and she sighed in relief.

"Mo, he feels kind of warm," Aria said.

Morgan instantly brought the back of her hand to Messari's forehead. Bash rejoined her.

"Is everything okay?" he asked.

"I think he's running a temp," Morgan said.

Bash took Messari and held his face to Messari's cheek. "I think you might be right."

"I have to get him home," Morgan said.

"You can't leave, Mo. This is your event. You worked hard to bring this together. Your friends are here all the way from Michigan. I'll get the twins home. I have the pediatrician on speed dial. He'll make a house call. I'm sure Messari can wait until morning to go in, but to ease your mind, I'll have the doc meet me at home. You do your thing."

"No. I need to go with him," Morgan protested.

"Baby, just stay. If you leave, all these people leave, and all the energy you put into this is for nothing. I'll call as soon as I have news."

Morgan nodded reluctantly, but tension formed a knot in her stomach so tight that she placed hands on top of it to try to calm her fears. Morgan had always been a selfish type of girl. Everything had always revolved around her. Not until she became a mother did she truly invest into someone else. Their needs, their wants, their everything trumped her. She was ready to say fuck this entire charity to be there for her baby.

"Hey," Meek said, jarring her attention. "He's probably just teething. Babies run fevers when their teeth are coming in."

"Nigga, how you know?" Isa piped up.

Morgan chuckled, and it relieved a bit of her anxiety. The laugh. Meek's logic. They were both needed.

"They do, you're right," Morgan said, nodding. "Let me at least carry him to the car," she said, eyes misting.

"Here, let me," Meek stated, taking Yara from Bash without permission and then walking side by side with Mo toward the exit. Bash trailed behind them, already placing the phone call to the doctor.

"Damn, Mo, you're really somebody's mama," he said in amazement.

Mo smiled, rubbing the top of Messari's head. "I am."

"It suits you," he stated. "Parenthood."

Morgan nodded toward Yara, who was resting comfortably in his arms, head positioned in the middle of Meek's chest. "You're not so bad at it yourself. Let me find out you got a baby mama tucked out here somewhere." She smirked.

"Nah, I ain't got that," he returned. "I wouldn't mind one of these, though . . . one day."

"You'd have to settle down for that to happen, Meek," Mo said.

"I'd settle down. Not for just anybody, but if I caught a real one, I'd be with the shits."

Morgan rolled her eyes and kissed the top of Messari's head.

Meek laughed as they reached the valet.

Bash came up behind them.

"The doctor will be there when we arrive," he informed her. He walked over to the valet attendant and handed the young man the ticket. The car was retrieved in minutes, and Morgan tucked her son into his car seat.

"Be good for Papa, okay?"

Messari's wet kisses made Meek frown, but to Morgan, they were golden.

"That's a part of the job, huh? The drool?" he asked.

Morgan nodded. "The very best part." She took Yara from him and strapped her in before turning to Bash.

"I'll be home as soon as I'm done here," she promised.

"We'll be fine," he assured. "Take your time and enjoy the spotlight, Mo. You earned it. Just take one of the black cars back. A driver has already been instructed to wait for you."

She nodded and watched as he hopped into the Range Rover, then drove away.

She turned back to Meek, who extended his elbow to her.

"See, a nigga know how to boss his shit up for the right one," he said.

Morgan smiled—genuinely smiled—and it had been so long since she'd done so that it felt foreign.

"Don't leave me hanging, Mo. You got me out here on

some suit-and-tie shit. The least you can do is take a nigga arm and pretend like you believe I'm good enough to be in your world," he said.

Morgan placed a hand to his elbow and leaned her head against his shoulder. "You're good enough, Ahmeek," she whispered.

Morgan worked the room with Meek at her side, and it felt good. It felt familiar, like she could compete in this circle, like she could handle anyone approaching her because she had backup . . . she had a goon on her team. He made her feel secure, protected, and by the end of the night, Morgan had raised over a quarter million dollars in donations.

"You should be proud of yourself. This is dope. Two years feels like forever ago. You're the same, but you're different too. You were a girl back then. You're a grown woman now, a fucking mother. Shit's crazy," he said, sitting sideways in his chair and leaning onto his elbows while looking up at her over his tense brow.

"I'm glad you came, Meek. Thank you for coming all this way. I haven't felt like myself in a long time. You reminded me of who I become when I feel confident." She paused. "You made me feel strong tonight."

"You're strong as shit, Mo," Meek stated. "Stronger than anybody I know. After what you've been through. Your whole life has been hard, and this is where you end up? That's strength. I'm proud of you."

Morgan blushed, twiddling her fingers to avoid looking at him. She had never been nervous around him before, but just his eyes gracing her filled Morgan with anxiety. "Thanks, Meek."

The band began to play a Stevie Wonder classic, and Mo looked toward the dance floor.

"Do you want to dance?" she asked.

"Nigga, no," he said. "Your ass ain't crying or nothing. You ain't sad. I ain't got to do no cheering up. Fuck no."

Morgan's eyes crinkled tight as her lips spread wide in amusement. She remembered the night he had hustled with her all those years ago, just to get her to feel better. It had been right after Messiah had deserted her. She had been pregnant and lonely, the saddest she had ever been, and he had tucked his gangster vibrato away to entertain her with one dance. She loved that part of him. He was hard, but not cold. Gangster, but not cruel. It was the day she discovered he would do anything to make her smile. "I mean, I can squeeze out a tear or two if it'll make you say yes," she countered.

He rubbed both hands atop of his wavy covered Caesar. "Man, where the fuck is Isa? It's time to break out." He chuckled.

"Knowing Isa and knowing Aria even better, they're having sex in a bathroom somewhere. Sex that they will later deny ever took place," she said, standing. "So, you have nothing but time to dance."

She pulled Meek to the center of the dance floor as the singer went into the first verse of the beautiful ballad.

Oh, so long for this night I prayed
That a star would guide you my way . . .
To share with me this special day

Morgan placed her hands in Meek's as the words carried her across the hardwood floor, following his lead, which she knew would be smooth. Meek was just a smooth-ass nigga. The things he said, but even more what he didn't say . . . smooth. The way he walked . . . smooth. The way he commanded . . . smooth. The way he pulled her closer and tapped on the small of her back as they danced . . . effortlessly smooth. Morgan swooned as she followed his lead, side to side, swaying like a couple. Only they weren't, but damn if they didn't look couple-ish. He was a hood nigga in all his hood nigga glory, but he was top shelf. VSOP. He knew when to turn it off. Taking him in didn't come with a bite. He was smooth. An effortless gang-ster. Morgan turned her face to the side and rested her cheek against his chest. She totally understood why Yara had taken the position against him now. It was comfortable. It felt safe . . . safe enough to close her eyes. The way he held her made her feel protected, like he would die before he ever let anyone get close enough to do her harm. She hadn't felt this secure since Mes-siah, and it snuck up on her, beguiling her into a comfort zone with a man she should not be comfortable with at all.

"I'm really glad you're here. I needed you and didn't even know it," she whispered.

Her words jarred him. They stunned her. She had no idea where they had even arisen from. He leaned his head back, fore-head wrinkled as he looked in her eyes. She knew he was search-ing for understanding. She hoped he found some, because she needed it too. He captured her in those dark orbs. She hadn't meant to say it aloud. It was supposed to stay trapped in her head where an explanation wouldn't have to follow, but they had slipped and now he was probing her, now he was wonder-ing. Now he knew that her refuge was in his arms. That the comfort she felt even after removing herself from his life for two years was overwhelming. Morgan was swallowed by confu-sion because she had never felt anything for him before. Sure, they had been friends, but her emotion was so bound by Mes-siah that she had none left over for anyone else.

He reminds me of Ssiah. My mind is playing tricks on me. My heart wants what it can't have, so it's beating for Meek because he's the closest thing to him. Morgan wanted to pull back because the connection frightened her, but she fit perfectly in Ahmeek's embrace. She was lost in the melody of the live band, in the darkness of his eyes, in the gentle rhythm as they swayed. The way he looked at her, like he couldn't find words, like his stomach was in knots, like restraint was evading him, made Morgan turn red, but she was in too deep to turn away from him, so he witnessed every moment of her reticence as they stared at each other. Morgan felt like she was floating. She planted her head against his chest and sighed, releasing every single piece of angst that plagued her body. It was such a pretty song. It just made her feel lighthearted like it was two years ago, and every fiber of her body had been kissed by love, only a different set of hands were holding her now. How was it possible to feel this again with someone else?

The tug of her elbow reminded her that there was a roomful of people around them. It was like someone had awakened her from a good dream, abruptly snatching her from that golden place, burning her soul with desperation to linger there just a moment longer because she was almost to the good part. She turned to find Christiana's eyes burning her, marking her with disdain.

Christiana held up a cell phone and accompanied it with a lifted brow of displeasure. "Bash has been trying to reach you."

Meek took a step back, and Morgan took the phone quickly.

"Is he okay?" she asked. Worry pierced her for a beat, and then she sighed in relief. "No infection? Just teething? Is he sure?" Another pause, and then her anxiety eased. "Thank God. Okay. Kiss them for me. I'll be home when I finish up here." She hung up the phone before he could say *I love you*. She always did, blaming it on a quick trigger finger, but Morgan hated to say it. It wasn't that she didn't care about Bash, because she did. She was growing to love him, but she wasn't in love.

Being in love felt different. She felt something for him, but it wasn't that. She handed the phone back to Christiana.

"Perhaps a bit of space between you and your friend," Christiana whispered to her. "You don't want people getting the wrong idea. You are a wife-to-be now."

Morgan nodded, flushing in embarrassment, then turned back to Meek. "You were right. He's going to be fine." She looked around the crowded room and back at Meek. "You want to get out of here? Find Isa and Aria and just go somewhere . . . somewhere fun?"

"How does Morgan Atkins have fun?" Meek asked.

"Meet me out front and I'll show you," she said.

Morgan left him on the dance floor and then sent a text to Aria to meet her at the door.

"A dance studio. This is fun?" Meek asked as he followed Morgan inside. She flipped the light switch, and it came to life.

"This is always fun," Aria said in excitement.

Morgan pulled a bottle of tequila from her tote bag. "This makes it even better."

Aria pulled out her phone and pressed Play. A gutter, old-school classic filled the air.

"You a goon, Ali . . . DMX, huh?" Isa snickered.

Aria smirked and hit a cute four count in her formal dress and heels. "Act like you know, boy," she said, snapping her fingers. "Pour up."

"We don't have cups here," Morgan said.

"We straight from the bottle with it," Meek said. "I know you all the way across the pond, Mo, but you Flint bred, baby." He cracked it open and lifted it to her lips. Morgan took the shot and grimaced as it traveled down her entire body, warming her instantly.

"Ugh!" she said, sticking her tongue out. "That's horrible."

Meek smirked, then took a shot without the dramatics before he passed the bottle.

Morgan clapped her hands together and bobbed to the beat. She looked at herself in the mirror, then kicked off her heels.

What type of games are being played
How's it going down?

Morgan took off, moving her body with aggression, aggression she wasn't allowed to show on a daily. In Bash's world, she was expected to be demure, to be the woman behind the man, to be the lady representing her family at tea parties and shit.

Meek took a seat on the floor, leaning his back against the mirror, propping elbows to his knees. He was her audience, and although Aria was right beside her, Morgan was all he saw. Isa joined him, and they passed the bottle between them while enjoying the show. It was like Aria and Morgan had never stopped dancing together. They picked up on each other's energy so well, falling into a freestyle that looked choreographed because they were so skilled. Meek held up the bottle for Mo, and she took a quick break to indulge in another shot. She laughed as it spilled down her chin. She held the bottle in the air and grooved.

She passed the bottle, then closed her eyes, getting lost in the music.

London was a new life for her, but she was still so Flint at her core. Keeping that part tucked, stifling her voice so that Bash could feel heard, so that he was secure about his position in her life, sometimes made her feel like she couldn't breathe. She was breathing deep tonight, and her lungs expanded, pulling it all in because it tasted like freedom.

Let that nigga play daddy, make moves with me

Meek shot her a wink, and she smirked as she let her feet work like only she could. Only Mo could make a Crip walk seductive as she snapped her pretty fingers. Aria stopped dancing and pulled out her phone, going live on social media with Morgan.

"Bitch, you ain't missed a beat," Aria said, laughing as the song ended.

Morgan shrugged. "God, this feels good. It's been a minute since I've just danced for no reason."

"Why don't you do the show with me in a few weeks?" Aria said. "You'll be back home by then, right? I feel like you've moved over here. Home is still Michigan, Mo. You can come back."

"I know," Morgan said. "Who knows? I just might." She shrugged, taking a seat between Isa and Meek.

"You should," Meek said. "Michigan misses you."

"Is that right?" she asked, smiling. It felt good to be missed . . . to be thought of . . . by someone who didn't consider others easily. By someone who didn't really know how to let emotions show. It made her feel special. To be missed.

Aria sat and slid her phone across the floor. "The fans miss you too."

Morgan picked up the phone and scrolled down the screen to see the comments. An outpouring of love. Heart eyes and exclamation marks. A few peaches and wet emojis. Morgan scoffed.

"Yeah, okay," she said, nodding. "I'll do the show. I'll be home anyway. Might as well, right?"

"Yo, Ali, I need to holla at you about something. Com'ere," Isa said, standing and walking out the building.

Aria stood and followed him, leaving Meek and Mo snickering.

"Are they always like this?" she asked.

"Man, bruh nose so wide open, it ain't even funny," Meek admitted, shaking his head.

Mo laughed. "What about you? Which of your ten girlfriends has your nose open?"

"I don't be entertaining these girls, man," he denied. Tattooed hands swept down his head. "What about you?" he asked, picking up her left hand and thumbing the diamond ring. Morgan had almost forgotten it was there. "You getting married, Mo?"

She shrugged, and her eyes went dark, like Meek had flipped a switch to turn the light inside her off. A heaviness returned to her chest. A doom occupied her stomach.

"I can see you're not happy, Mo. If he can't, it's because he doesn't want to or because he don't know you," Meek stated.

Morgan lifted stunned eyes to meet his. "You're talking like you know me."

"I pay attention," Meek said. "I know you don't want to get married."

Morgan blew out a deep breath. "Yeah, well, we don't always get what we want. I've tried love. Love didn't work. Even before Messiah died, it fell apart. It started off with a lie. It would have ended eventually anyway. I still question if he ever even loved me."

"He loved you, Mo. That much I'm sure of," Meek stated.

"I don't want to talk about him. I never talk about him," she whispered.

"Maybe you should. Not with me, but like with a professional or some shit . . ."

"Why? Because I'm crazy? I guess I went a little crazy, huh? You've seen me key cars and bust out windows." She shook her head and buried her face in her hands.

"You still owe me for that shit too," he said.

Morgan grimaced and threw her head back to the sky. "It wasn't my best moment. I was so fucking mad. I can't believe I did that. I can't believe y'all let me!"

"Fuck was we gon' do? When the queen come through to burn shit down, you just let the queen burn shit down," Meek stated, licking his lips as amusement filled his eyes.

"I've grown," she said.

"I can see that." He nodded. "Little Morgan a grown-ass woman now and wearing that crown real well. I'm proud of you."

"Little Morgan is twenty pounds too heavy and barely keeping up with two toddlers," she said, shaking her head.

"The weight is nothing; that's bitch shit," Meek stated. "A real nigga gon' appreciate that shit . . . he gon' replace your fucking wardrobe every three months anyway so you ain't even gon' stress that shit. A nigga can see from a mile away that you got it. Always had it, never lost it, no lie."

Morgan's face warmed, and she placed her stare in her lap because looking at Meek was dangerous. It was like driving around a sharp curve at night at fast speeds. Men like Ahmeek should come with warnings. Proceed with caution. Danger ahead. Slippery when fucking wet.

The vibrating of his phone broke through the intensity.

"One of your hoes?" Morgan asked, lifting a curious brow as she snatched his phone. She shook her head when the nude photo popped onto his screen. "Whoa!" she said as she covered her mouth with one hand. "How do you even get women to send you shit like this?" She turned her head sideways, gritting her teeth as she turned the phone upside down. "Is that a banana? So you eating bananas out of bitches' pu—"

Meek snatched his phone back. "That mouth too pretty to be so dirty, Mo."

Morgan erupted in laughter. "Bananas, huh?"

Meek blushed and crinkled his nose in denial. He licked his bottom lip.

"Seriously, what does one say to a woman to get her to do that?"

She knew she was being a hypocrite because she had seen her fair share of days where fruit was used in unconventional ways. Messiah had sucked an entire strawberry out of her before. She knew the exact type of man it took to make a girl go crazy.

"I don't be gaming women, Mo. They do what they want. I don't ask for shit like this. They searching for attention," he answered.

She pulled his phone from his hands again. "What's the passcode?"

"One-one-two-eight," he said without hesitation.

"Bet if I was your girl, you wouldn't be giving that code up so quickly." She snickered.

"If you were my girl, I'd give you the passcode, the safe code, the social security number, the ATM pin, all'at," he replied.

"Mmm-hmm . . . you talking good." She nudged him with her shoulder as she opened his photos. Just as she suspected, it was filled with different women.

"Okay, what's wrong with her? Why not settle down with her? She's pretty," Morgan said.

"She got ugly feet," Meek answered.

Morgan laughed from her soul. Only a man would judge a woman for something so miniscule. They tended to pick women apart, to erode the confidence of a woman without even really meaning to do harm. She shook her head and flipped to the next photo.

"And her?"

"She's shallow as shit. Stay on some did you see this on Shaderoom type shit? Did you hear about such and such? I ain't with the gossiping. My bitch got to move like I move," Meek answered.

"Your bitch?" she asked, challenging him.

"My bad, Mo. My woman," he corrected. "I prefer the private type."

"And her?" Mo flipped to the next one, holding it up to his face.

"She can't take dick," Meek stated bluntly.

Morgan shook her head and handed him his phone.

"These women would probably love you so good, Meek. No one woman has everything. Choose one and build with her," Morgan stated.

"Every woman ain't like you, Mo. They ain't worth building with," Meek stated.

Morgan met his stare. "I hope you find someone worth something to you one day, Meek," she whispered. "You deserve to know what that feels like. Loving one woman more than anything else in the world. Having someone you would kill for . . . die for . . . without thinking twice."

"That's what love is? Being willing to die behind something? What I need a girl for? You give me that. How I'ma find a girl that understand that? That I'll lay a nigga down for Morgan Atkins? What girl you know gon' accept that?" he asked.

She shrugged. "I did. I understood about Bleu."

"That's because you're the shit," Meek stated. "You're one of one, Mo. That fiancé of yours is a lucky man."

Morgan sighed because just the mention of Bash had brought her back to reality. Meek had her head in the clouds, and reality had grounded her. This might have felt like old times, but they weren't. Time had moved on, and she had a life to return to.

She checked the time on her phone. "It's late. I should go," she whispered. He stood and reached down to help her to her feet.

"Thank you for coming all the way here to see me. You don't even know how it helped," Morgan admitted. "You guys remind me of a time in my life when I was happy. It feels like forever ago. I'm sorry I pushed you away after Messiah died. You called a thousand times. I just couldn't answer. I didn't trust you. I was looking for someone to blame, and it fell on you . . . it fell on Isa. I didn't know how to feel. I went from hating him for lying to me about who he was to grieving him because he was gone," Morgan said. She shook her head in dismay. "I don't know. It was just a lot. You guys were his best friends . . . I thought you were my friend, and I was embarrassed because you knew about his plot to hurt my family. I felt stupid, like I was an inside joke."

"You weren't a joke, Mo, and a lot changed for Messiah after y'all got together. A lot changed for us all. It wasn't just him. We all loved you. We all felt fucked up about how it was going down," Meek admitted. "We still got love for you, Mo. If nothing else, I would like to be able to call Morgan Atkins a friend. I'm sorry for everything I did to contribute to your hurt, Morgan . . . to make you change into what I'm looking at, because what you were before was perfection. For that, I'm sorry."

She nodded and swiped away the lone tear that had escaped. She sniffed as he pulled her into him, wrapping arms so strong around her that she melted. She wrapped her hands around his waist and cried on his shoulder, releasing two years' worth of misunderstanding, of confusion, of uncut pain. For years, she had held resentments against him, against Isa too. It was one of the main reasons she spent so much time in London . . . avoiding them. They were the new kings of her old city, and she hadn't felt like she belonged . . . hadn't felt confident enough to show her face after the humiliation and the loss.

"Thank you for being my friend, Ahmeek," she whispered.

"Always, Mo," he said, kissing the top of her head. "I don't fuck with many, but I fuck with you, and I know time has passed, but there wasn't a day that went by that I didn't think about the apology I owed you."

"Thanks, Ahmeek," she whispered. "When do you leave?"

"Isa and Aria are here for a few days. I'm on the next bird out in the morning."

The disappointment that filled her was surprising, and she took a step away from him.

"When you come home, hit me up. I'll drop whatever I'm doing," Meek stated.

"You mean whoever you're doing," she teased.

He shook his head. "You don't cut a nigga no slack." He snickered.

"Not ever," she admitted, smiling. She reached for his hand and gave it a squeeze. "Bye, Meek."

He held on to her fingers like his life depended on it as she walked away. Distance was the only thing that forced him to let go. Morgan glanced back one final time before pushing open the door and walking out into the night.

3

"Why you won't fuck with a nigga, Ali?" Isa said as he walked Aria to her hotel room.

"When are you going to stop calling me that?" she asked, laughing.

"You still knocking bitches out without thinking twice?" he asked.

"When they get disrespectful," she answered.

"Then you'll forever be the greatest . . . Ali," he said. "Now answer my question."

"Why would I fuck with you, Isa?" she asked as she turned to face him, leaning her back against the door. He placed a balled fist above her head and leaned into her, licking his lips as he lifted her chin with the tip of his finger.

"Because it feels good," he said. "You don't even know how bad I want to fuck you."

Aria frowned and moved her chin out of his grasp. "And that's the problem," she said. "You're kind of disgusting, Isa. Like for real, the shit you say to women. I'm sure other girls eat that shit up, but I'm not them."

Isa swiped a hand down his face, blowing out a breath of exasperation. "Here we go," he said. "You know I argue with you more than I argue with my main."

Aria craned her neck back. "Your main?" she scoffed. "Now there's a main? Why are you here, then, Isa? If you have a girlfriend?"

"Because this where I want to be," Isa said. "And I do what the fuck I want to do."

He was so damned cocky. Aria felt like knocking his head off. She had always known that Isa kept females around. He switched them out like Gucci belts, a different one for every day of the week, but she had never heard him speak of one specifically. She didn't know why it bothered her, but the word *main* distinguished one among the crowd.

"Your main," Aria sneered. "So, what, I'm a side? Somebody you think you about to slide through, then swerve afterward?"

"You know better than that. You talking crazy. You know what it is."

"I don't know anything. What else do you want from me? I know you want to fuck me. Everybody wants to fuck me. I sell sex onstage. Every nigga in every venue I perform in want it."

"Every nigga in every venue can get they shit rocked too, Ali. Stop playing with me," Isa said, jealousy dancing in his eyes. "I'm the only one driving that."

"Boy, you don't even have a key to this. You couldn't even start my engine."

"Well, you better put that bitch up for the winter until I find the shit. Let another nigga touch my whip and I'm airing shit out." He didn't yell. There was no need to. He meant what he said, and he reaffirmed his words with action. He was with all the gunplay. Anytime.

Aria crossed her arms and shook her head in disbelief.

"You're possessive, but meanwhile, you have a girlfriend?" Aria asked, cocking her head to the side, a frown on her pretty face.

"I ain't got no fucking girlfriend," he said, sneering like he smelled something, like the concept of having someone that he was committed to made him ill. "Quit making shit up."

"Well, what the fuck is a main?" Aria asked.

"Not a girlfriend," Isa countered.

"And what am I?" she asked.

"A fucking tease," he snapped.

The words landed on her chin viciously. He may as well have slapped her the way she recoiled. "You know what? I think you should hop that flight home with Meek tomorrow."

She slid the key card into the lock and entered her room, but Isa was right behind her.

"Isa, good night. Go to your room," she said, waving him off, tired of the circus act. She was growing bored with the back-and-forth. She liked Isa, but no way would she do anything other than what they were doing, and she didn't even know what that was. She enjoyed his company, but she knew it was only because he wasn't hers. He didn't owe her any loyalty, any explanations. He spent money, took trips, spent time with her at her whim, all without a physical connection. They were friends, and although the attraction was there, Isa was a ladies' man. She didn't want to be the girl trying to train a dog because at the end of a day, a dog was going to do what a dog was designed to do . . . chase pussy. "I'm exhausted, and you're on some bullshit."

"I'm on some bullshit? You got me flying you across the world, racing up and down the highway to fuck with you, hopping flights to show love at your shows—"

"That's what friends do!" Aria said.

"Fuck you. Don't nobody want to be yo' friend with your high-maintenance ass. I'm trying to pop that."

Aria lifted one foot to slide her red bottom off, and she chucked it at his head.

"Fuck me? No, fuck you and your girlfriend, nigga! Get the fuck out my room!"

"Throw something else at me," Isa threatened, pointing at her from across the room and flinching every time she lifted her other shoe. He snickered a bit, licking his lips. "On God, when I hit that shit, I'm tearing that shit up. I'ma murder that shit."

Aria tossed her shoe aside and stalked over to him.

"Call her," Aria demanded.

"Call who?" Isa asked.

"Don't play stupid," Aria shot back. Fire blazed in her eyes, daring him to deny her. Isa pulled out his phone, and Aria snatched it from his hand. She typed in his passcode, fingers striking across the screen like lightning.

"Yo, you wild for knowing my code. What you, the feds?" he muttered, his words laced in sarcasm and discontent as he sat on the bed. He leaned forward, elbows to knees, rubbing his head as Aria went through his phone. She frowned as she read his text messages. "So you just think of something cute to say and send it to four different women? You better not ever say this shit to me."

"I wouldn't say the same shit to you," he answered. The sorrow she heard in his tone pulled her eyes to his. Like a magnet, he captured her stare with those light brown orbs. She couldn't look away if she wanted to, and God, did she want to. There was just something about this rude, foulmouthed man in front of her.

"But you do, Isa. Maybe, not word for word, but you come at me like I'm an object. Like it pisses you off that you haven't had sex with me yet. Like the expectation is that I just trust you with my body. I'm not that girl. I was going to have you call these women and tell them you're done . . . tell them not to call you, but for what? I'm not doing that. A man that wants to lay between my legs wouldn't even put me in a position to feel like I need to do that. I'm work," she said. She shrugged. "You've got to work for me, and I'm not talking about spending money. You've got to show me that you're worth my time and that you're worth my energy. Sex is more than physical. I want you." She held up his phone and then tossed it to him. "Not all of them. I don't want their energy infecting me."

She walked to the door and held it open. "Now good night," she said.

He took his time standing and then walked over to her. He stood directly in front of her, leaving no room between them. He placed both hands around her face, cupping it. Aria tried to maneuver out of his hold, but he pulled her back. She closed her eyes.

"I don't even know why I do this with you," she whispered, shaking her head.

"Yeah, you do," he said, picking her up. Aria wrapped her legs around his waist, and he carried her away from the door toward the bed. He sat her down at the edge of the bed, gripping her chin in the U of his hand and causing her lips to purse. Her heart was so tender it ached. She felt every beat as he took her lips, stealing kisses that he knew she was too stubborn to give. They were soft, gentle . . . his kisses were everything he was not, and Aria felt like an idiot when she lifted hands to his face to kiss him back.

He pulled back. "I'm sorry. I hear you."

He kicked off his shoes and removed his suit jacket before pulling her down onto the bed. She turned and tucked her body underneath him. It was a position they had taken many times before. Aria would call him just so he could warm the other side of her bed. She felt better with him around. It was the only time she could close her eyes without nightmares.

He eased her soul, even with all his women, and even with all his bullshit, Aria valued the odd bond they shared. He never pushed her limits, never let a hand slip where it didn't belong. He just held her, and in that moment, none of the other girls mattered because he wasn't doing this with them.

"I hate you," she whispered.

He craned his neck backward so he could look in her eyes, then he placed a kiss on the tip of her nose. "I hate yo' ass too. Hate you like a mu'fucka."

4

"Keep going, youngblood. You don't want it. Keep pushing that shit. To the limit . . . to the fucking max. How bad you want it? How bad you want your old life back?"

"Agh!" Messiah roared in pain as the old man beside him added another one-hundred-pound plate to his back. Four steel plates threatened to level him as he continued to power through the push-ups.

"Fifty push-ups, a minute plank, let's get it . . . let's get that shit. Eat that shit! All the way to a thousand! Mind over body. That's your mind telling you to quit! That's your brain telling you to stop. You survived worse. Keep pushing that shit!"

Messiah gritted his teeth and locked in on the picture in front of him. Morgan Atkins. The love of his life. The only person he had ever hurt that he held regret over. It was too late to get back to her. He was dead to her. He had made sure of it. The hardest thing he had ever had to do was disappear from her life, but it was the only way to get her to grow, to get her to move on. Morgan was a butterfly. Messiah had been her cocoon. He had wrapped himself around her so tightly and protected her so fiercely that she had flourished when she was with him, but cocoons were temporary. It was inevitable for Morgan to transform into the next phase of her life. He had let her fly free because he had cancer, and he didn't want her to watch his sickness take him under. No way could he let her ride that disease out with him. He wasn't even supposed to be breathing. The doctors had given him only weeks to live, but one specialist, one surgeon, Dr. Buscemi, had convinced him to let her try one more time, to cut out the cancer and take him through a treatment so intense he would wish he were dead. Messiah had been through hell the past two years. She had taken him from the hospital and declared his status as *null* in the system. He'd been transported all the way to Maryland, where she practiced at Johns Hopkins. They had cut his body to pieces, removing infected muscle and even shaving down bone to remove every cancerous cell in his body. The pain had been unbearable. The solitude alone was enough to bring a man to insanity. He had begged her to kill him. Through tears, he had cursed her name because who the fuck delivered this type of excruciation and called it *healing?* Then the chemo had eroded him. It had been worse than the cutting. It was poison. It was the devil's serum running through every fiber of his being. It was a year of living on the brink of death as Dr. Buscemi tried to keep him hopeful. Messiah had counted up every dollar to his name and sent a check to Morgan. One million dollars. It was everything he had hustled for over the years, and it was hers. She deserved every red cent for what he had put her through. If he died, she'd get another million from his insurance policy. It was enough to set her up for a while, and although he knew she didn't need it, Messiah felt responsible for contributing. He had been her man, and a man took care of his. She would forever be his, despite the miles that separated them.

When he made it to one thousand, the weight was removed from his back, but the mental heaviness that he lived with daily remained. Those steel plates were lighter than all the burden he carried around with him.

"Looking strong, young," the man in front of him stated, giving Messiah a firm pat on the back.

"I don't feel it. The cancer could come back at any time," Messiah said, breathless as he lifted a water bottle to his mouth. He gulped down the liquid relief, wincing from exhaustion.

"You're right, but you got to keep your mind strong. Get your body as strong as you can to get ready for the war when it comes. Right now, you're cancer-free. Thank God for that. Celebrate the small wins. Eight months cancer-free, and you've built your body up well. A strong mind, strong body. Remember that."

Messiah nodded and snatched up the towel from the weight bench in front of him. His trainer walked out, leaving Messiah to his thoughts. He snatched up the picture of Morgan and his phone, then opened his Instagram account. He went to her page, something he did daily, sometimes for hours. He never liked anything, but today he had an overwhelming urge to connect to her, to communicate with her even though he knew she wouldn't know it was him. He went through every single image, clicking the little heart beneath. He snickered, shaking his head, because only Morgan could have him on some sucker shit. The liking of pics and heart eyes and such. He clicked the message icon. He had never slid into a DM in his life, but Morgan was always the girl to get him out of character. He typed two words . . .

Pretty ass.

Morgan's phone buzzed as she pushed the twins in their stroller through the busy airport.

"Are you sure you don't want to just wait until I can come with you?" Bash asked.

Morgan shook her head as she pulled the phone from her pocket. She stopped walking and opened her notifications. She frowned as she saw the name. *MurderKing810*. Her thumb moved down her screen as she saw how many pictures had been liked.

Such a creep.

"Mo?" Bash called, jarring her attention back to him.

"I'm sorry, what?" She shook her head and focused on Bash.

"Taking the twins through the airport alone on a ten-hour flight. Why don't you just wait a couple of weeks and we'll go back together?"

"No, I've already told Ethic I was coming home. Bella's birthday is coming up. I have to be there. You stay and handle your business at Cambridge. I'll be fine. Join me when you've wrapped things up," she said.

She appreciated the way he worried about her. He was accommodating. He was caring. He was honest. He was handsome. He was ... *fucking boring*. After loving someone who made her soul feel like it was on fire, being with Bash was mind-numbing. The uneventfulness of their lives, the routine, was growing old. She hadn't realized it until Aria and the crew had come to visit, but since then, she had been dying to escape.

Morgan hoisted the diaper bag onto her shoulder, accepted the goodbye kiss from Bash, and then slid her phone back into her pocket. She maneuvered through the masses of people, then handed her ticket to the agent standing at the security checkpoint. Her stomach was in knots. She hadn't been home in a long time, and what awaited her there was terrifying. Old wounds, ghosts of lovers past, and she would never admit it, but Meek was there too. Flutters filled her mind just thinking about him, and as she waved goodbye to Bash, she knew that she should turn around. Flint was trouble. Meek was trouble, but he made her feel again . . . he listened . . . he was the only one who could see that she was drowning in a roomful of people. He noticed the vacancy in her eyes when she smiled. So instead of turning back, she was like a moth drawn to the flame . . . Morgan was tired of running. She just wanted to go home.

5

There was something about being in the city of Flint, Michigan, that made Morgan's heart swell. It had declined over the years. Its cruddy city blocks and boarded-up homes looked worthless to others, but to her, it was home. When she stepped off the plane, pushing sleeping babies and struggling with a diaper bag, she breathed deep. Anxiety filled her as she made her way to baggage claim. She hadn't realized how much she had missed home until the plane had touched down. She had secluded herself and her babies from her family, and she was desperate to make up for lost time. Morgan struggled with a sense of belonging. With two dead parents and a sister in a grave beside them, she never felt like she had true family. Family was supposed to share your blood, and although Ethic had adopted her when she was a little girl, he hadn't been able to fill that void. Being away from him had caused her to rethink things. He had done all he could do to nurture her. She hadn't understood how potent his love for her was until she gave birth to the twins. Over the past two years, she had learned a lot about love. As much as Morgan had taken Ethic through, he should have given up on her a long time ago, but he was still hanging on, loving her through it all. The only love that could endure her type of defiance was parental. Ethic was her father, and no matter who came into his life, he always would be. It had taken her a while to grasp that. His marriage had made her feel threatened once upon a time, but the twins had made her realize that the bond between parent and child was forever.

As Morgan exited the elevator, her eyes scanned the crowd anxiously. She would recognize him from a mile away. He stood tall and strong, facing the conveyor belt window. One hand was tucked in his Nike joggers, the other held his cell phone to his ear. She wasn't sure why she felt relief, but Ethic's presence soothed her aching soul. As if he felt her nearing, he turned in her direction, and Morgan left the stroller to run into his arms. She cried, clinging to him for dear life.

"Shhh, Mo, I'm right here," he whispered as he gripped the back of her neck and wrapped a strong arm around her. "You're okay." He moved his hand to the back of her head and rubbed gently. "You're okay, Mo." He held her for minutes, minutes that felt like hours, as Mo struggled to compose herself. It was overwhelming to be back. It brought back memories, and they all invaded her brain at the same time. The thoughts attacked her, making her panic, telling her to turn around and go back to London because running was easier than facing her losses. "Come on, Mo. Let's get your bags and get the babies to the car," he whispered, kissing the top of her head. She nodded and sniffed away her distress, rolling her eyes to the ceiling as her pointer fingers cleared the mess from her face.

Ethic motioned to a young man standing nearby, and he sauntered over with eager eyes, rubbing his hands together smoothly as he bit into his lower lip.

"Keep your eyes down, homie, before I rip 'em out your head," Ethic said, snickering.

The young man blushed in embarrassment. "No disrespect, OG. I wasn't—"

"You were, but you won't again, understood?" Ethic asked.

"You got it, big homie," he stammered.

"Grab her bags, and meet us at the car," Ethic stated.

"It'll be the Louis Vuitton suitcase," Morgan added.

Ethic shook his head. "You just got back, and it's already starting." He snickered. "It's always the ones that work under me." He laughed, pulling her under his arm and then heading toward the stroller. He grabbed one handle, and she clutched the other as they pushed the twins through the crowd.

"I missed you, Ethic," she said, leaning her head on his shoulder as they walked. Ethic kissed the side of her head.

"I missed you more, Mo. Welcome home."

"Look, we have a guest in the studio today. He needs dancers for his video shoot this weekend, y'all, so get it right. It's high tempo. It's fast, but it's not hard. Your hands are doing the choreography; your hips just roll. Hips roll slow, hands move fast. The choreo is all up top, then you hit the split. If you can't split, then, I mean"—Aria waved her hand dismissively—"why are you even here? This is upper echelon, ladies and gentlemen," Aria coached as she went through the moves she'd arranged. Her white biker shorts were knee length but skintight, and her cropped white hoodie revealed her new tattoo—angel wings right on her rib cage.

The popular rapper stood in front of the mirror, arms folded across his chest.

"Umm, bruh," Aria said. "Some people like to watch themselves have sex. My dancing is like sex, and I like to see myself cum. You want to slide to the side?"

The group of dancers laughed, and he snickered but lifted

hands in surrender and moved away from the mirror. "I want to see that too," he said. The group of dancers chuckled.

"It'll be the last thing you ever see, G."

The threat accompanied nothing—no snicker, no titter, no joking banter—because it was 100 percent truth.

Aria saw Isa break through the crowd of dancers, swaggering toward her with a contemptuous stare, pulling up his pants.

"I'm so sorry, give me a second," Aria told the rapper. She hurried toward Isa.

"What are you doing here, Isa? I'm kind of busy," she said.

"I don't give a fuck, Ali. Why you ain't answering my fucking calls?" he asked, towering over her. Aria could practically feel the rage permeating the space around him. He was angry. He was used to receiving attention from women whenever he wanted it. Aria had put him on ice, and while she knew he thought she was playing games, Aria was just tired. The exchange of energy with Isa was too much. She hadn't dated anyone in the past two years because she had gotten caught up in their friendship. She was being faithful to a man that wasn't even her man while he was entertaining a flock of women. She didn't have time to play games. She was graduating college soon, booking tours with Stiletto Gang in the meantime, and turning down eligible men, and for what? She was pulling back, and now that she had made herself unavailable to him, Isa was livid.

Aria looked around at the roomful of curious eyes that were on them.

"Isa, I'm working. Can we do this later?" she asked, placing her hands on her hips.

"Nah, we doing this shit right now. Fuck is the problem?" Isa asked. "We been back for a week, and a nigga ain't heard from you. I take issue with that." He pointed a finger in her face, and Aria knocked it out of the way.

"I don't really care what you take issue with. Don't you

have a roster? A main? What you want with me? Your hands are already full. Go play with one of them, because that's all you're doing with me. Playing me. I'm not with the games," she said. "And I'm busy, so goodbye." She turned back toward the mirror, and he grabbed her hand, spinning her around. So aggressive. Dominant.

She blew out a sharp breath.

"What you want me to do? Huh? It's been a week, Ali! A week of no fucking contact. I'm blowing you up, and you buttoning me and shit like I'm one of these lame-ass rappers you be giving the runaround." The last part was a shot to the artist in the room, and he raised his voice to make sure it was heard.

Aria rolled her eyes in protest at this ego trip. She wasn't naïve enough to think it was anything more. Isa's feelings were hurt because she wasn't the one calling, she wasn't the one wondering where he was and hoping he'd pull up. That had never been her thing. Chasing a man. Her mother had taught her long ago that men were built to hunt. Aria knew the game. If she was too accessible, too interested, too approachable, men would come fast and leave with even more haste, so Aria flipped the game. She was hard to get and, therefore, harder to let go of. Once a man captured her, he felt like he was getting a prize. No one had been awarded the trophy yet, and she could see it in Isa's eyes, hear it in his tone, and feel it in his touch . . . he wanted to be the first. "You ain't even calling me to pull up at night. That's fucked up."

Isa was bothered. What had started as a way to help her sleep at night had become a routine that helped him rest his weary soul. In Aria's bed, he found peace. He didn't feel the need to sleep with one eye open. Their connection, although not sexual, had affected him. She had gotten under his skin. The smell of her skin, cocoa butter, was missing in his life. She put it on so much that he would walk around smelling it for days. In his bathroom, on his sheets, on her sheets, in his car. The scent had faded, and he was pissed.

"Y'all, take five," she said. She bumped his shoulder as she walked past him and out the front door. He pushed it so hard that the bell above the door broke and clattered as it fell to the cement below. She spun on him when hustling ears were out of reach. "How dare you come here spazzing on me, making a scene! Do you know who that is in there?"

"Yeah, I know who that nigga is. Corny-ass song playing on a loop on the radio," Isa mumbled. "That's the type of nigga you want? A rapper that play gangster? You got a real shooter in front of you, Ali."

"Isa! You are not my man!"

"What am I, then? I'm flying your little ass to London, paying your rent, buying you shit. What that sound like?" he asked.

"Like you my main," she said, rolling her eyes. "But you played your hand wrong, and now I'm no longer interested."

Isa snickered. "That's what this is about? The bitch in my phone?"

"Plural, Isa. The *bitches* in your phone. I don't play the back or the side or the front. If a nigga can't make me his only, I remove myself. I replace you."

"So you fucking with somebody else?" he asked. "That nigga in there?"

"You don't get to ask questions about who I keep time with. Which is not him, by the way. I don't shit where I eat, but even if I did . . . you don't get to trip on me and run up on me with the rah-rah. I don't belong to you."

"What I got to do?" he asked.

"What?" she asked, frustrated as she frowned in confusion.

"To be your man, Ali. To hit that shit every night? What I got to do?" Isa asked.

"You're unbelievable. That's all you think about," she muttered.

"Have you seen you? That's all any nigga think about when he look at you, and your little ass done had me on ice for two years. That's the first thing I think about. I think about other shit too, though, Ali. You got me fucked up. I think about you. I think about a lot when it comes to you," he said, lowering his voice and leaning his back against the brick wall. He looked off in the opposite direction, blowing out a breath of exasperation.

"Like what, Isa?" she challenged.

"Like what it would be like . . . ," he started. He flicked his nose and kept his eyes up the block, too embarrassed to look at her. "To come home to you. When I'm done mobbing. If you were there at the end of the night to take some of that off my soul. I think about you, Ali."

Aria was floored. Her mouth fell open, but no words came out. She snaked her neck back and scoffed. She swept a hand through her hair and turned around to walk back into the building.

"What I got to do?"

His words stopped her, froze her where she stood. She didn't want to give into Isa. She knew him. He would get what he wanted and then move on to the next.

"You'd have to marry me, boy," she said, shrugging. "That's the only time a man can come and go in my life as he pleases. He'd come with a ring and a last name, and I'd pop that shit for him whenever he wanted, however he wanted, wherever he wanted."

"Man, go get your shit," Isa said, rubbing the top of his head, brows lifted, overwhelmed.

Aria shook her head, face scrunched in irritation. "Did you not just hear me?"

"You want a nigga name or not?" he barked.

Aria jerked her neck back so hard it hurt.

"Don't make a big deal, man," Isa groaned. Aria's face broke into a smile, then laughter. When Isa didn't crack a smile, she stopped.

"You're serious . . . ," she whispered. "Isa!"

"What, you don't want to? First you want to, now you don't want to? I swear to God, man . . ."

"This isn't a proposal," she said. "Are you serious?"

"I ain't getting on my knees and shit, Ali. You said that's what it takes, so that's what it takes. Let's go."

Aria walked up to him and stood directly in front of him. She looked up at him in disbelief. Isa was 100 percent certified. He was born and bred in the gutter. It wasn't romantic, it wasn't planned, she was sure he hadn't thought of it at all, but she was also sure that he wouldn't have ever uttered the notion if he didn't want to. Her heart swelled. "Isa, we can't . . . this is crazy."

"Yeah, well, I'm a crazy mu'fucka, so what's good? You gon' let me get that?"

If Aria's skin weren't so rich, she would have been red. She bit her bottom lip, and he reached down, holding her under her arms and picked her up so that she was his height. She placed her hands on the sides of his face.

"You want to marry me so you can have sex with me?" she asked.

"I want to marry you because I hate yo' ass," he responded. He pecked her lips, then set her down on her feet.

She reached up and pulled him down to her mouth, kissing him so sensually that he groaned in contentment. "I hate you too," she whispered.

• • •

"Meet you where?" Mo screamed into the phone. "Aria! That's insane!" Morgan looked around at her family. It felt good to be home around the people who loved her. Bella and Eazy were on the living room floor playing with Yara. Ethic was asleep with Messari napping on his chest, and his wife, Alani, was baking. "What do you mean married? Like *married* married?" Alani looked up from across the table as Aria filled Morgan's ear with details. She took the phone away from her ear.

"Would you mind watching the twins for me tonight?" Morgan asked.

Alani nodded. "Of course," she said. "You don't ever have to ask. We always love spending time with them. They'll be good practice for Ethic." Alani snickered, and Morgan smiled, admiring Alani's swollen belly.

"I'm really happy for you, Alani. You deserve this. You both do."

Alani's eyes welled with tears, and Mo's lip trembled. They had been through a hard time. Connecting with and accepting each other had been a journey, but Morgan's heart swelled when she looked at Alani now. Alani reached across the table and held out her hand, and Morgan grabbed ahold of it. Alani just emanated love, and Morgan felt it transferring to her through Alani's fingertips.

"Thank you, Mo," Alani whispered. "He's going to love you so much. I love you so much."

"I love you too," Mo said.

She stood and walked around the table, bending down to hug Alani and then kissing her pregnant belly. She put the phone back to her ear. "Okay, Alani's watching the kids. I'm on my way, I guess. See you soon." She hung up the phone and grabbed the keys to her car. She made light work of the short fifteen-minute drive into the city. She parked curbside to the county courthouse, and quick feet carried her inside. As soon as she entered the building, she saw Aria pacing the length of the lobby.

"What the *hell?*" Morgan asked, her eyebrows raised in disbelief. "Married!" She looked around Aria to Isa. "Married?" she shouted at him.

Isa shrugged. "That's your homegirl. Got me buying the whole fucking cow just to get some milk."

"Tell me I'm not crazy for doing this," Aria whispered, shaking her hands in front of her. Aria was freaking out. "I'm only twenty-two years old. My family is going to kill me. This is a bad idea. A bad, bad, bad idea, right? I should have just fucked him."

Morgan laughed sympathetically and pulled Aria into her arms. She hugged her and then pulled back, placing her hands on Aria's shoulders. "Do you love him?"

"I hate him," Aria said surely, nodding in a panic and rolling her eyes to the sky. She stomped her feet, throwing a mini-tantrum. "Mo, I hate him so much."

Morgan shook her head.

"Ali . . . ," Isa called.

"Be my maid of honor?" Aria asked. She blew out another nervous breath. "I'm going to throw up."

"And I'll be there to hold your hair. That's what maids of honor do." Morgan smiled. There was a nagging in her heart because Aria was affiliated with Isa through her. It had all started with Morgan and Messiah. She had always thought she would be the one being reckless, running off into the sunset to get married behind Ethic's back. She would have done that with Messiah. She would have done it without thinking twice. Maybe that was the problem. She hadn't thought with him. She never paused to question anything. She just believed in him. She had followed him blindly.

• • •

Aria sucked in air, and Isa held out his hand for her. Aria walked over, grabbing it tightly as Morgan followed behind.

"Yo!"

Meek's voice erupted through the building, bouncing off the high ceilings and echoing off the walls. Morgan froze, and an ache in her heart stopped her breath.

"Somebody order a best man?" Meek asked as he walked into the building. Dark denim, Christian Louboutin spiked black sneakers, and a black fitted V-neck T-shirt. "You called me an hour ago, bruh; I ain't have time to throw on a suit. Apparently, neither did you." He snickered. Meek slapped hands with Isa, and they embraced. Meek kissed Aria on the cheek.

"Hey, Meek," Aria greeted. "This is insane, right? Tell him this is crazy."

Meek smiled, licking his lips. "It's not the most logical shit, but I'm here for it." Meek reached in his back pocket and pulled out a velvet box, tossing it to Isa. Isa caught it out of thin air.

"Three karats should be about right," Meek stated.

"My nigga," Isa stated, putting two fingers to his forehead in salute.

Morgan's head was spinning, and it wasn't even her last name on the line. It was all happening so fast. The spontaneity of it all put butterflies in her stomach. She knew Bash would give her the grandest affair when their day came, and it wouldn't even be close to being as passionate as this. Isa and Aria had met through the association of her and Messiah, and she couldn't help but feel that this was supposed to be her. That this passionate, irrational love affair was a page out of the book of M&M. It made her miss him. It made her hate him. Messiah. He lived in her. He haunted her. He was a ghost that wouldn't leave, and in this moment, Morgan felt like crying. She was happy for Isa and Aria, but their impromptu wedding did something to her soul. It dug up bones she had buried. Unearthed the heartbreak like it was brand new.

Ahmeek placed eyes on Morgan. The way the outer corners of his eyes creased and his forehead relaxed as the corner of his mouth lifted in appreciation made Morgan look away. She couldn't figure out where these fucking butterflies were coming from. He had never made her feel like this two years ago. Her entire stomach disappeared when he marked her with that stare. Out of nowhere, she became antsy, nervous. Her chest lifted as she drew in a breath.

"You're home."

She shrugged, lifting her shoulders as if it were no big deal. "I am."

"How long?" he asked.

"Who knows?" she said. "At least until graduation."

He nodded. "Congratulations on all that. It's crazy that you finished in two years, Mo. You've been working your ass off."

"I like to keep my mind busy, so I can't think about other things. School is a distraction," she said in a low tone that held so much sadness that Ahmeek didn't know how to respond.

"We're up," Aria interrupted.

"Okay," Morgan said with a heavy sigh. "I guess this is really happening."

Meek smirked. "I guess so," he answered.

The pair followed Aria and Isa into the courtroom. Morgan aligned herself behind Aria, and Meek stood behind Isa.

"I'm Judge Franklin. I'll be administering the ceremony today." The white man stood in a black robe. "Do you have the marriage license?"

From his back pocket, Isa pulled the folded piece of paper that he had purchased in the lobby and handed it to the judge.

"I'll need both parties to sign. Both witnesses too," the judge said, holding a pen out for them. "Then we can begin."

Aria took the pen first and bounced on her tiptoes, her anxiety eating her alive as she stared at Isa.

"You're going to break me, aren't you?" she asked.

Isa shook his head. "Nah, Ali. I ain't gon' never do that," he said.

They stared at each other for a moment, and then Aria leaned down to sign the marriage license. Morgan felt her eyes mist. The dysfunction of Aria and Isa was a power struggle between the two. Two people terrified to love each other, going through the motions of pushing and pulling to see who would fall in the middle first. Today, they were taking the plunge together and Morgan was overwhelmed with an emotion she couldn't identify. She was happy for them—ecstatic, in fact— but envy lived in her. She had jumped into love before; jumped headfirst without a life vest, and she hadn't survived. Seeing her friends make this leap into the next phase of their lives without thinking twice reminded her of the reckless ways in which Messiah used to love her. It reminded her of the days and nights they had spent doing things that others wouldn't understand, because they no longer lived in the real world. Their love had resided in an alternate world. M&M-ville where the only rules that applied were the ones they set for themselves. *Messiah* . . . Morgan didn't even realize she was crying until the air-conditioning inside the room hit the tear on her face. She swiped it away and shook old memories from her mind as she gave a flat-lipped smile. Isa took the pen next, and his hand lingered over the paper. A beat passed. Another. Then another. He set the pen down and stood.

Aria recoiled, and her entire body tensed as Morgan placed a hand on her friend's shoulder.

"We not doing this," Isa stated, shaking his head as he swiped one hand down his face. He pulled the velvet box from his pocket. "Man, this is some corny shit," he uttered before lowering onto one knee. "If we gon' do it, I want to do it on some G shit. Some real proper shit. My niggas in suits, you in white. This courthouse ain't good enough for you, Ali."

Aria smiled, and one tear fell from her stubborn eyes. She didn't require much. Aria was young. A fourth-year undergraduate with a fetish for bad boys. She didn't need Prince Charming, she didn't need romantic. This courthouse and the spontaneity of it was enough for her, but the notion that he wanted to give her more, that he wanted to try to give her a standard that he thought she wanted was enough to make her heart swell. She didn't want to change him. She didn't want to grow him up. She didn't want a man in tailored suits and a briefcase in hand. She wanted the shooter. She wanted the man that would pull triggers behind her, that was so tatted up that he had to turn city blocks into a million-dollar enterprise because no way was he ever sitting in anybody's boardroom. She wanted a hood nigga. A gangster that could tame her mouth and ignite her body. This indecent proposal was perfect for her. She was bourgeoise enough for the both of them.

"The fact that you're willing to do it like this tells me this ain't a mistake. I ain't shit, probably won't ever be shit, when niggas speak my name they gon' remember one of two things. That I'll shoot the shit out of a nigga and that I get money around this bitch. I'm good with that. It is what it is. I wasn't trying to change a thing, then I stepped into that small-ass college club and saw you. You fuck me up, Ali. Make me feel like if I look at you too long, a nigga can touch me because I get weak like a mu'fucka. You're better than I'll ever be. You make me look like I'm worth something . . . like if you fucking with me, I got to be worth something. Got niggas looking at me like, 'Damn, how he bag that?' You wanna take a nigga name and hold on to it for a while? Maybe do something good with it, Ali? Make it worth something?"

It was the best worst proposal Aria had ever heard. The vulnerability in his voice left room for only one answer. Aria's smile broke through her coffee-colored skin and lit up the entire room. "Yeah, I can do that," she whispered.

Isa rushed her. "My nigga!" he shouted, causing her to scream in surprise and delight as he picked her up, hands under her ass while she wrapped her legs around his waist. She laughed as he carried her out the door.

6

It was a brisk spring morning—barely morning, in fact. The darkness from night had yet to retreat, and Messiah was the only person in the park. He was three miles into a five-mile run. Every morning. It was necessary. It was hell, and the burning in his lungs felt like fire, but the pain also reminded him that he was alive. He was here to feel the pain, and he was grateful. Sweat drenched him as his feet conquered the pavement. Five miles was a feat because there had been days when he couldn't take five steps to cross a room. He had withered away to a mere one hundred pounds of nothing. He had felt like a child, too weak to do anything for himself. Months of being carried to the bathroom by nurses, of having his body rubbed down with soapy sponges because his legs wouldn't hold him up in the shower. The physical pain had been unbearable, but that mental pain had been worse. The emotional pain indescribable. So, these five miles, while hard, were a privilege to run. Every morning, because if he was going to go back for his girl, he had to be the man she remembered. He couldn't be weak. He couldn't look like what he'd been through. When she saw him, he wanted her to see the same man that she remembered. He knew their goodbye had been a bitter one. It played in his mind every night before he closed his eyes to sleep. She had cried so many tears. She had begged him to stay. Messiah wished he had handled things differently . . . that he had handed her with care. It was too late to take it back. He couldn't change the mistakes he'd made. He only hoped she would be the same . . . that the damage he had done hadn't stolen the light from her eyes because that light helped him find his way out of the darkness every time he saw her.

He pushed himself all the way to the finish, and when he burst through the door of his loft apartment, he had to sit at the bottom of the stairs. He'd pushed himself too hard. He always pushed past his limits, and his limbs shook as he gulped in air. He felt the bile building in the back of his throat, and he burst back out the door as a mixture of food and poison raged from his mouth. The chemotherapy treatments had lessened, but they were still needed—one a month, a lower dosage—and still it was the only thing keeping him alive. Cancer multiplied in him. The cells flipped like Messiah used to flip bricks. He could turn twenty to forty, forty to eighty. Give Messiah a bag, he would always double that shit. Apparently, cancer was the same. Always doubling, always bouncing back, always multiplying. The shit was destroying him, but he was alive. He was breathing, but it was getting harder and harder to live without his reason. Without Morgan.

He struggled through his door and climbed the stairs to his loft. The loft he could barely afford. He had sent Morgan every dime he had to his name two years ago. A million dollars. Every penny he had ever made in the streets. She deserved it. She deserved the world, and he hadn't been in a position to give it to her because of his diagnosis. Leaving had been easier than telling her. Abandoning her had been simpler than taking

her through unbearable pain. Messiah had been facing death.
He didn't want to make a widow out of Morgan. She had only
been eighteen years old. She was too young for such grief. He
didn't want the images of what cancer would do to his body
to be ingrained in her mind forever. No, he had left her to remember him as he was. Her king. He realized she would hate
him. He knew that it had hurt, but it hurt less than watching
him die, so he was okay with that. He wanted her to live, and
if she watched him die, a piece of her would become infected
with that image and it would rot her slowly until she took
her last breath. He didn't want that for her. If she lived, if she
smiled, if she conquered the world, it would mean he was doing
all those things too, because one place where he would never
die was in her heart. So he walked away. It crushed him. The
bruise to his heart had been unbearable, but still he did it. Then
medicine had saved him, had prolonged his life, and he couldn't
stay away. If he had more time, he wanted to spend it with her
because Morgan Atkins was the love of his life.

Messiah made his way to the bathroom and shed his
clothes before stepping into the shower. The water streamed
over his body. If it weren't for the scars that the surgeries had
left him with, no one would be able to tell he had been through
hell. He peered down at the artwork on his inner forearm.

M&M

His entire body was a tribute to Morgan Atkins. In addi-
tion to that piece, her face was etched over the defined muscles
of his back. Her first name and his last name over the left side of
his chest. And a butterfly was lost in the art-filled sleeve on his
leg. Every single time he thought of a new way to pay tribute to
her, he did it. It made him feel close to her; it made him remember what he'd felt when in her presence. He hoped one day her
lips would grace them, because Morgan had been infatuated
with kissing his body, with tracing his tattoos with her tongue

as she made her way south to his dick. Head wasn't just head with her. It was a trip to an art museum, and Morgan appreciated every single exhibit before wrapping her pretty lips around his flesh. Just the thought made him go brick.

Two years without a woman was torture to a man like Messiah. Before Mo, random pussy would do just fine. After her, it wasn't even an option. He wanted Morgan so bad he dreamed about it. His hand around his need. Her image in his head. Messiah lowered his head and gritted his teeth as he came off memory alone. He needed Mo like he needed air, and his body was begging him to reunite with her. Messiah's heart raced as he climaxed, and he closed his eyes, bracing himself, both hands against the tile as the shower rained over him. He felt so much angst in his soul. Being away from Morgan was unbearable. Knowing she was out there in the world without him hollowed him. He just wanted his girl back. God could keep the rest. The money, the status, the power . . . he could do without it all, except her. He lathered twice, rinsed, and then stepped out the shower, knotting a towel around his waist and grabbing his phone. He stepped out onto balcony, and the sun sat bright in the sky, knocking off the chill of the early-morning hours. He sat at the table as the wind kissed the beads of water that still lingered on his body, sending a chill down his spine.

He slid the lock bar on his screen to the right and opened his Instagram app. He had never been so concerned about another person in his life, but in the past two years, he had become obsessed. He kept up with Morgan from afar, often using her pictures as focal points during the times he felt like he wouldn't make it. She had no idea the ways she sent him strength. On days when she posted her man and her kids, those images tore through Messiah like a bullet. She had two angel-faced kids, and each time he saw them, jealousy seared him. Those faces that matched hers exactly should belong to him. It was a dream they had shared, but she had fulfilled it with someone else. Another man had proved that he deserved her more, and Morgan had given him what Messiah craved most. Family. And not just any family. A bloodline to her. A connection to Shorty Doo Wop. A family with anyone else just wouldn't do. He clicked on her profile, and the black-and-white selfie penetrated him. Her eyes were different from how he remembered. Morgan Atkins put up a good front for everyone, but he knew her, and the sadness he saw in the windows to her soul was undeniable. The hurt he had put on her had changed her. Scarred. By him. Morgan's eyes told the story of their tragic end. The caption read, *There's no place like home.*

Was she talking about him? She had told him he could always come home . . . that she would always be home. He wondered if it were still true. If he returned, would she unlock her doors, unchain her heart to let him back in? He tapped the little heart beneath the photo and went a step further to leave a comment.

A shot to a nigga heart.

A butterfly landed on his phone screen, and Messiah stilled, not wanting it to fly away. His eyes lifted to the many more that bounced their beautiful wings nearby, floating over the small rooftop garden that grew just a couple of feet away. He rented the place from his trainer, working in the gym, speaking to the young boys that came in and out from the neighborhood, and tending to the garden. It was how he kept a roof over his head, and the butterflies were his roommates. What at first was a nuisance had become a source of peace for him over the past two years. They reminded him of Mo, and he took pictures of them every day. An odd habit, but one he was unable to stop. The butterfly flew to his knee, and Messiah slowly opened his camera and focused on the orange beauty that sat fluttering. It was so delicate, so fragile, that even the slightest disturbance could harm it. Even if unintended, Messiah had the power to kill something so beautiful. That butterfly was Morgan Atkins. She was fragile and beautiful all at the same time. Messiah clicked the picture and then posted it to Instagram, adding it to the collection of other butterfly pictures he had taken. It was the only thing present on his account. A symbolic image of the love of his life. Messiah's heart was shattered. It was severed because Morgan had it in her possession. Those butterflies were his best attempt to turn the pain into something beautiful . . . to turn those broken pieces to art because their love had been a masterpiece.

The notification went off, and he felt like a clown when his heart lurched in his chest. Every little interaction with her moved him. Even something as simple as a comment.

I hit my target every time.

Messiah snickered. *Cocky ass,* he thought. The type of crazy that made Messiah both grateful and angry that she was flirting online. He slid into her DMs.

MURDERKING810
You should stop being so friendly to niggas online. Might fuck around and get caught up.

He stood and walked back into his room, sitting on the edge of the bed.

SHORTYDOOWOP
Nah, I keep a couple shooters handy so that'll never happen.

Messiah's brows lifted. *Cocky-ass Morgan Atkins.* He snickered because he knew she wasn't lying. Ethic could call out an entire army on Mo's behalf on any given Sunday. He had no idea of the true shooters she spoke of. The crew he'd left behind that were loyal to her off general principle alone. He had disappeared from her life, but Isa and Ahmeek were present. Two killers who were just a phone call away and would step it to anybody that crossed her path with the intention of doing harm. Morgan would never be short of shooters whether Ethic was involved or not.

MURDERKING810
Pretty girls like to talk tough.

Messiah waited, and he wondered what had distracted her. His chest tightened, and he grew possessive at the thought of Bash interrupting their conversation. Three entire minutes passed before she replied.

SHORTYDOOWOP
This pretty girl know how to walk tough too. Be careful with me.

Messiah's dick bricked. Little Morgan was big Morgan behind the safety of her social media. The anonymity of it had given her moxie, and Messiah wanted to fuck her. He liked that shit. The confidence . . . the borderline arrogance that she had developed. He remembered she would get that way after performing onstage, when she felt most in control, she would exude a power and poise that was so strong he would need to tame her instantly. He bit his bottom lip and tossed his phone onto the bed before dressing. *Witcho pretty ass.*

It was time to go home. He couldn't keep watching from

afar. If his doctor didn't clear him, he would just have to transfer his treatment back to Michigan. The distance was killing him. The solitude was agonizing, and he was ready to run down on little Morgan and shake shit up. He didn't care about anything but her, and he was determined to get her back.

7

"King me, bitch," Meek said as he slid the king of spades onto the table. He slouched in the chair of Mo's dinette set. The Nike jogger's set hung from his black skin perfectly as one hand finessed his beard. The other held his hand of cards deceptively, facedown against his knee as one leg stretched out comfortably in front of him.

Morgan's manicured hands scooped up the books.

"I swear y'all be using sign language or some shit. Mo ass be cheating," Isa complained.

"I have a sign for you, Isa," Mo said as she stuck up her middle finger.

Aria burst into laughter and tilted the shot glass to her lips.

"But I'm a G. We'll hit the shot with you losers since you're talking cash shit," she said.

Meek's brow lifted. "Yo, Mo. Don't write a check your ass can't cash," he said. "I ain't fucking with that cheap college shit y'all drinking."

"Last time bruh had 1800, we aired the whole fucking

club out." Isa snickered. "Cuz a nigga stepped on this pretty nigga Buscemi."

Laughter filled the room, and Meek blushed as he shook his head in embarrassment. "One too many, G," he mumbled. "I ain't proud of that."

"I think I have dark," Mo said. She lifted from her seat and walked the short distance to the kitchen. She reached for the cabinet above her stove and stood on her tiptoes, barely able to reach the top. The scent of Tom Ford cologne enveloped her, announcing Meek's presence before she even felt him push into her as he reached to grab the bottle of Hennessey with ease. Morgan steeled and gripped the edge of her sink. He took a step back and turned to open another cabinet, retrieving a glass. Morgan turned to him.

"I can't believe they're getting married," she whispered. "Like they almost said, 'I do,' today." Morgan covered her mouth with one hand to conceal her laughter.

"Shit's wild as fuck," Meek answered, snickering. He opened the bottle and half filled two glasses, handing one off to her. "You ain't missed a beat. One day you're hosting charity events, the next you're talking big shit over cards. You were always able to turn your hood on around us."

"What you mean turn it on? You don't think I'm hood? How you know I don't turn it off when I need to?" she asked, frowning.

Meek shook his head. "Nah, you ain't hood. You were around the way, but you not from around the way. That's how it's supposed to be. You're removed from the bullshit."

"And somehow it still touched me," she whispered. A pain filled her, and her eyes fell to her feet because she didn't want him to see how affected she was. She had lost everything, and although Morgan looked like she was doing okay, she was lost on the inside.

Meek lifted one of the tumblers, and she wrapped her dainty fingers around it. He lifted his own, and she connected hers to it before lifting it to her lips taking a sip. She pretended to gag.

"Oh my God! Meek! This is going to make me grow chest hair!" she protested.

He laughed, smiling wide, a rare sight because he hardly gave up more than a smirk.

"Kill that shit," he said. "You've always been dainty and shit."

"I am not dainty!" she said defensively. She took the words as a challenge and frowned while lifting the cognac to her lips again. She grimaced as she took a bigger sip.

"Dainty as fuck." He smirked as he finessed his beard. "I ain't mad at it. I ain't mad at it at all, Mo." He said it like he was appreciative. Like he enjoyed every single line that filled her face from the bite of the potent libation. Like it was too strong for something so pretty, it made her weak quick. She made him weak quicker.

She grabbed the bottle and led the way back to the table.

"So, we have to toast," Aria said as she lined up four shots. Three tequilas. One cognac. Mo reached for one and held it in the air.

Aria looked Isa in the eyes. "To love . . ."

"Fuck love," Mo piped up. "I'm not toasting to that."

She looked across the table, and Meek's eyes were on her. Dissecting her. She meant those words. She couldn't toast to something she didn't believe in . . . to something that had broken her . . . to something that had convinced her to lower her guards only to be deceived. Love had left her burned. No, Mo would never toast to that.

"To friendship," Meek said.

There was a time when she had resented Meek. When she

had blamed Isa for being privy to the secret that had destroyed her, but deep down, she knew they weren't to blame. Here they were two years later, sitting, laughing, like nothing had changed. Only something had. Her heart. The bully named Messiah that never played but sat with a watchful eye on her kitchen countertops was gone, and only a foursome remained. She loved each of them for different reasons, and even through the loss, they all had tried to reach out to her to make sure she was okay. She could toast to friendship. They touched glasses and swallowed the shots.

"Bring it right back," Isa said, pouring another round.

The second shot went down smoother.

"I'ma need food, bruh," Isa said. "Ali, you gon' cook something? That's wife shit."

"Not this wife. Let's be clear. I don't cook. I can feed you, though, baby, a mouthful of something real natural with your vegan ass," she said.

Meek snickered and stood from the table, placing a hand on Isa's shoulder, patting him sympathetically before heading toward the bathroom.

"Yo keep talking and you gon' be coming off that shit tonight, Ali," Isa stated.

"I might bless you," she answered, a sly smirk on her face as she propped her elbows onto the table, making a bridge with her hands and resting her pretty face atop it.

"We about to break out," Isa said, eyeing Aria like she were prey.

"What? I thought we were kicking it," Morgan protested. "I have two kids. Do y'all know how long it's been since I've been out? Since I was able to let my hair down?"

"Sorry, Mo," Aria said, still locked in on Isa.

Morgan looked on appalled as her friends stood from the table.

"I'll call you when I get home," Aria said as Isa snatched her hand, pulling her toward the door.

"She ain't going home," Isa said. "She'll call you tomorrow."

Morgan laughed, shaking her head as she watched them walk out. Such an unconventional pair. Aria and her beast. She stood and grabbed the empty glasses from the table. Meek emerged from the bathroom.

"Party's over, I guess," she said, shrugging. "You think he's serious? About marrying her?"

Meek shook his head, then blew out a breath in overwhelm. "When he called me earlier, I thought he was bullshitting. When I got to the courthouse, I realized he wasn't. When Isa lock in on something, he doesn't ease up until he gets it. The fact that he couldn't get her made him want her more. I think he's securing that. Aria's a good one. She'll be good for my nigga," Meek stated, smiling. He grabbed his car keys from the table and headed toward the door. "You good? You staying here or going back to Ethic's?" Meek asked. "You want me to follow you?"

Morgan pulled her sleeves down over her hands and folded her hands across her chest. "It's late. I'll grab the twins in the morning. It's been a while since I've slept in an empty house. When I have them, I complain about having no me time; now they're gone, and I'm a little afraid to be alone. Gives me too much time to think." She gave a weak smile.

"What you thinking about, Ms. Atkins?" Meek asked.

"How I lost control of my own life," she answered. She leaned against the back of the couch, placing her hands beside her. A heavy sigh fell off her lips. "I don't even know who I am anymore, Meek." She lifted her left hand and pulled the pretty ring off her finger. She twirled it between her fingers "This. London. It's not me. It's a great life, but it doesn't feel like *my* life."

"So why stay? Why pretend like that's what you want?" Meek asked, leaning against the door, one foot kicked up behind him, one hand locked around the opposite wrist.

"I mean, what else is there? There's nothing here anymore. The memories haunt me, Ahmeek," she said, eyes glistening. She looked down and slid the ring back in place. "Do you miss him?" The question was nothing more than a whisper. She said it like she was ashamed to, like she was embarrassed to even think the thought. The possibility of missing Messiah, of acknowledging that he even existed, but it was hard for Mo not to . . . she looked into his eyes every time she looked at Yara and Messari. They were constant reminders, keepsakes of the man that had broken her heart. She was mad at him for dying because it made her feel wrong for hating him, but damn, she did. She hated him so much.

"Every day, Mo. He was my brother. I followed him into a lot of wars. Some we won, some we lost, but it was the Ls that made us men. The three of us were rocking for a long time before he died. He ain't have a lot coming up after his pops got sent away. His mama didn't give a fuck. I used to sneak breakfast sandwiches and shit out the house for him, to take to school for him. My mama used to beat my ass because I would lose pairs of sneakers and shit, but I wasn't losing them shits. I was giving them to bro, because he ain't have shit. If I had a dollar, he got half of that shit. Different mothers, nobody-ass daddies, but somehow that nigga was my family. We may not have been blood, but we were brothers. Isa too. Shit will never be the same, Mo."

The tear slipped down her nose, itched her skin before falling to the carpet.

"It's okay to miss him. It's okay to love him, Mo."

"No, it's not. That's not okay. After the things he did, it's not okay at all. He didn't love me," she shot back.

"He did, Morgan."

She looked up at Meek, and the tension in his forehead and gloss in his dark eyes put a knot in Morgan's stomach.

"Do you want to stay?" she asked. "Talking about Messiah. It brings up bad things in me. Really dark thoughts. I hurt myself after he left . . . after that day at Bleu's. Thinking about him makes me feel . . ."

"Like you're going to hurt yourself?" Meek interrupted. "What does that mean, Mo? I know I got to be misconstruing this shit because I know you're not talking about . . ."

The tremble of her lip caused him to stop speaking, and he placed a hand to the left side of his chest. His face collapsed in ruin as the realization of her admission crushed him. "You didn't do that, Mo. Don't tell me that. Nothing's worth that."

She was humiliated, and she tore her eyes away from him, turning her head to the side before placing her lips to her own shoulder. There were very few people who knew about that day . . . about her attempted suicide. Just her family and Aria.

"Can you just stay?" she asked.

Meek nodded and took a step toward her. "Yeah, Mo," he answered. "Whatever you need."

"I'm fine. I'm not crazy. I just get lonely sometimes," she whispered. "I'm in a roomful of people every day, and no one hears me. No one gets me, and then I think about him and I want to die."

"No, Mo," Meek stated. "You not on that no more. Fuck that. Whenever you feel fucked up, you hit my line. I don't care how late it is. I don't care if you're halfway around the world with that corny-ass nigga. If you feel like that, you call me first. You call me so I can listen. I won't judge you. I'll just listen so you can get it out. Can you do that for me?"

Morgan nodded and tilted her head back as tears rolled

out the sides of her eyes. He pulled her hand, and she submitted, falling into his embrace.

She closed her eyes and held on tight, staying there until she was done crying. He was patient and rubbed circles into her back until she calmed. He knew better than to rush her somberness. He had held his mother a lot of days as a child as she cried, and he had learned to let a woman cry until she couldn't anymore. To empty her soul into exhaustion.

They stood in the middle of her apartment clinging to each other, rocking slightly back and forth as he rested his chin on top of her head.

"No more Henny for you. You get to crying and shit."

Morgan burst into laughter, grateful for him breaking the ice. He laughed too and then pulled back, swiping a hand over his wave-covered head.

"You don't have to stay, Meek," she said.

"Shut up, nigga. I'm staying," he concluded. He walked to the couch and grabbed the remote control to her television. She plopped down onto the love seat diagonal to him as he clicked on Netflix.

"I'm not watching anything except *Grey's*," Morgan said.

"Fuck is *Grey's*?"

Morgan sat up off the couch. "You don't know what *Grey's Anatomy* is?" She stood and leaned to snatch the remote control from his hands. He shrugged.

"I don't watch TV. I'm never home. I keep up with the scores and shit . . . ESPN, so I'll know what teams to bet big on, but that's about it," he said, snickering at the look of shock on her face.

"Season one, episode one," she said. She walked to the hallway closet and pulled out two blankets, tossing one his way.

"Yo, if it's on some soap opera shit, I ain't fucking with it," Meek protested.

"Boy, just watch it," she shot back, laughing as she got comfortable.

Meek kicked off his shoes and tossed one leg onto the couch before covering his lower body with the blanket. Morgan was already tuned in. She hit Mute on the television.

"Hey, Ahmeek?" she called.

"What's good, Mo?"

"Thank you, for staying."

8

Aria emerged from the bathroom wearing Isa's Versace robe. It was big for her, hanging off her frame, revealing one chocolate shoulder and cleavage that looked good enough to eat. Beads of water clung to her skin, and her wet hair curled beautifully. Isa was gone on a food run. Three o'clock in the morning and Aria wanted lobster, so lobster he was sent to retrieve. She was high maintenance and uncompromising. She wanted what she wanted. Her requirements weren't optional. Isa had been fulfilling her desires for the past two years. Spoiled. Aria was spoiled rotten, and she hadn't even had sex with Isa yet. She heard his keys in the door and then listened as his heavy footsteps carried down the hall. He pushed open the bedroom door carrying two large brown paper bags.

Aria sat on the edge of the bed as he neared, sitting beside her.

"Thank you," she whispered. She stared at the ring on her finger. "I would be lying if I said I'm not afraid of you, Isa."

He placed a finger to her chin, turning her head toward him. "You should be, baby, I'm a fucking monster."

Aria didn't retreat as Isa leaned forward and sucked her bottom lip into his mouth. He stole her breath away. Fucking thief. It was the most expertly planned heist he'd ever executed. A two-year job. The mission to steal her heart. He pushed her back onto the bed and slid light fingers up her dark thighs. Her pussy felt like silk. She was wet for him, soaked for him, and he pushed two fingers into her cavern, letting his thumb linger on her clit.

She gasped. "Isa . . . I have to tell you something."

"What's good, Ali?" he groaned while kissing her neck.

He smelled like liquor, weed, and Creed cologne. A combination that made her intoxicated. He had blown one in the car on the way back, and the way he was playing her instrument made her join him in a mental high. She was running from his hands, so she could only imagine the ways he would fill her with what she felt hardening against her thigh.

"Damn, boy," she whispered. "I . . ." His tongue was behind her ear, tracing the *A* she had tattooed there. "Isa . . ."

"Hmm?" he groaned in reply, moving down her body. He untied the robe with one hand, still working her middle with the other, and freed her breasts. Areolas so dark they looked like Hershey's Kisses greeted him. He pulled one erect nipple into his mouth, and Aria's back arched as a grunt of bliss pushed from her tense stomach. It felt like lightning was striking through her body as his tongue trailed down the middle of her stomach, dipping into the pothole of her belly button and lingering there, kissing there, before going lower. She tensed, breathing tensed, mind tensed, whole damn body went rigid as he licked the crease that separated her thigh from her vagina.

"I need to—" She paused. "Hmm." She placed her hands on top of his head as he came up the other side of her left thigh, licking the other crease. "Tell you something . . ."

He removed his fingers, offering momentary relief, but her

body was on fire. He put his hands under her hips and lifted before wrapping his lips around her swollen clit.

"Isa!" she shouted. Her eyes closed, and colors exploded. Fucking fireworks to accompany the fire-ass head he was blessing her with. "Isa, nooooo."

"Mmm-hmm," he moaned, pulling the flesh between her southern lips and wrapping his tongue around it. He was kissing her middle like he had been dying to for twenty-four months, and he had. He had imagined what she would taste like, and no disappointment existed now that he was indulging. He planned to get his fill.

"What the fuck! Isa!" She reached out to the side and gripped the sheets. It felt so good that she couldn't take it. Pleasure so intense wasn't right. Her body wasn't supposed to feel like this. She placed a hand on his forehead, forcing him back. "*Wait.* Isa, there's something you should know."

"Damn, what, Ali?" he asked, irritation burning through those light brown eyes.

"I've never done this before, Isa," she panted. "You have to slow down."

Stun painted itself over Isa's face. "Word?" He finessed his lips with his tongue, then pulled her halfway off the bed. "You been saving this pussy for a nigga, Ali?" he asked, kissing her inner thigh. She craned her neck to look down at him. "All that big-girl talk, and this shit brand new?" He smirked, biting her thigh in the same place.

"I don't fuck for free, Isa. You've got to pay me in emotion," she whispered. "Men are cheap, and the price of admission was too expensive. Until you. Until now. Is this for real? Me and you?"

"Yeah, it's for real, girl," he answered, kissing her middle, slowly, being gentler than he had before.

"Are you mad?" she asked. "Ssss."

"Mmm-mmm," he groaned. "I'm about to put my name all over this shit. Can I have it?" he asked. Aria squirmed beneath him, barely able to take the pleasure. She placed her hands on top of his head, tilting his head up so she could look him in the eyes. Aria came up on her elbows.

"I want it to mean something, and I want it to be with you, but I don't know. This whole engagement. It just feels like a joke. Like you're doing it to get what you want, and as soon as I give it to you, you're going to pull out on me. I know you."

She sat up, and he kneeled between her legs, coming up to kiss her lips, then pulling back to look in her eyes.

"If you knew me, Ali, you'd know better. I ain't going nowhere," Isa said. "I'm tired of waiting, though, baby. Let me just put the tip on it. I won't even put it in. I just want to touch it. Let a nigga feel something wet on it." His face was back between her legs, and he kissed it again. He was chipping away at her resolve because he was making her feel so good and she wanted to be bad for him.

"I can't, Isa. It's important . . ."

"Just the tip, Ali, I promise," he whispered. He took his fingers and opened her wider, pulling back the hood of her womanhood and taking a flat tongue to it. His lips pulled it into his mouth, and she melted. The robe was nonexistent, pooled in luxury at her feet, which were pointed against the floor because she was tense from the pleasure Isa was causing.

"Yo, Ali, I swear to God, you're pretty than a mu'fucka. Your skin is the shit," he groaned.

He pulled off his shirt. He was a skinny-ass nigga, but Isa had never gotten complaints because his trigger finger was buff. His body was like a museum . . . a wall of art decorated every inch of his upper body. A sleeve covered each arm, murals covered his stomach and chest, and a boxing glove with the word *Ali* covered the left side of his chest, over his heart. Aria was his heart. He had never told her, but she'd known it. No man of Isa's caliber put up with the amount of stress she caused without love being a factor. Aria set rules that he complained about, but followed. She slapped hoes behind him, popped shit under comments of girls' pictures who tried to claim him. Aria stayed kicking up dust with the women he rotated. His jump-offs. She disrespected them every chance she got. It was on sight with them until they got the point: Isa wasn't worth the trouble. She caused his love life havoc, and he loved that shit. He claimed to be single, so women kept chasing him, but he clearly had something with Aria. A situation . . . a celibate-ass situation . . . until now. He pulled a condom from his pocket, then shed his jeans. He peeled out of his boxers and rolled the rubber onto his need. Aria eyed the ripped wrapper. *Magnum.* The word terrified her. Aria's body instantly tensed as he positioned himself at her doorway. He pinched her chin.

"Yo," he whispered. She brought timid eyes to his.

"You're going to break me, Isa," she whispered.

He didn't respond. He kissed her so deeply that she didn't have time to take a breath, and then he pushed into her, slow, inch by inch by inch by . . .

All that can't fit in me.

Aria's body was wound so tightly as she put hands to his stomach to try to stop him. How a man this skinny could carry so much weight between his thighs was beyond her. Aria was terrified. She anticipated pain.

He's going to knock my fucking cervix out, she thought.

"Wait, Isa, I can't take it all," she said in alarm.

"Damn, I know, baby, but how a nigga supposed to stop now? You're dripping, baby," he groaned. He pulled out and then pulled the condom right off. She was a virgin. There was no need for it. He got tested every month like clockwork because he knew he was a hoe and he strapped up with every woman he had ever hit, but not tonight . . . not with Aria. With pussy this pretty, he had to feel it without limits, without a barrier. He wanted to feel her. Her clit peeked between her lips. He focused there, smearing the mess she was making, her own damn wetness. Spreading it around with the tip of his peanut butter–colored tip. The sight of his light skin against her darkness made Isa suck in air. She had the prettiest sex he had ever seen. If it were a beauty pageant—scratch that, a pussy pageant—Aria would be crowned the motherfucking queen because it was exquisite. It was rich and dark, like every other part of her skin, but when he opened it, the pinkest center he'd ever seen awaited him. Isa already wanted to kill niggas behind her. No-motherfucking-body could have this shit after him. He would kill every man that tried. Period. Hell yeah, he was marrying her ass.

"Isaaaa," she moaned as he pressed on her button, turning her on.

He applied pressure to it, sliding his girth up and down, letting her southern lips clench him, gripping him as the tip of his dick mashed her clit. It was fucking amazing, and he hadn't even entered her yet. White teeth broke through dark lips, and her chocolate cheekbones rose as she moaned in bliss. She was soaking wet . . . leaking everywhere. His lips wrapped around her nipple, and one hand pulled her into him as he inched into her. She gasped, gripping his back so tightly that her nails dug lines in his skin.

There was pain, a burning, like Isa was stretching her too far, and she panicked. "Isa . . ." He steeled, but didn't withdraw.

"Ali . . . *fuck*." Her name on his lips jarred her attention. He was always hard, never vulnerable, always strapped, never unarmed mentally, emotionally, or physically. She had caught him slipping. She could hear it in the sound of his voice. He had disarmed himself for her . . . for this moment. He arrested

Aria as his eyes lightened, going from light brown to auburn. She wondered if they did that when he was in the throes of passion. When he was with other girls. Or was he letting her glimpse into his soul? Was he letting her in?

He lowered to kiss the tear that pooled at the corner of her eye, then pulled back and stared at her. "Trust me." She nodded and wrapped her arms around his back.

He grinded into her, deeper, and deeper, and deeper, pushing her limit further and further until she felt the door to her womanhood break. Her legs trembled uncontrollably, and Isa rested there. He didn't move, he just lay on top of her, inside of her, elbows propped around her head as he rubbed the top of her crown.

"You okay?" he asked.

Aria nodded as one tear fell from her eye and rolled down the side of her face, pooling in her ear. He pulled out, and insecurity filled her.

"What are you doing? Why'd you stop?" she whispered, a little frantic, thinking she'd done something wrong.

"Your first time got to feel good, Ali. It ain't about me. The door is open. I'll walk through it later. I got the key now, so a nigga gon' come and go as he please. Tonight, I just want to make you feel good," he said before sliding down her body and disappearing between her thighs. Aria's stomach tensed because she was unsure of what came next, but then she felt his mouth on her.

"Oh my God," she whispered. He sucked her clit like he was eating something sour. Aria talked a big game, but no one had ever touched her there. The only attention her sex had been given was from her own fingers, but this . . . this euphoria that Isa had her wrapped up in was different from anything she had ever experienced. She was insecure about his face being buried in her intimacy, but the way he groaned in satisfaction eased her troubled mind. He ate her like she was his last meal, savoring her, getting comfortable between her thighs while she lost it beneath him. Aria bit into her lip, trying to keep her cool, but her stomach kept collapsing as new waves of pleasure washed over her. It was the best form of torture.

"Okay, okay, Isa, I can't . . . I can't . . . it's too . . ."

But he wouldn't stop . . . couldn't stop. It was like someone had poured Hershey's chocolate all over her and Isa was cleaning up the mess. Her flavor was rich, the most potent cocoa he'd ever had. She was the sweetest he had ever tasted—the only kind he'd ever tasted, in fact, because Isa didn't do this for just anybody . . . in fact, he hadn't ever done it at all. He might have been the first one to pop her cherry, but she was the first to feed him hers. Fair exchange wasn't robbery.

Aria reached for the pillows above her head and covered her face with one as her thighs parted more.

Aria lifted her entire ass off the bed, pressing herself into his face. Isa applied more pressure, sucking her soul dry as she screamed his name. She heaved, spent, as she removed the pillow from her face and hit him over the head with it.

"What did you do to my body?" she asked, groaning, bewildered and confused as aftershocks made her quiver. She couldn't understand why she still felt the sensations long after he'd stopped.

"Made it mine, Ali," he said. He planted his fists around her head, denting the bed as he hovered over her. "And I don't share well with others."

"Yeah, well, neither do I," she said. Worry lived in her eyes. "Isa, be for real about me . . . about this. The other women, they can't exist. They just can't."

"I'm done with all that. Everybody before this is no longer an option. I need this shit, Ali. You . . ." He reached between her legs and palmed the face of her sex like he owned it, like he was the owner of that storefront and he needed to put padlocks on it to keep it closed until he was ready to open it. "This. I only want this."

"You promise."

"On my mama," he answered.

Aria didn't know how she'd gotten sucked up in this type of man, with his hood colloquialisms and his gun-toting, multiple-women-having, aggressive, leave-a-nigga-leaking mentality, but she was all in. She was stuck. She only hoped he didn't leave her with a broken heart in the end.

9

Knock! Knock! Knock!

The heavy pounding on the door caused Morgan's eyes to flutter as she fought against the fog of the heavy sleep. She frowned as her lids lifted, giving her a view of her bedroom. She closed her eyes.

Knock! Knock! Knock!

Popping her eyes back open, she lifted her upper body from the mattress, saying goodbye to dreamland for good.

"Mmm," she groaned as she swept messy hair from her face. *How did I get in here?* She remembered falling asleep on her love seat. She had tried her hardest to keep her eyes open as she and Meek made it through episode six of her favorite show. *A fucking soap opera.* She smiled without even opening her eyes because it had been like pulling teeth to get him to watch more than one episode. She had opened a bottle of wine to accompany the popcorn she had made, and they had made it through the entire bottle before passing out. Her stomach churned, and the light hurt her eyes as she attempted to open them once more. Hungover. A result of last night's escapades. She climbed from her bed, gingerly placing her feet on the carpet. She grimaced as she stumbled toward the front door. Every single step made it feel like an earthquake was destroying her brain.

She noticed that Meek had folded the blanket he'd slept with, and the mess they had made was cleaned up. She hurried to the door and glanced out the peephole. A white man carrying a plastic bag came into view.

"Can I help you?" she called through the door.

"I have your Uber eats," he answered.

Morgan frowned and pulled open the door. "What?"

"Your food. A lobster roll, sweet potato fries, with a side or ranch, side of barbecue sauce, and a seltzer water?" The man held up the bag for Morgan, who accepted it in shock.

"Who ordered this?" she called after him.

"Ahmeek Harris!" the man shouted over his shoulder without stopping.

Morgan smiled, scoffing at the accuracy of her order, and then took the food inside, locking her door before heading to her room. She snatched her phone off the charger and did something she'd never done before . . . call Ahmeek.

"What up, Mo?" he answered as if he'd been expecting her to call.

"So that's what you do? Show a girl a good time and then leave before she can tease you about crying during *Grey's Anatomy?*"

"Get the fuck out of here." He chuckled. "That was your ass boo-hooing every time a patient died and siding with O'Malley's whiney ass."

"George is my fav and Alex is an asshole," Morgan defended.

She heard the amusement in Ahmeek's voice as he said, "I'm team Alex. Alex is a real nigga."

Morgan laughed as she popped open the Styrofoam container. "Thank you for the food. My stomach is appreciative. I'm a picky eater. How'd you know what I like?"

"I pay attention, Mo. I've known you for years. I know not to serve the queen no bullshit."

"What's up with you and this queen stuff?"

"Rule number one . . . know who you're addressing, Ms. Atkins," he answered.

"What are you doing today? You didn't have to rush out," she said.

"Unfortunately, I did, Mo. The money don't wait, love," he replied.

"Neither does the queen," she shot back as she lifted the lobster roll to her mouth.

"My bad. Playa fuck up. The queen comes first," he said. "I'll keep that in mind from now on. The queen requires undivided attention."

"Now you're learning, Ahmeek." She snickered.

Morgan smiled. This felt a lot like flirting, and she knew she was walking a fine line, but she would be lying if she said it didn't feel good. Meek was easy to talk to, and she could hear the smile on his face through the phone. He was hard, but not hardened, thuggish, but not damaged, and motherfucking fine. He was *foine.* He was *foine foine,* and Morgan felt giddy when he looked at her. That smile and those eyes. God had done his very best when creating that man. He was beautiful, and the way she'd seen him charm his way into the hearts of random women, she knew that he knew it. Meek didn't play fair.

"I don't mean to rush you, Mo—"

"Then don't," she said.

"I swear if I could, I would partake in all things Morgan Atkins right now, but—"

"You're busy," she finished. "It's cool, Meek. Thanks for the food." She hung up the phone. She didn't know why her feelings were hurt. He didn't belong to her. Of course he wouldn't stop his entire world to cater to her. She had been selfish to expect him to.

"Let me go get my babies," she whispered. She ate her food, finding relief in the ease of her unsettled stomach as she coated it with the meal. She showered, pulled her hair up in a messy bun, and threw on diamond stud earrings, black leggings, and a brown-and-tan Fendi sweatshirt before sliding into vintage Jodeci boots and matching high Fendi socks. She rushed to her apartment door and pulled it open.

"Agh!"

She placed a hand to her heart. "Meek! What are you doing here?" She shouted the words as she placed the hand that curled around her keys to her forehead. "You scared the shit out of me! I thought you had business to handle."

"I do," he said. "But the way you hung up the phone told me to get my ass back here before I catch a fade."

Morgan laughed, shaking her head in disbelief.

"You didn't have to come back, Meek," she said.

"That's what the words mean, but that tone . . ." He finessed the side of his face as if he wanted no problems. "That mean something different. What is it with pretty girls and their demands? Y'all difficult on purpose? Is it like a secret society where y'all agree to give niggas a hard time?"

Morgan smirked. "So, you think I'm pretty, huh?"

"The world thinks you're pretty, Mo. Quit fishing for compliments with your difficult ass," he shot back.

She hollered at that. If only he knew what those compliments did for her self-esteem. Morgan was known for her beauty, but if people could see on the inside of her, they would know she was full of insecurities.

"I have to get the twins. I didn't know you were coming.

I've already called Ethic and told him I was on my way," she said.

"Come on. I'll take you," he said. He took a step back so that she could exit and lock her door.

They walked to the car in silence, and he placed a hand to the small of her back before opening the passenger door. The BMW was nice and spotless. She could tell a lot about a man by the way he kept his car. It told her that Meek was meticulous and that he had never had nice things coming up, because once he got them, he never forgot their worth. Morgan, on the other hand, had gum stuck in the bottom of Birkin bags. She had been spoiled all her life, so she tended to take luxury for granted. Not Meek, however. He had earned every dollar he had ever counted, and he coveted his success dearly. He appreciated everything he had, never taking a single thing for granted.

"So, which girlfriend did you spin to come back? What lie did you make up?" she asked.

"I have friends that I keep time with. No girlfriend, though, so explanations aren't necessary. When I pull up, I show them a good time; when I pull off, it's over. No promises made, no expectations to maintain," he said.

"Them? As in more than one?" Mo probed. "You are a whole hoe, Ahmeek."

Meek pulled out of her parking lot, fisting the steering wheel with one strong hand and rubbed the hair on his chin with the other. "I'm really not. I don't know where you get that from. I'm a single man. I enjoy women, but I'm not a bad dude. I play my role, they play theirs."

"And do they know that there are multiple women auditioning for the same part?" she asked.

"I've never lied to a woman a day in my life. That's not my thing," he added. "Why are we talking about that anyway? You called me back to give me a hard time about women that I'm ignoring for you right now?"

Morgan looked out the window and forced herself to be quiet. She wouldn't nag him. He wasn't hers to nag. The car was silent, and Morgan didn't mind. She had spent a lot of her life in induced silence. She was comfortable there. Most people spoke because the taciturnity was too loud. Saying nothing spoke volumes. Morgan would rather let stillness fill the space between herself and another person to see if they could handle it . . . to see if it unnerved them. Meek leaned against his door, finessing his lips with his left hand while steering with his right. His phone rang through the Bluetooth, filling the car, and Morgan's eyes darted to the screen on his dash.

Livi.

She watched him hit Ignore, and she smirked. "Glad you know better," she said, rolling her eyes out her window as a small smile flirted with her lips.

He snickered, and the silence resumed all the way to Ethic's house. She leaped out the car when they pulled up. She was halfway up the driveway when she realized Meek was still behind the wheel of the car. She frowned, walking back.

"So you know, you can't pull up here and not get out to speak. Ethic doesn't receive disrespect very well," she said.

Meek blew out a breath of angst, then climbed from the car. "I don't know if I'm welcome inside, Mo. Everything ain't kosher with Ethic. The nigga don't forget a face or a motive. My motives weren't always good."

"Meek, I wouldn't have brought you here if I didn't trust you. It's fine," she said.

She turned, and he followed her up to the massive brick home. She used her key to enter.

"I'm back!" she called out.

Alani hobbled into the room, carrying Yara in her arms.

Her swollen face and round belly made Morgan smile. Pregnancy was doing a number on Alani but she radiated.

"Why'd you have to come so early? We wanted the day with them. We were going to take them to the zoo," Alani said.

"I swear, you and Ethic are such an old couple." Morgan snickered. "Just like grandparents, I tell you."

"Well, somebody made us grandparents early as hell," Ethic stated, swaggering into the room. He pulled Yara from Alani's arms. "She's too heavy for you, baby. The doctor said take it easy."

"I've been taking it easy, Ethic. I can carry her just fine. I won't break," Alani answered. She looked to Mo. "Your dad is going to drive me crazy with this pregnancy."

Morgan smiled because she knew that Ethic's protection could border on controlling, but with all the couple had been through, she also knew Ethic was afraid of losing another child. He would never say it, but she knew it. She could feel his tension, she could interpret the permanent lines that creased his forehead. She noticed the way his eyes locked in on Alani, following her around the room waiting, anticipating, her need for his protection. She knew him. He would be on edge until Alani gave birth. If anything went wrong with this pregnancy, it would be a devastating blow to their entire family, but no one would feel it like Alani.

"Ethic, this is—"

"I know who he is," Ethic deadpanned. "Why is he in my house? Why are you in his possession?" Ethic held no punches. There were no niceties spoken, no hospitality granted when there were none felt.

Morgan looked Ethic square in his eyes, one of few people who had the ability to do so . . . to bypass the intimidation and stand their ground. He had taught her that. To look a person in their eyes.

"He's my friend, Ethic. He'll be where I am sometimes." She wrapped a hand around his waist and put her head to his shoulder. "Be nice."

Meek extended his hand. "Good to see you, man. Long time."

"Long time? I've never seen you," Ethic answered without acknowledging Meek's hand. He kissed the side of Morgan's head. "Where's the corny nigga? Bash?" he gruffed.

Morgan turned red. It was clear Ethic didn't approve of this new friendship.

"Ezra . . ." Alani was the leash on Ethic's gangster. She kept it in check. Kept him reeled in, because if she let him off it, he wandered out the yard—and when that happened, it was dangerous for everyone. So she kept him on her porch, loving him, so he wouldn't be provoked to do harm.

"Call me when you get home; let me know you made it safe," Ethic stated. He stopped at the threshold. He turned, marking Ahmeek with his glare. "Fucking get them home safe. You trying to fill shoes that ain't made for you, homie. One scuff and—"

Messari ran into the room, interrupting Ethic's clear threat. Children were the perfect tension breakers, and Morgan thanked God for timing.

"*Mommy!*"

"Mommy's Ssari!" Morgan just beamed whenever her son was in her presence. Her twins were day and night. While Yara's love was soft, Messari loved her hard . . . his love was like his father's, and Morgan needed that more than her son could ever understand. "Pop-Pop says him takings us to the soo." Messari both signed and spoke the words.

"Pop-Pop is an old grumpy man, so Mommy's going to take you." Morgan both signed and spoke as well. It was important to never leave Yara out of their interactions, so they spoke dual languages all the time.

Alani snickered, and Ethic lifted one side of his mouth in a half frown, half smirk, to show his disdain as he swiped a hand behind his head, rubbing stress away. Always so serious.

"Thanks for keeping them," Morgan said. Alani wobbled over to the closet and pulled out the twins' diaper bag and then handed it to Ahmeek.

"I'll unlock the door to the truck so you can grab the car seats," Alani said. Ahmeek took the bag, nodded, and opened the door for Morgan, standing back so she could ease out first. Messari held her hand, and Yara was in her arms.

"Yo, Ahmeek Harris . . ."

Ethic's voice stalled, and everyone turned, surprised that Ethic was addressing Meek at all. Alani reached for Ethic's hand, lacing her fingers through his, and Morgan waited, holding her breath.

"Walk light," he said.

Ahmeek nodded in full understanding. Ethic was displeased with his presence, with his relationship with Morgan—whatever it may be—and he had been warned. Fuck up and there would be repercussions. Morgan and Ahmeek made their exit.

"That could have been worse, right?" she asked, snickering as Ahmeek escorted her to the car. Ahmeek shook his head and finessed the side of his face, brows lifted from the pressure of it all.

"I've never held my tongue for a nigga a day in my life, but a nigga like his tongue. I'd like to do a few more things with it before Ethic rips it out."

Morgan laughed aloud and paused to wait while Ahmeek opened the door to Ethic's Range Rover to retrieve the safety seats. He managed the load with ease and opened the back door to his car for her.

He installed the car seats, and then Morgan loaded her kids inside before climbing into the passenger seat. He was patient, waiting to close her door before entering the car himself.

"The zoo?"

Morgan placed shocked eyes on him. "Meek, you don't have to. I can take them. Seriously. There's a zoo like fifteen minutes from my place. This isn't your job."

"It's no problem, Mo. I already canceled niggas today. You have me at your disposal. Besides two car seats, that big-ass stroller, diaper bags, and two babies. That has to be hard. I'm help. Accept help. Use me, Morgan Atkins."

10

"When's the last time you've been to the zoo, Meek?" she asked as she climbed out of the car.

Ahmeek shrugged. "Shit, never."

Morgan lifted Yara out of her seat and looked at him, stunned. "Really? Never? How is that even possible?" She frowned.

"Last thing I remember about the zoo is my fourth-grade field trip. I wanted to go, but it was twenty dollars and my mama didn't have the shit, so I couldn't go. I remember feeling fucked up over it, and by the time I got my bread up to take myself, I was too old for the shit. I just never got around to it."

"So, your first time at the zoo is with me," she said, smiling. "We've got to make sure you have a good time, then. Create a memory or two. Can you grab him, please? They'll have a wagon we can rent inside."

"Come on, man," Ahmeek groaned as he bent down to pick up Messari.

He lifted the toddler onto his shoulder, and the foursome headed inside. Messari beat on Ahmeek's head like it was a drum, and Ahmeek took every lick, grimacing, as Messari's hands went to work. When he felt the moisture from the teething two-year-old hit his head, he laughed. He lifted Messari from his neck and flipped him over his shoulder, eliciting laughter. "Yo, homie, I'm trying to be cool in front of a pretty girl, and you drooling all over a playa," Ahmeek said, lifting Messari into the air and looking up at him. Messari laughed from his vantage point as Meek shook him playfully.

Morgan smiled as Yara rested on her hip. Yara patted Morgan in excitement and pointed across the courtyard at a peacock casually strolling by.

"That's a peacock, Yolly Pop," Morgan both signed and spoke. "Can you show me the sign for *bird?*"

Yara's little hands moved on cue, and Morgan beamed. "That's right. Now you both try *peacock,*" she said, repeating the sign.

"Beacock!" Messari yelled while signing.

Yara signed the word, and Morgan pursed her lips. "Give Mama kiss," she signed. Yara leaned in and pressed her lips to Morgan's before wrapping tiny arms around Mo's neck.

"They're smart as hell, Mo. Did you know sign language at two?" Meek asked, looking on in amazement.

Morgan nodded. "My parents found out I was deaf when I was born. Everyone in my family learned from that day forward," she said. "Most people would be sad about having a daughter who's deaf. I love it. I connect with my baby so much, but I also know what it feels like, so I can pour all the confidence into her in the world. I can do things that my parents missed and that Ethic missed because he couldn't fully understand how I felt inside."

"She's a lucky little girl," Meek said.

"No, I'm a lucky mom. I just want to do the very best job I can with them because they were made out of love."

His brows lifted, and Morgan's heart plummeted. She hadn't meant to let that out. "We can rent the wagon here," Morgan whispered, changing the subject. She rushed to the window. "Hi, can we get one of the double wagons, please?" she asked.

Ahmeek removed his wallet and put a platinum Amex on the booth countertop.

"I've got it, Ahmeek," she said, sliding his card back to him and pulling out her own.

"Yo, Morgan, you got me real fucked up, love," he said, snickering as he removed her card from the counter and slid it in his back pocket. He pushed his card forward. "I'll give it back to you after the day is over. Fucking pulling out your money when you're with me . . ." He said it like he was disgusted, like he was offended. "You know better." He leaned back and looked Messari in his eyes. "Your mama showing out, homie," he said.

Morgan smirked and then placed Yara in the wagon as Ahmeek bent down to place Messari next to her. Yara reached for him.

"Yolly Pop, you have to sit, okay?" Morgan signed and said.

Yara's bottom lip bulged as her eyes welled with tears. She was so accustomed to getting her way. She was so pretty that everyone always doted, always spoiled her.

"How the fuck can you say no to that?" Meek asked, scooping Yara.

Morgan chuckled. "Her and that lip. She's a master manipulator. When she gets heavy, you'll put her down."

Yara smiled and held on to Meek's neck, hugging him tightly before sitting up in his arms and pointing ahead.

"I guess she's the boss," Meek said, then headed in that direction.

Morgan grabbed the handle of the wagon and pulled Messari as she walked next to Ahmeek. He wrapped his free arm around Morgan's shoulder and pulled her toward him, kissing the side of her head before releasing her.

She turned to him, shocked, and her feet halted like someone had put her in park.

They stood there in the middle of the path as people maneuvered around them. She stared at him, eyes peering into him, heart fluttering, stomach sinking, common sense leaving.

"You're going to ruin my life," she said. "I can see it coming."

His eyes melted in amusement, warming at her assumption, and he ran the pinkest tongue Morgan had ever seen across his chocolate lips. He trapped his bottom lip between white teeth. "Nah, I can't see that."

"I don't think you'll mean to, but I know better than to expect anything else. I didn't know better before. I know better now. So whatever this is—"

"It's friendship, Mo. It's an apology. It's a blessing."

"A blessing for me to have you in my life, huh? You're cocky, Ahmeek. Who says I'm staying? Who says I want you here?" she asked.

"A blessing for me, Mo," he answered, disarming her.

"Bears, Mommy! Bears!" Messari shouted. Morgan stole her eyes away from Ahmeek, struggling to focus on her son as she glanced back to him. Yara placed her hands on the sides of Ahmeek's cheeks, and he inflated them for her, only for her to squeeze the air right back out. Morgan blushed. His ability to be childish for her kids, to be patient as they drooled on him and probed him curiously, made Morgan smile.

"Okay, baby boy, let's go see some polar bears," she said.

They moved through the exhibit, balancing two kids, diaper changes, snack time, a few temper tantrums, and grape juice spilled down the front of Ahmeek's Burberry shirt. He didn't seem to mind. The smile never left his face, and the patience never dissipated from his tone. Yara stayed tucked in Ahmeek's arms, and as she grew sleepy, she refused to lie in the wagon. Instead, she made a pillow of Ahmeek's shoulder, forcing him to carry her the entire time as Messari dragged Morgan around the entire zoo.

As they made their way back toward the exit, a man dressed in stripes approached them. "Would you like your picture taken?"

Morgan picked up Messari as Meek stepped aside. "Say *Mommy's Ssari!*" Morgan baited.

Messari practically leaped out of her arms. "Mommy's Ssari!" they both screamed, eyes bright, smiles wide.

"Now let's get Dad and the sleeping beauty in the picture," the man said, motioning for Ahmeek to join in. "You have such a beautiful family. We've got to get a group shot."

"Oh, he's not . . . we're not . . ."

Morgan felt her face flush as she turned to Meek. "I'm sorry. You totally don't have to." Ahmeek stepped up and gripped her chin.

"It's just a picture, Morgan. It's fine," he said, calming her. She nodded.

"Say *cheese!*" the photographer baited.

Morgan felt Ahmeek's hand loop her waist, and she held Messari on her hip as she leaned into him and smiled.

"Beautiful!" the photographer said. He handed her a ticket. "You can purchase the photos on the way out."

"Yo, my man, can you take another one?" Meek asked, sliding the man a hundred-dollar bill and his phone. Morgan tucked herself right beneath Meek, and Messari kissed her cheek. The man snapped it at the perfect time. Morgan was mid-laugh and absolutely stunning.

"Good man," Meek complimented, shaking the man's hand and giving him a firm pat on the back. Meek sent the picture to Morgan's phone and then tucked his in his pocket.

"I should get them home," she said.

They made the long trek to the car, laughing and talking. Morgan couldn't believe how carefree it felt. He was like a cool breeze on a scorching summer day. She had never seen him be so lighthearted. Ahmeek the street king had a weakness for little girls who smelled like baby magic, little boys who liked to roughhouse, and sweaty mothers who had frizzy edges and swollen feet.

They stopped for one more diaper change before loading up and heading home. When they arrived, Ahmeek walked Morgan upstairs. The twins were grumpy and exhausted, causing a ruckus as they went straight to the living room where their toy chest was located.

"I'm going to give them a bath and put them to bed. You can stay if you want. We can finish season one of *Grey's?* I mean, you don't have to. I know you're busy, and I've taken up your entire day, but—"

"I've got to spin through the hood, Mo. Money can wait, but it normally don't. When I'm done, I'll call you, if that's cool with you. Can I call you?" he asked.

"I don't really do easy, Ahmeek. Calling is easy. Texting is easier. I'm with the face-to-face. I need to see your eyes when you tell me something, so I can see if it's bullshit," she said. He heard her resentment. It wasn't caused by him, but it was certainly aimed at him. Morgan didn't trust people . . . men in particular, and he knew why.

"I don't bullshit," he answered. "When I tell you something, you better believe it's bond. Give me your phone."

She rolled her eyes and took her phone out of her crossbody purse. He FaceTimed himself, then answered.

"Face-to-face," he said. "You can play *Grey's* while I shoot this move. Give me the play-by-play, so I don't miss shit."

She blushed, then a smirk spread on her face as she stubbornly snatched her phone. "That's technically not face-to-face."

"The fuck it ain't," he protested. He held up the phone and backpedaled. When he was at the door, Yara came running in his direction, crying. She was already attached. Ahmeek had spoiled her all day. Yara had found a new sucker. Ahmeek's heart melted as he bent to pick her up.

Baby Yara put her head on Ahmeek's chest, and he rocked her side to side.

"Now I've got two pretty girls giving me a hard time about leaving," he said. "Y'all Atkins girls don't play fair."

Morgan smiled and lowered her eyes to her feet. "I'm being a brat. I know. I'm used to getting my way." She pulled a resistant Yara from his arms. "Thanks for keeping us company."

"Anytime, Mo. It was a good time. I've been chasing paper since I was twelve years old. Never really took the time to do something so simple. It felt easy."

"Yeah, it did, didn't it?" she whispered. They stared at each other, wondering, resisting, trying to figure out how he had become the one walking her to her door at night and gazing into her eyes. "Good night."

"Night," he said.

He stepped over her threshold and turned. Morgan closed and locked the door, then leaned against it as she kissed the top of Yara's head.

"Mommy's playing with fire," she whispered. She headed toward the bathroom. "Come on, Ssari. Bath time."

Morgan ran her babies a bath and then put them to bed.

"I wuv you, Mommy," Messari said and signed.

"I love you most, Messari," she returned. She looked at Yara. "Love you to the moon, Yolly Pop."

"Love you," Yara signed.

Morgan pulled out a book and leaned back in the rocking chair that sat between their twin beds. She opened it and signed while reading the words. Like usual, Yara's eyes closed first, and her stubborn boy lasted an entire half hour longer before giving in to sleep. Her phone rang, and Morgan jumped at the loud noise. She hustled out of their room. She couldn't stop the smile that spread across her face when saw the name . . . *Ahmeek Harris*. When had he become the one to make her smile like this? Better yet, *how* had he become the one to make her smile like this? She pressed the green button, and his face popped up on her screen.

"Face-to-face as promised, Ms. Atkins," he said when he saw her. "Y'all all settled? You need me to hit you back later?"

She shook her head. "No, I just put them down. They're sleeping."

"So, we doing this *Grey's* thing or what?" he asked.

"Over FaceTime, Ahmeek?" she shrieked. "You won't know what's going on. It's sweet of you to try, though. To keep your word."

"You want to see my face when I'm talking to you. You call the plays, Mo," he said. His phone was in an awkward position, sitting in his lap so he could drive and speak at the same time.

"Ahmeek, get off the phone before you die," she said. "I'd rather you be alive for me to give you a hard time."

The smile that broke across his stern face elicited one from her. "A'ight, Mo. Yo, thanks for the memories. The zoo. The little people hanging all over me. The pretty girl spending all my bread on henna and face paint . . ."

"I told you I would pay!" she protested.

"Never that," he shot back. "Sleep well, Ms. Atkins."

"I will. Be safe, Meek." She didn't know where he was going or what he was about to get into, but if he was still in the same business as he had been in two years ago, then he needed to be reminded. He needed to be prayed for. *God, please keep him safe.* Her heart sank to her stomach, because when did Ahmeek become the nigga she prayed for? Morgan's gut churned.

Her finger lingered before she pressed End, but he disconnected the call. Morgan flopped down on her bed and then let her back fall against her mattress. Eyes to the ceiling, head in the clouds, Morgan felt herself turning into a dreamer again. Morgan felt herself veering toward a danger zone, and she was speeding toward disaster.

11

The heart of a woman was like the ocean, so deep and full of caverns, where treasure lay in wait. It took a brave person to try to excavate those hidden places, to explore those depths, and Morgan could feel Ahmeek traversing troubled waters, trying to discover her riches. His charm was unintentional. It was natural for him to bleed charm onto women. It was as natural as breathing to him, and Morgan could feel the agonizing attraction sparking inside her. Her phone rang, and she answered it so quickly she didn't bother to screen the call.

"I need to talk to you . . . ," she said, the words rushing out in a breathy jumble as if she were tired, running. Because she was. She was running from this feeling, from the butterflies that filled her at just the idea that he was on the other line. Just the thought that the sixty seconds that had passed since they'd hung up had unbearable for him too.

"I need to talk to you too, beautiful. I've been thinking about talking to you all day."

Morgan frowned as she pulled her face away from the phone, looking at it, checking the name on her screen.

"Bash . . ." A sigh of disappointment left her lips.

"I just wanted to call and tell you good night," he said. "I'm going to try to get over there soon. Wrapping up a few things at Cambridge, and then I'll be free to travel."

"Yeah, of course. No rush," she said.

His voice and the making of plans and such reminded her that she belonged to someone. She had a life, and a man, and he had a plan for her life, an itinerary for her to follow. A ready-made royal family for her to join.

"I love you, Morgan," he said.

"You too," she answered. Always *you too.* Never *I love you too,* because she didn't want to lie. It wasn't that she didn't love him, but the type of love Bash was expecting, she couldn't reciprocate. She wouldn't ever be able to.

"I'll call you tomorrow," he said. He was gone before Morgan could say more, but he had brought her back down to reality.

Morgan turned off her phone, showered, and then put on a satin black robe before getting comfortable in bed. After a long day of adulting, it felt great to rest her body, but her mind wouldn't comply. Seeing Ahmeek handle her children with such ease, seeing his gangster soften almost to putty when dealing with them, made Morgan emotional. They didn't even belong to him, and the interaction was breathtaking. She wondered what life could have been like if Messiah were still alive. If he were in their children's lives. He had been so damaged that she didn't know if he had the capability of being a father. She had thought so, but after discovering his truths, she truly didn't know at all. *Everything happens for a reason. If he was supposed to be here, he would be here. He was no good for me. He wanted to hurt me. God, how could he have wanted to hurt me when all I wanted to do was love him? I was such a fool.*

The television played, but it was watching Morgan because

she couldn't focus. Two hours of overthinking was torture, and sleep was a joke . . . she hadn't slept in years. The unexpected knock at her door pulled her to her feet. The clock shone that it was close to midnight, and she sat up in bed, slightly alarmed. She hustled to the door before the sound could wake her twins. Eye to the peephole, her breath caught in her chest. She opened the door.

"So, you think you no longer need permission to pull up, huh?" she asked, unable to keep up the resting bitch face that would make him think she was serious. Her heart lightened at the sight of Ahmeek.

"Nah, I don't think that, Mo," he said. He gripped a greasy paper bag in his hand. It smelled divine.

"Did you handle your business? Livi, I think it was?" she asked.

Ahmeek licked that bottom lip and put his free hand behind his neck, rubbing, like the question was stressful, like his answer was important.

"I wouldn't leave you to handle that, Morgan," he said.

"I mean, you don't owe me no explanations. We're friends. I get it. You have a life. You have women. People who need you," she said.

"Morgan. Am I with them or am I standing here in front of you right now with shrimp fried rice, extra egg, extra shrimp—but only if the shrimp are deveined; otherwise, make it veggie fried?"

Morgan's eyes sparkled in amusement at the recanting of her difficult food order.

"How the hell do you remember the craziest stuff about me?" She laughed.

"You ordered it every Friday night. We had pizza. You had Chinese. I remember, Morgan. Now, you gon' let me in or what?"

She stepped to the side, and he slid past her, body so close to hers that Morgan couldn't breathe. He stopped directly in front of her, looking down at her.

"Your bourgeoise ass." He snickered. She pushed past him playfully, and he closed the door before following her to the kitchen.

"I'll grab plates and forks. We can eat in my room. *Grey's* is already on," she said.

Meek sat on the floor at the foot of her bed, back leaned against the mattress. Morgan climbed onto the comforter, belly down, putting her head at the end near his shoulder.

He opened one of the origami-type boxes and opened the chopsticks, breaking them apart, then passing them over his shoulder. He passed her food off next and then dug into his own meal. She leaned over his shoulder, reaching for his box.

"Nigga, gone. My shrimp got veins, greedy ass," he said, laughing.

Morgan hollered in laughter. "Give me some, stingy!" she shouted as she reached farther, falling off the bed and into him.

He chuckled as she held her stomach in hilarity. His baritone hopped around as he laughed too and that smile. White teeth. Chocolate skin. The kindest eyes she'd ever seen. Morgan felt a level of comfort that surpassed any she had ever felt before. Ahmeek was normally stoic, serious—glowering, even—but when it was just the two of them, he was playful. He was lighthearted, and she wondered who else had seen him this way.

"Here, man," he groaned, passing his pint of rice.

She smiled wide and stuck out her tongue, then dug her chopsticks into his carton.

"So fucking spoiled," he mocked, shaking his head.

She smirked. "People find it hard to tell me no."

"Soft niggas. I'ma tell your ass no often just so you remember what the fuck it sounds like," Ahmeek fussed.

"Then why am I eating your food right now?" she asked, frowning in curiosity.

"Because you're a fucking bully. You practically broke my damn shoulder diving for that box," he answered, laughing while wiping a hand across his bearded face and wrapping four fingers behind his neck.

Morgan laughed, such a carefree sound. She hadn't found a reason to laugh this hard in years. Who could laugh when it hurt so bad, but here she was laughing and shit?

"Here, boy. You should learn to share," she added, folding her legs Indian-style and sitting beside him. He scooped a bite of the rice and held it up to her mouth. Morgan opened up, then nudged him with her shoulders. Meek scoffed, shaking his head before taking a bite for himself.

She pressed Play on the remote control, leaned against him, grabbed her food, and then sighed as she got lost in a fake world. They ate, and Morgan cleared the mess away, rushing to the kitchen so she didn't miss a second of a show she'd seen at least three times already. She returned and grabbed all the pillows off her bed, making a pallet of discomfort right there on the floor.

He propped one hand behind his head, and Morgan lay in front of him because he was bigger and he would block her view. No hands, no touching. Just a friend to take some of the loneliness away. A friend who accepted who she was. A friend who didn't try to change her.

"Thank you so much, Meek, for coming back today and for the zoo and just being great," she said, smiling as she swept her hair behind her ear. "It just gets so fucking lonely sometimes."

"It's never a problem, Mo," he replied. "I can't believe you have kids. Seeing you today with them, in mom mode and shit. Like I've seen you all glammed up, I've even seen you in your school vibe, but man, seeing you with them. You're a good mother, Mo." He rubbed the top of his head, his thick eyebrows lifting in admiration while a chocolate hand traveled down his wavy head . . . he did all this before rolling those dark orbs back to her. "Are you happy?" He paused, and she dropped her stare, digging into her food, mixing it around. "With that cornball-ass nigga?"

Mo shrugged. "Nothing feels extreme with him. No highs or lows . . . just average . . . I'm coasting in the middle lane." Her words trailed, and her mind wandered to a time when every day of her life had been intensified. When she had given 100 percent of herself. She no longer did that. She would never do that again. She didn't trust anyone enough to ever give them all of her. That's how you ended up hurt. She wouldn't invite heartbreak a second time around. Bash loved her more than she would ever love him. It gave her the advantage in their relationship. She wasn't susceptible to heartbreak when it came to him.

"You ain't average, though, Mo. By far. I know that's the father of your kids and all, no disrespect . . ."

Her heart seized in her chest. It was one of the moments that she knew would come. She had anticipated it since the day Yara and Messari were born. To tell the truth or to lie. Bash had been by her side for the past two years. He was the only father her babies knew. They went to him when they cried. Smiled at him when he entered a room. He was good to them and for her. He was safe, and Morgan couldn't let anything get in the way of that. It was the smart choice, the sure bet. She couldn't blow up her entire world by admitting that the twins were Messiah's flesh and blood. She wasn't lying. She was omitting, and she would have to be comfortable with that.

"None taken," Mo whispered, still avoiding his gaze because looking in Meek's eyes made her feel transparent. She couldn't tell him that Messiah was the father of her twins. She couldn't tell anyone. Bash was making a legitimate woman out of her. He loved her. His family had accepted her. They were helping her get through school and setting her up for the future. They were supporting her. She had to keep up the façade. Let the world think he was the father and that they were in love. She loved him, but in love . . . Mo would never allow herself to be submerged in something as deep as love ever again. It wasn't Bash's fault. That injury had come before he had. It cut deep. She had almost drowned in love before, so she was afraid to swim in its depths again.

"Press Play," he said, lifting one side of those dark lips, revealing white teeth that broke through a lazy smile. On rare occasions when Meek allowed his guard to lower and he blessed a room with a smile, his eyes sparkled, and Mo got lost. It felt like she was gazing at stars. A hood star, but still something beautiful all the same. It was just the effect he had on women. All women from little girls to grannies. He was naturally charming—seductive, even—and Morgan shook her head. She grabbed the remote and started the show, grateful that he no longer felt the need to talk.

As the late-night hours ticked away, silence took over the room. Too tired to joke, they focused on the show. Morgan was all in. One show played after the next. She didn't realize how late it was until she heard Ahmeek snoring lightly behind her. She sat up and turned to find him sleeping, one arm propped against his forehead, lips slightly parted. She flipped her hair out of her face as her heart sank into her stomach. It never failed. This hour of night made her sick. Every night. For the past two years. It was the Messiah shift. The time of day she had carved out for him while they were together. The sun never saw them together. She had school. He had the block. But when the moon traded places with the sun's rays, Messiah used to push one hundred down the freeway to get to her. She worked him for an entire eight-hour shift, and he wouldn't leave until dawn. They had made love in those midnight hours not just physically but mentally, emotionally; they had figured out how to manifest love, and it had felt so pure . . . until one day it proved poisonous. Fraudulent, even. Morgan's eyes prickled as she pushed up from the floor, covering her mouth so that her sobs wouldn't escape. Every night. Like clockwork, she cried. She rushed into the hallway, pulling her bedroom door closed before leaning against it in angst. She pushed forward, peeking in on her twins, eyes leaking unstoppable tears, before heading to her living room. Morgan pushed her couch backward, making a space in the center of her floor, directly in front of the mirror. She had to get this out. She had to dance this out. This pain. It was crippling her. Shaky hands pulled her iPhone from her back pocket, and she connected it to her Bluetooth speaker.

Play.

The soft melody filled the room. Summer Walker. She stood in the middle of the room and tilted her neck backward until her eyes met the ceiling and tears cascaded down the sides of her face, pooling in her ears.

Honestly . . . Honestly, I'm tryna stay focused

Morgan's body moved. Eyes still to the ceiling as she gripped at the hem of her satin robe and moved it, pulling it as she moved her hips, slowly . . . a seductress . . . a show woman.

Morgan's body glazed over the beat, sensually, like she had composed it herself. The mirror in front of her was her audience, and she was seducing the crowd as her hands moved over her body, ending at her hips. The way she rolled with the music was passionate like she had a point to prove. Slow. Methodic. A little off beat because Mo just couldn't catch it like everyone else caught. She rode it differently. No other dancer processed music the way Mo did, and it made her better than everyone else. She felt her tears on her face and didn't even bother to wipe them. They only replenished anyway. She had been crying for years. She danced them away in the middle of the night because it was the only time she could do so without Bash judging her.

Give it to me like you need it, baby
Want you to hear me screaming, heavy breathing, I
*   don't need a reason, baby*

She saw Meek emerge from the bedroom. He stopped in the hallway, gripping the header of the doorframe. He lingered there, and Mo kept dancing. Kept crying. He had already seen her, so why stop? She couldn't if she'd wanted to.

Her face was destroyed, emotion painting the torture that she felt on the inside onto her features. She was so damned sad, so angry, so lonely. The worse she felt, the better she danced. Her choreo was otherworldly. The way she put one move in front of the other, connecting a sequence so unique it explained the story of her heart without words. She was art. The way her body moved was like a paintbrush over canvas. Morgan painted a pretty picture just with her presence, but when she felt the beat in her bones and danced, she became a masterpiece. She bounced slightly, lowering to the floor. She prowled slowly across the hardwood floor as the song changed and a sultry voice sang about shame. Mo was an expert at that. Shame. Being ashamed. Those silent sentiments raining down her face as she came to the base of him, coming up on her knees, fingertips climbing his body, until she was on her feet.

You see right through me
You see through the smile
You see straight through me

He looked down at her, and she placed her hands on his chest and dug her forehead in the center of it, crying. Meek kept his hands where they were, above his head, gripping the header. They were safe there. They couldn't disrespect there.

"Mo," he whispered.

"Don't say anything, Ahmeek!" she cried. "Just shh."

Meek looked down at her. He was struggling to keep this thing friendly, to keep it about her, but she was so fucking pretty, so alluring . . . putting need into the atmosphere, a need he was more than capable of filling, but he was fighting the urge because she didn't belong to him.

"Yo, we can't," he said.

"I know." Morgan barely whispered the words as she clung to him, gripping the T-shirt he wore. Her heart raced, and he brought his hands down to cup her face, swiping his thumbs across her cheeks like windshield wipers to clear the pain. Anxiety tightened her stomach, and guilt forced her eyes closed. Meek was her friend. Meek was *his* friend. They couldn't take it there. They shouldn't, but she was so lonely, and he was here, dripping in danger and aggression, with a tablespoon of finesse. God, Meek was a legend in the city, and the power, the authority, the influence . . . it called to her. She was made by a hustler, bred by a hustler, no way was she supposed to be with anyone other than a hustler. It was in her DNA. Like Raven Atkins and Justine before her, Morgan was purposed to sit on the throne beside a king. Trust fund money didn't spend the same; Morgan wanted to blow a bag. She now wished she had sent Meek home. Proximity made them vulnerable. They couldn't be regulars in each other's lives because lines would get blurred. They were already blurred. Morgan was crossing all types of boundaries, but Meek smelled so good, he looked even better, and he made her heart race.

"Meek, I need you to walk away because I can't. You're

making me feel something, and I don't want to feel this. I can't feel this."

Morgan felt his hands pinch her chin and lift it. She snapped her eyes closed because he was setting her up, forcing her to look into eyes so gorgeous she knew they would trap her. His stare was a cage, one she would get locked inside.

"Ahmeek, no!" she cried as a sob escaped her. "No, Meek, please, please leave."

"It's your world, Mo," he said as he lifted hands in surrender and took a step back. "I'ma go."

She nodded frantically, unable to form words, unable to think straight, unable to suck in breath. She both hated and loved what she was feeling all at the same time. Meek gave her butterflies.

No, you can't do this. Butterflies are bad. They're dangerous. He's off limits. You're off limits. He's Messiah's friend.

Temptation turned up the temperature in the room, and she felt him move around her. She squeezed those eyes tighter, struggling as she heard his heavy footsteps walk toward the door. They echoed against the wood and resounded in her vacant soul. She hated that with every thud her heart ached a little.

"Ahmeek?"

He stopped in the doorway.

"If I had met you first, would you have broken me? Would you have torn my heart out my chest?" she asked.

"I won't kick dirt on my nigga name. He loved you, Mo. I don't know what I would have done, because it wasn't me. That was then. This is now. All I know is what I want to do now."

"And what's that?" Morgan asked.

"Some shit I shouldn't even be thinking about doing. Some foul shit, Mo."

"And what if I'm thinking about it too? What if I've been

walking around dead inside for the past two years, but with you
I feel alive?" she asked. She walked toward him and stood in
front of him. He swiped at her tears. "I'm like a robot. My life
is a routine. I've memorized it, and I just keep doing the same
thing every day, all day, but I feel this. I feel you, and I hate it. I
hate you for making me feel things I haven't felt since . . ."

"Look, Mo. You're vulnerable. You're looking for me to
make you feel what you felt with Messiah. I'm not him."

"I know that. I don't want you to be him," she sniffled, wiping her nose with the back of her hand. Meek looked down the
bridge of his nose at Morgan, leaning against the doorframe.

"What you want, Mo?" Meek asked.

"It's wrong . . ."

"Say it," he ordered.

"This is wrong," she protested, shaking her head, ashamed
that the thought had even manifested in her mind.

"Say it anyway," Meek said, licking his lips and making
Morgan's heart skip beats as his eyes probed hers. She felt transparent, like he could see straight through her. He was waiting
for her to say what he already knew. He was adamant, pressing,
and Morgan was weak. The way he squinted at her, doubtfully,
like he wasn't buying the bullshit she was selling, made Morgan's thighs clench in yearning. If they were going to speak on
it, he wanted to hear the truth. The energy was already spilling
into the air, but he needed the words to come from her mouth.
To tell him that the attraction was mutual. That his presence
was wanted.

"I can't, Ahmeek." She whispered the words like it pained
her to let them slip from her lips. She was at a disadvantage. It
was Friday too. Fine nigga Friday, and this damn god of a man
was standing in front of her, looking at her like she was a delicacy. Like he was ready to hear her heavy breathing in his ear
and feel her nails in his back.

"Fucking say the shit, Mo." There it was . . . aggression . . . frustration . . . He wasn't afraid of her innocence. He didn't treat her like she would break. Morgan's heart raced.

Morgan closed her eyes and felt the chill of fresh tears as they ran down her cheek. Shame. Similar to the emotion oozing out the speaker. She felt it all, but she still opened her mouth to speak. "You, Ahmeek. I think I want you." The words were so treasonous they blew her entire heart apart as they transformed from thought to fruition. She could deny them if they lived in her head. She could fight them, but now they existed. She had brought them to life, and before she could even lift her lids to witness his reaction, she felt his hands cupping her face.

"Can I touch you, love?" he asked.

She couldn't open her eyes because she was afraid of bearing witness to whatever happened next. She expected a kiss to her lips, but instead . . . a gentle peck to the tip of her nose. Her nose. Of all the places he could have indulged in . . . her nose. It was the sweetest place she'd ever been kissed. It wasn't sexual. It was appreciative. It was endearing. She sucked in air, holding it, dying a little on the inside because that single kiss traveled down her spine, then through the channel between her thighs, then farther south to her toes. His hand fell to her hip, then rounded her ass, gripping the cuff, pulling her into his aggression. If the feel of his body against hers was any indication of how aggressive he was, then Meek was big mad, big Meek. He was hard for her, and Morgan's body came alive as her mind yelled, *Free Meek!*

Her desire dripped, moistening her southern lips, begging her to indulge in what they both wanted. His stare was intense, luring her shame-filled eyes up to his, and her neck craned back as he took her lips. A fist in her hair kept her in place, but even without it, she wasn't going anywhere because her legs wouldn't work. The remnants of something sweet infiltrated her tongue as he devoured her. Her clit pulsed like someone had revived her sexuality because she hadn't felt that heartbeat between her thighs in years. She didn't even know her body could work like this again. She had thought it was a secret that only Messiah knew, because Bash never made her body weak like this, but damn if Meek didn't know the secret too. They had been friends. Had Messiah betrayed her again and told Meek about the ways he used to make her cum? Had he shared the manual? Had they discussed her? Had they laughed about how stupid she had been to believe the lies? Morgan placed timid hands on Meek's chest, then pulled back.

"Meek, wait," she stammered.

"My bad, Mo," he returned, pinching his lips. "Damn."

"What are we doing?" she asked.

"Whatever the fuck we want to do," he answered.

He said it like he had no worries. Like they had no one to answer to. Like he could do what he felt without thinking twice. Damn, how Morgan wished she could be so bold, so brave, but this wasn't right. No matter how right it felt, it was an illusion. It was dead wrong. It had to be. Her heart wasn't supposed to race like this for him.

"I have a fiancé," Morgan whispered. She turned and fisted her hair in dismay. Nerves ate away at her. Guilt weighed on her shoulders because she would have to live with her Meek-stained lips. She would have to kiss her babies with those lips. Kiss Bash with them too. She wondered if he would taste the hint of chocolate on them, because that's what Meek was made of. God had constructed him using Godiva fucking chocolate, so smooth that not one blemish lived on his body besides the ones he had put there on purpose. Ink that held deep meaning.

"I don't give a fuck about that nigga, Mo. He can become a memory like that." He snapped the fingers on his left hand while the right rubbed the top of his fade. There it was. His aggression. He was more skilled than Messiah at keeping it hidden, at controlling it. He kept it tucked like the 9 mm pistol on his waist, but it was there. He buried it beneath the pretty-boy looks and the charm and that smile that made Morgan's stomach hollow. Morgan knew Meek's threat wasn't just talk. He had the ability to make Bash disappear without a trace, and with lust dwelling between them, he now had a reason to.

"I have two kids, Meek," Morgan added. "Is it *fuck them* too? I'm not little Morgan anymore. I have responsibilities. I have a family."

"I know that, Mo—"

"So, what are we doing?" she interrupted. "Playing?" Morgan's brows lifted as she probed for a reaction. She saw the makings of regret all over him. He was the man she would have and then immediately wish she could take off her hoefax, because no way would Meek stick around. When he didn't respond, she nodded, scoffing in disbelief. "Yeah, that's what we're doing . . . we're playing with fire . . . with people's lives. Bash has been good to me."

"He ain't the only nigga that'll be good to you, Mo."

"You want to raise two babies, Ahmeek? Cuz I highly doubt that you do. You out here getting money, flying free, moving fast. My life isn't fast anymore. It's slow. It's steady. It's boring, and you are butterflies."

His brow pinched as she continued, "You don't seem like the potty-training type. We could do this, and it would be amazing, it would be fun. I'd feel sick to my stomach every time I smelled your cologne because looking at you right now I can barely stand, but you're not here for the long haul. You won't be there to enroll my kids in school. You won't come to softball games, or pack school lunches, or help me send them to college. We'll have sex, and I'll like it. Hell, I'll love it, then you'll leave. Just like he did." Morgan felt a nagging in her soul. Meek was

Messiah all over again. He would be interested until he wasn't, only this time she had Messari and Yara to think about.

"I told you a long time ago, no woman has ever asked me to do more. If that's what you want, that's what I'll give, Mo. But do you want it? Do you want it with me? You say yes, and I'll handle the rest. You don't even got to pack your shit. We'll grab the twins and break out. New nigga, new life, new throne, but you got to want that shit."

Morgan couldn't think. She was overwhelmed. Meek would be her undoing. She had finally gotten to a stable place in her life. It had taken her years to piece herself back together. To learn to hide the emptiness she felt after losing Messiah. She had convinced herself that it didn't matter if she were happy as long as she looked happy. Walking and talking the part was enough, but Meek was making her forget all that she'd rehearsed. He was chipping away at the picture frame full of lies that she called her life.

"Is that what you want?" she asked, confusion plaguing her. "You say it like it's so easy. Like our common denominator isn't Messiah and like this isn't wrong. You want me? Since when?"

"Since for-fucking-ever, Morgan," he admitted.

The answer snatched the logic from her mind because it made no sense. She had been in his space too many times to count. How hadn't she picked up on his attraction? Then her mind flashed to the night in the club ... the night she had pulled him onstage ... then the night he had defended her when she was pregnant. She had thought he had done so out of respect for Messiah, but he had done so out of disrespect for Messiah ... out of something deeper, an emotion that he had harbored for her. He had danced with her just to make her smile. Murder Meek had allowed himself to soften for her ... for no one, but her.

"He trusted you," Morgan uttered. "You were his best friend."

"And you were his girl, but before you were his girl, you were *the* girl that every nigga in the hood wanted. You were the one niggas used to try to get in position for just so he could have his paper right when he came at you. You thought niggas didn't speak to you because you couldn't hear. Nah, niggas couldn't speak because they weren't ready. I wasn't ready. I needed to boss up a little, but it's always been you."

Morgan was speechless. Messiah and Meek had put her on pedestals before she even knew her own worth. She was still working on that part, but Meek was standing in front of her professing her greatness without thinking twice. If he could only see her broken parts, he would know she was damaged goods.

Meek nodded and rubbed a hand down his face before pinching the bridge of his nose.

"Meek . . . ," she whispered. There was consolation in her tone, sadness, perplexity. She didn't even know how they had found themselves in this position. She couldn't have him. It didn't stop her from wanting him, because—like it or not—he filled a void in her, a void a similar man had left behind. It would be easy to slide Meek into that spot, to let him try to repair the devastation that occupied that place, but Morgan's conscience was working in overdrive. Her mind was spinning, tossing around the reasons why she couldn't allow this to go further.

"I know," he said. He placed both hands on her face, cupping it in his palms, his thumbs caressing her cheeks softly. "I know," he repeated. "I'ma break out."

Morgan lifted her hands, catching his wrists so he wouldn't withdraw just yet. She closed her eyes, enjoying the flutters inside of her because she knew once he walked out the door, they would fly out with him.

"Take care of yourself, Mo," he said. "Lock the door behind me."

It felt like a punch to the gut when he walked out. The remnants of his cologne lingered, and Morgan drowned in it. She bowed her head and placed a hand to the wall to steady herself.

"You can't have him," she whispered to herself. She flicked the bolt on the door and slid down until her butt touched the floor. Morgan was in trouble. She was with one man, yearning for another, all to try to fill the hole Messiah had dug in her soul. The damage he had left behind was irreparable. She would never be okay.

12

"I can't believe you proposed," Aria whispered as she lay on Isa's chest. The smoke from the blunt he pinched between his fingers clouded the air. He brought it to her lips, and Aria hit a toke, holding in the smoke before lifting her neck and pushing out of pursed lips.

"Shit, is it too late to take that shit back? I was high than a mu'fucka," he said. Aria punched him, and Isa snickered. "I'm just fucking with you, Ali."

"So, you know you've got to meet my family now, right?" Aria said.

"I ain't marrying them, I'm marrying you. A nigga need permission for that?" he asked, lifting a brow and looking down at her. Aria stared up at him as he put the blunt to her lips once more. Inhale. Exhale. High. Her mind was floating.

"Not permission. I'm going to do what I want to do regardless, but an introduction is necessary. My brother will want to meet you," Aria stated.

"Your brother?" Isa asked.

"Nahvid," she said. "My half brother. He's my whole world.

He's kinda like a father to me because I never met ours. He got locked up when I was a baby. So Nahvid basically raised me. Everything I know, everything I am, he put in me. Crazy, right?"

"Not crazy, Ali. That's everyday life in the hood. What about your mom?" Isa asked.

"She moved to Atlanta when I came to Michigan for college. She owns a salon down there. Nah bought it for her," Aria explained. "What about your family? Your mom? Do you have sisters? Brothers? How are we getting married and we don't know anything about one another?"

"Cuz I ain't interested in nobody but you. I don't give a damn about none of that shit. As long as you're here, Ali, I'm gucci," he said. He lifted her chin, and Aria climbed on top of him. She removed the weed from his hand and put it out in the ashtray on the nightstand. Then she went lower, kissing him so deeply she pulled a groan from his soul.

"You been playing it real safe with me. I want you, Isa." She reached down, rubbing, groping, grabbing what felt like a blessing just from size alone. "I'm ready," she whispered between kisses. She could feel him rise beneath her. She knew he wanted it too.

He placed hands on her hips and lifted her off him before climbing out the bed.

"Don't you got class and shit? Ain't you gon' be late?" he asked.

"Graduation is three weeks away. Whatever I haven't done by now isn't getting done." She chuckled.

"And what about rehearsal? You skipping that too? Don't you got to perform tonight?" he asked.

She frowned and came up on her knees. "What are you, nigga? Alexa?" she questioned. "You got my whole day planned out in your head. I'm trying to throw you some pussy, and you throwing it back. Am I bad at it or something?" A bit of insecurity crept into her. He had a reputation for being with women, more than one, often all at the same time. He wasn't accustomed to mediocre sex, and Aria tensed. She was so new at it, she wondered how she compared. "You didn't like it?" she asked.

He approached the bed, picking her up, forcing her legs around his waist. "Hell yeah. I love that shit. You got pure dope between these thighs, Ali," he whispered. "I'm just trying to be different with you. I ain't no gentleman. I like to fuck. I like to dominate women in bed, and you're not ready for all'at. I don't want to hurt you, Ali, so I'm going slow. Trying to develop some manners."

She smirked because she constantly told him that he lacked them. He was trying. He was making an effort to be what she liked. "Ain't no rush. I got it for forever, so I'ma break it in slow like a new pair of Guccis or something. Stretch it out a little bit before I go beast on you. I'm your man, I got to act like your man. You don't need to be skipping class. You didn't do it before, so don't start now. I ain't the nigga that's gon' let you fall off. Go to class, go to rehearsal, and I'll do backflips in that shit later. A'ight?"

He placed her on her feet and then lifted her under her armpits like she were a child. He brought her to his lips. She was so short that it had become a habit of his . . . one that she liked.

"Will I see you tonight?" she asked.

"Yeah, I'ma pull up," he assured.

He set her down, and Aria reluctantly put on her clothes. "I guess I should go. I have no clothes here. I need to stop by my place first," she said.

"You'll have a closetful by the time you get back," he assured. "Send me your sizes."

"Okay," she said. She hurried into yesterday's outfit and then cupped his chin in one hand, planting a sensual kiss on his lips. His dick against her stomach, then a hand to her ass, pulling her into him as she groaned.

"I hate you, boy," she whispered.

"I hate you like a mu'fucka," he responded. She turned, and he slapped her ass. Aggressive. In need.

"Quit playing if you ain't gon' do nothing with it," Aria said before rushing out the door. "I'm going to be late," she said to herself as she hopped in her car and pulled away from Isa's house. She had been in a bubble with him for two days. Since the day he had proposed, they hadn't left the house. Nothing else had existed. Not even Ahmeek and Morgan could interrupt their bliss. She barely wanted to leave, but Isa was right. She couldn't let him throw her off from everything she had worked hard for. She promised herself she wouldn't get lost in his world. She couldn't lose herself trying to find love. She refused to. Aria was halfway up the highway when her phone rang.

She smiled as Isa's face popped up on her screen. She answered on Bluetooth. "Hey."

"I thought you forgot about me. I've been blowing you up all weekend."

Aria frowned when the sound of a female's voice drifted through her speakers. She picked up her phone, double-checking to make sure it was Isa who had called.

"You here now, ain't you? You came to complain, or you gon' do something useful with that mouth?"

Aria's brows lifted, and her heart sank. Isa's rude-ass voice filled her car, and her stomach hollowed.

Aria was so silent she could barely breathe. She gripped the steering wheel in angst.

"Hmm, I missed you, boy," the girl moaned.

"Daddy missed you too," Isa groaned. "Shit, baby, suck that shit."

Aria didn't even look first before she crossed over two lanes to catch the upcoming exit.

She wanted to hang up the phone, but she couldn't. She had to hear every single second of Isa's exploits. She wanted to know every detail so she could remember never to fuck with him again. She felt like she would throw up, and her eyes prickled. *Lying-ass nigga. Such a fucking liar. Why would you trust him? You know how he is!* She scolded herself the entire way, trying to put some courage in her spine, trying to fill the hole that was digging through her body along the way. She was shaking, she was so angry. Her feelings had never been so hurt. When she pulled up to his house, she parked directly behind the Chevy Malibu that sat in the driveway. Whoever was in the house wasn't leaving until Aria allowed her to.

Aria hopped out the car and tried the front door. It was locked. She picked up her phone and dialed Isa's number. When he sent her to voice mail, Aria saw red. She lifted one Chanel sneaker to his front door and kicked.

Boom! Boom! Boom! Boom! Boom!

She knew his temper would cause him to open the door without looking because she had come knocking like the police. He was so predictable. The door flung open, and a shirtless Isa stood in front of her. Sweatpants hung low around his waist, so low that she could see wiry hair peeking up from his waistline. Evidence that he had thrown them on without drawers, proof that he had been naked before she knocked and had only put the pants on in haste to answer. The look of irritation on his face disappeared as soon as he saw her face. A girl stood behind him in her panties and bra.

The shit don't even match. Aria scoffed and shook her head in disgust. *Fucking arrogant-ass nigga.*

"I'm a fool," she said. She had come with the intentions of wreaking havoc, but seeing him there with this random girl deflated her. He had bigged her up, made her feel like they shared something, convinced her that she was different just to treat her the same. His guilty eyes rang in alarm.

"Ali, let me talk to you for a minute," he said.

She shook her head and took a step away from him. Her legs barely held up. Devastation made her weak . . . so much regret filled her because she had known all along that he would do this . . . why she had convinced herself that Isa could be good to her . . . that he'd meant it when he said he loved her . . . she didn't know.

"No. I'm good. What's understood needs no explanation," she answered. Her voice trembled, and she hated it. She hated that she was hurt. She hated that he knew she was hurt. She had known better. She knew how Isa operated, and she had trusted him anyway. She had given him her body, and he had taken it knowing what it meant to her. "You and I . . ."

She couldn't even finish her sentence. She just shook her head in disgrace as she headed back to her car.

"Yo, Aria!" he shouted as he followed, frantic and desperate because she was walking away like she wouldn't come back.

She didn't stop. She made it all the way to her car. She opened the car door, and he closed it. She opened it again; Isa closed it. Aria's eyes were welling with tears, and he wrapped a hand around her waist, planting his lips in her hair. Aria refused to face him, but the kiss sent a quiver down her spine.

"Look at me, Ali. Don't leave me, baby," he whispered.

He was a world-class actor, motherfucking Denzel, because the sincerity in his tone made her half believe that he wanted her here. Her body was rigid.

"Let me go, Isa," she said. "Go back to your main. That's what she is, right? That's her?"

His silence was all the admission she needed. Isa turned her around, and her chocolate face was filled with an emotion he couldn't identify. Disgust. Disappointment. He had spent an entire weekend staring into her eyes. They had been hopeful. Happy. Now they were dark. Now they were injured, and he was to blame. If she had come to his door with this very expression, he would have been ready to push it to a nigga for making her so sad. He was to blame, however. No one else but him. He had hurt her.

"I'm sorry, Ali," he whispered.

Aria didn't say anything to him. She looked past his shoulder, steadying her gaze on the house behind him, trying to maintain control of her tears. She made him wait, her silence making him uncomfortable, making him nervous. Finally, she asked, "Who is she?"

"She's nobody," he said.

Aria was silent. Her mouth pinched tight in disdain, her hands crossed over her chest, and her eyes on the house with the red chipped paint.

"Ali—"

"That's not my name," she said, her tone flat and unforgiving. Aria wasn't the girl to give a million chances. You either got it wrong or right on the first try.

"That's your name, baby," he whispered, placing hands on her hips. "I named you, Ali. What else I'm gon' call you?"

"Nothing at all. You won't need to call me anything, because we won't be talking. You won't be seeing me. I'm good on all this. I'm done," she said. Her lip quivered, and she pulled it into her mouth. She was angry at herself for even caring, for giving him this power over her emotions.

His brow dipped. "Fuck that supposed to mean?" he asked. "You're wearing my ring, Ali. That means you're staying. Through whatever. I thought you was riding for a nigga."

Aria's brow lifted. "Wrong girl. I'm not riding for you. I'm not dying for you. I'm not ignoring cheating and lying and disloyalty." She pointed to his house where the girl in the mismatched panties and bra was standing, peering nosily out the door. She looked like she wanted to say something, and Aria hoped the bitch made one peep, just so she could have a reason to knock her head off. "And the disre-fucking-spect," Aria finished. "For what? Ride or die for what, Isa? Just to say that I belong to a nigga that don't belong to me? You were on your knees proposing days ago, and you're already in there fucking the next bitch. It hasn't even been a week since we got engaged and you're already on some bullshit! Did you even change the sheets after I left? I came all over those sheets hours ago, and you slid the next bitch in my spot without thinking twice!" she shouted.

Isa rubbed the top of his head and blew out a deep breath. "I'll make her leave, Ali. She's fucking nobody. Just a little bitch from around the way. If I'm choosing, I'm choosing you," he said.

Aria shook her head. "If only it was yours to decide," she said. "You're lucky I didn't beat the brakes off that bitch." She pushed by Isa and opened her car door.

"Ali . . . ," Isa said.

"That would mean I saw something worth fighting for, and I don't. Whatever I thought this was, it isn't. I made a mistake with you. Lose my number, Isa. You butt-dialed me, by the way. Might want to lock that phone, playa."

"Aria!" he shouted.

Aria got in the car and drove away, leaving him standing in the middle of the street, speechless.

She didn't allow herself to break down. Her chin quivered, but she clenched her teeth, driving through tears so heavy she could barely see. She refused to let even one fall.

Fuck him, she thought. She had a performance to get ready

for, and nobody stopped her art. She was a hardened girl, but the stage was the only place she allowed herself to be vulnerable. Dancing allowed her to cry, it allowed her to weep for every little fucked-up thing that had ever happened to her. Ever since she was a child, music had helped her purge pain from her soul, and now Isa had added more that she needed to get out.

Aria lifted one stiletto boot to the chair and leaned over to roll the leather up over her leg, then past her knee until it stopped at her thigh.

"Bitch, you trying to kill shit tonight, huh?" Mo asked.

Aria stood and pushed her titties up and licked her lips before flipping her long ponytail over her shoulder. It sat on top of her head and was so long it kissed her ass as it swung behind her. Her makeup was flawless. All black everything. It was lights out for these niggas tonight because Aria was back on the market.

"I got to bag something new," she said, and she smudged her lipstick, then finessed her baby hair before squinting. "I see you on your Aaliyah vibe."

"I'm on my Morgan shit," Morgan replied, smirking.

"Bitch, that's vintage baby girl. Give credit where it's due. Aaliyah was the queen, but you making it work though baby mama," White Boy Nick added. "I mean, you could show a little more skin, though. What's the point of having all that ass if you ain't gon' show it?"

"Look, y'all lucky I'm even here. I haven't been onstage in two years."

"This ain't a stage. This is practice. This little club is nothing. Relax. Just pretend its rehearsal. It'll warm you up for Vegas," Aria said.

"I never agreed to Vegas. This is a onetime thing. I'm just filling in," Mo protested. "Bash doesn't even know I'm here."

"And? He ain't your parole officer, Mo!" Aria shouted. "Just do what you do. You know you miss it."

"Let's go, hoes, it's time to stroll!" Nick yelled, interrupting their petty argument.

Aria was focused as she walked out onto the stage.

"*Detroit,* what up, *doe?*" she shouted in the microphone. The crowd turned up instantly. Aria was a whole damn mood. "Can I get some love? I'm trying to put something on y'all real quick. I'm looking for the realest in the city. Where he at? Nigga got to be heavy, though, cuz I don't do nothing light. Y'all gon' show Stiletto Gang some love?"

The crowd erupted.

"I got my girl Mo' Money with me tonight! She ain't been on the stage in a minute. Y'all missed her?"

Mo strutted her pretty ass on the stage like she was in a Miss America pageant.

The crowd showed love. They were so loud that Aria's ears rang.

"I'ma let her rock this shit first," Aria said. "Mo, get your pretty ass out here. DJ, drop something for her."

I want a slim, fine woman with some twerk with her

Morgan rode that beat like the music had infected her soul. She didn't even care that she couldn't breathe. Every inch of her body moved. Every move was exaggerated. Her hair stuck to her face as she worked up a sweat. Her nose turned up, and her brow deepened as her lips curled.

Morgan's hands were balled like she was gripping drumsticks and she was in a drum line. On every offbeat, she banged on 'em. The crowd went crazy. Morgan popped pussy like it was her profession. She was so arrogant onstage that not a dancer in sight could keep up. Aria came close, but Morgan's ears, her interpretation of music, made her incomparable.

Do it, baby, stick it, baby, move it, baby, lick it, baby
Suck up on that clit until that pussy get a hickey, baby

Morgan didn't half step. Those dainty hands went to the front of her womanhood, and she moved them in a circle right over her clit. Then locked her fingertips before flicking her hand to the crowd.

"*Bitch!*" Aria screamed, jumping up and down off to the side. She was always Morgan's biggest hype man, and Morgan stopped dancing as she fell into a laugh. She snatched the microphone from Aria.

"DJ, run that back. Y'all want to see her act up now?"

Aria pulled the mic back.

"Okay, okay, we all know Mo Money got it. White Boy Nick, where you at?" Aria shouted.

He came out flamboyant and turned to the crowd twerking.

His fans screamed and egged him on. Morgan had just been the introduction. The warm-up. It was game time. The trio was about to tear the roof off this club.

Aria paused when she saw the crowd begin to part. Isa and Ahmeek made their way through the club. Aria was so livid it was like they were moving in slow motion. She heard her heart beating in her ears, and her stomach hollowed. Ahmeek bit his lip and dapped up someone he knew on the way to VIP, hitting Morgan with a two-finger salute of acknowledgment. Isa trailed him, chewing on gum, and taking pause to laugh with another man along the way, showing love, shaking hands, before making way to an empty booth. Two fine-ass niggas had just elevated the temperature in the room. Their status was unspoken. Kings. Plain and simple. The crew had entered the building.

What is he doing here?

She turned eyes to Mo, then rolled them back to the crowd. She didn't miss the shooters the duo put on the door. Isa and Ahmeek walked directly into VIP. A group of men were already seated at the booth they chose, and they dapped up apparent friends before getting comfortable.

"If you see something you like, show me. I'm choosing tonight. Let's go!" she shouted. She placed the microphone on the DJ booth and bopped to the beat as it dropped. She was center stage. Mo stood to her right, a step back, Nick rounded out her right. Aria turned on like a light. A quick sixteen steps made the crowd buck. The City Girls track set the tone. It was twerk time. Aria held no prisoners as she turned and rotated her ass like a DJ rotated a track. Her ass didn't miss one 808. Normally, Morgan ate the stage. Her twerk sessions were legendary, but tonight, Aria had a point to prove.

Itty bitty pretty, I'm the realest in the city

Aria butterflied her pretty chocolate thighs so hard that they quaked. She was throwing all 140 pounds of her body all over the place as her hands hit her knees and she popped her body. She was so angry that her temper flowed out into her choreography. She lifted her hands, bit her tongue, and moved that thang like her life depended on it. She could see Isa's frown through the crowd. He sat there, surrounded by groupies. They were coming and going, flocking like birds, but his eyes never left the stage. By the time the set ended, he was on his feet, gripping the railing to the loft area and hawking her every move.

"What type of shit you on tonight? Where that come from?" White Boy Nick asked. "You started getting dick and you a whole new bitch!"

Morgan snickered as Aria laughed. The crowd gave it up, and even though the set was over, Aria bounced into the crowd. She pulled Morgan and Nick to the dance floor, grabbing a bottle of Moët out of the bucket of a random table on the way. Aria tipped the bottle to her lips as she freaked it.

I do, what I like I do, I do.

Aria was in a zone as SZA sang her life. She did whatever she wanted to do when she wanted to do it. Isa was about to learn an important lesson about her. She refused to stress over one man when she had her pick. She turned and saw a girl hanging all over Isa. Aria's temper flared. *He got me fucked up.*

"Let's grab a booth!" she shouted to Mo and Nick over the loud music. She made her way to VIP and took the booth that the owner kept reserved for them. Three bottles were already on ice. They were close enough to the crew to witness the fanfare, but not close enough to take part.

The DJ mixed in the smooth sounds of Jhené Aiko, and Mo grabbed a bottle of champagne from the bucket.

Baby, while we're young

She stood on the cushions of the booth and lifted the bottle to her lips, then into the air as she snapped fingers on one hand while gripping the bottle with the other. Her body floated softly, swaying side to side to the melody. Her eyes closed, and her brow pinched, because she felt this shit. Every word, every pretty note. Nick stood in front of her, and Morgan wrapped her arms around his neck, laughing as she sang the words to him and he sang back. She pointed at him, opening her palms and exaggerating each movement.

Telling everybody you're mine and I like it
And I really hope you don't mind, I can't fight it

The lyrics reminded her of Ahmeek. She hated to admit it, but he had infiltrated her brain. She tried to fight it, but her thoughts drifted back to the zoo. The memory they had made. An absolutely flawless day.

Yes, Jhené was singing the desires of her heart, desires she was having a hard time coming to terms with. Ones she still wanted to deny because it felt so wrong. It was against the rules, and Morgan was naturally obedient. She was terrified of the feelings that were attached to that day. They were so inappropriate, but still she kept them locked away inside a chest inside her heart.

I'll go everywhere you go

Aria joined her on the cushions and wrapped her arms around Mo's shoulders as they grooved. They were the sexiest duo to bless the club. They always sold sex. Always exuded confidence. Cookies and cream. Aria's coffee-tinted skin against Morgan's fairer complexion was beautiful, and the way they danced—eyes closed, hands roaming, completely comfortable with each other—was like a spell. They were lethal together. Men wished they possessed the confidence to even approach them. Ahmeek glanced her way, and the girl vying for his attention became invisible. He didn't stare. Smooth-ass Ahmeek didn't play his hand that way. Morgan would have never even known his eyes had graced her if she didn't feel it. His eyes on her was like stepping into the sun. Her entire body warmed. It was a millisecond of his attention, and it felt like a lifetime. He turned his eyes back to the woman in front of him. He and Isa were stars wherever they went, and tonight was no different. Isa sat across from Ahmeek, a pretty, round brown straddled him, whispering in his ear. The smirk that broke out over his face made Aria's brows lift in disbelief.

"I swear this nigga is trying me," Aria said.

"Fuck him, Aria. We're young, we're fly, we're popping. These people came out to show us love. This is our scene. Isa want to play, let's play," Morgan said with a wink. She grabbed Aria's hand and held it up. Without hesitation, Aria freaked the beat, grinding on Morgan. If anyone hadn't been watching before, they for sure had eyes on them now. Aria and Morgan were an entire vibe. Aria and Mo left no space between them, dancing so close that their lips almost touched. A show. A damned good one. Rated R, no kids allowed.

"Stiletto Gang putting on a show in VIP!" the DJ shouted.

Their two-step was effortless, and Mo turned the bottle up to her lips once more, closing her eyes. When she looked down, she had Ahmeek's full attention. Morgan and that tongue, she ran it across her bottom lip, then bit it before flipping Aria's hair over her shoulder and planting a kiss on the back of her neck. She could have sworn she saw him blush. He was amused but tore his eyes away from her, shaking his head while trying his hardest to contain the smile on his face. She loved that smile. That smile made her river rage. She wondered if he could handle her rapids. Inappropriate. Her thoughts about Ahmeek Harris were just inappropriate.

The tempo of the music changed, and Morgan knew the wrong song had come on. She didn't even recognize it. It was so old that she couldn't identify it, but when the energy in the club transformed into aggression, she knew it was an anthem. Aria threw up balled fists and bounced to the beat like she was ready to fight.

> *Knuck if you buck*
> *Knuck if you buck*

Aria had a bottle of her own now, rocking to the beat. They had transformed from vixens to thugs with just the change of a beat. When she set her eyes on Isa and saw the *same* girl was still in his lap, the fire in her chest intensified. The girl ran a tongue down the tattoo on Isa's neck, and Aria saw red. "Oh, he got me so fucked up," she said, climbing down off the couch.

"Aria!"

Aria heard Morgan behind her, but she was already making her way across VIP. Her heart thundered when she saw his tattooed hands travel up the skirt of the girl before him. She couldn't get to him fast enough. Before she could even stop herself . . .

"Bitch!"

Aria threw the glass bottle like she was on third base and she was trying to take a nigga out. Aria was on Isa's groupie before she even knew what was going on. Aria didn't care if the girl was clueless. Isa knew better. If he didn't, he was about to learn.

"You hoes gon' learn one way or a-fucking-nother!" she shouted as she snuffed Isa's groupie, holding the girl down by her hair as she threw vicious blows. Aria may have been little, but she was a fucking bully. Nothing about her was nice. When her heart was on the line, she came to punish. This wasn't even about this girl. It was about Isa. It was about the way he had shattered her feelings mere hours before. Aria felt something wet on her hands, and when she pulled back her balled fist, she saw blood. Every stiletto nail on her hand was broken. She didn't care if the blood belonged to her or not; it didn't stop her. She kept swinging, cocking that fist back as far as she could before connecting.

"Bitch! I'm. Not. Playing. Games. Behind. This. Nigga!" Every word came with a blow to the face. The girl couldn't shake Aria loose because all twenty inches of her weave was wrapped around Aria's fist.

Mo was right behind her with the assist. She didn't have a choice. They were one band, one sound-ass bitches. Aria had started it; Mo had to finish. Ahmeek moved to intervene, but Mo snatched out of his grasp.

"Bitch!" Her blows came next as she caught one of the girl's friends before she could sneak Aria. It was melee in VIP, but Mo had hands. She hadn't thrown them in years, but it was like riding a bike. She wasn't even sure why they were fighting, but it didn't matter. She didn't need a reason to act a fool over Aria. She was like a sister to Morgan. Even when Aria was wrong, Morgan was riding.

Whop! Whop!

Aria felt security grab her, but she wouldn't let go of the girl's hair. She yanked it so hard that it tore from her scalp. Aria was the tiniest thing in the fight, but she was roughhousing bitches, flinging the girl by her hair as if she were a rag doll. The security guard snatched her, but before he could even detain her, she heard Isa's baritone interrupt the confusion as he hemmed the security guard against the wall.

"One fucking finger on her and I'ma cut your lights off, my nigga," he said, putting his burner under the man's chin.

"That's you, Isa? I ain't know, G! No disrespect, fam! I just need them to bring it down. I'm just doing my job. Please, G.

Just get them out of here before the police come shut it down. No disrespect. It's love, god. It's all love. I didn't know she belonged to you."

"Nah, I ain't his. I ain't his at all," Aria said, heaving as she pushed past Isa. He reached for her, but she pulled away, snatching her arm as she headed for the exit.

Ahmeek had Morgan trapped against the wall, arms extended around her to stop her. White Boy Nick stood on the cushions of the booth, swinging the wig he had snatched during the fight.

"I'ma need you to calm down," Ahmeek said.

Morgan nodded, but she wasn't focused on Ahmeek. Her temper was heightened, and her adrenaline fueled her. She was hardheaded, and she was in a mood. A beat-a-bitch-ass mood. She was too busy chastising the opps to follow directions. What was an ass whooping without the lesson? Pointing her finger, identifying her target.

"That's what happens when you're disrespectful, *hoe!*" Morgan barked. "You and your homegirl out here acting like mutts, sis, so I took that ass for a walk!" Morgan lunged for the girl, but Ahmeek's hold on her was too tight. Morgan picked up a glass ashtray, tossing it across VIP. "Fetch, hoe! I hear you barking—where that bite at, though? I'm 'bout that action!"

"Meek, get your bitch!" the girl shouted.

"Don't say his name, hoe! Niggas like this don't choose you! He's never choosing you! Say his name again and watch I snatch your tongue out!"

Ahmeek scooped Morgan, carrying her over his shoulder as she talked cash shit all the way out the club.

When they emerged, Aria was mid-swing.

"Yo, I promise you got one more time before I fuck you up," Isa warned.

"Nigga, I wish you would. On my mama, I will ruin your entire life with one phone call!" Aria shouted. She jabbed his ass again.

"Aria!" Morgan shouted as she stood on the sidelines.

"Mind your fucking business, Mo. I got her crazy ass," Isa said as he sat sideways on the seat of his bike, folding his arms across his chest.

"I trusted your dog ass," she said. "I knew better, but I went against my better judgment because you told me I could. You told me I was safe with you!"

Aria was a wreck. She had kept her cool all day, but she was just like a teapot, boiling, steam building, and after seeing the attention he got when he walked into the club tonight, the whistle was erupting. She couldn't hold this inside if she wanted to.

"You're bleeding, Ali, com'ere," he said, wiping one calm hand down his wavy head.

"Don't do that. Don't sit there calm and cool like I'm tripping on you. Don't act like you care. Fuck my hands; my heart is bleeding, nigga. You are tearing me apart!" she cried.

"Sex ain't love, Ali. These bitches don't mean shit. I like pussy. I get pussy. I like to carry bitches a certain way. I don't want to carry you like that, so I called one up. Shit didn't mean nothing," Isa stated.

Aria was livid. She marched over to Isa. "Shit means everything!" She lifted her foot and kicked over his bike, sending Isa stumbling. The expensive machine collided with the pavement, and Isa barely recovered, narrowly hitting the ground before regaining his cool.

"Yooo," Ahmeek said, swiping both hands down the top of his head while amusement lived in his eyes. Morgan snickered, covering her mouth with one hand in shock.

Isa and Aria were in the parking lot making a whole scene. Lights. Camera. Action, nigga. Aria was the leading actress. A shit show. Aria was causing a shit show.

He was on her ass like white on rice as she stormed off. He pulled her arm, spinning her, and before she knew it, one hand was wrapped around her neck. His hands were so big that one hand had the power to squeeze the life out of her, but Aria was fearless. The fire in her eyes dared him.

"You want me to fuck you? Is that it, Ali? You out here showing your ass because you want some dick? You want me to fucking beast on you like I do random hoes?" Isa barked the words as fire danced in his eyes. Meek and Mo stood among the crowd of gawkers.

"Should we stop this?" Mo asked.

Ahmeek shook his head. "Ain't no stopping this. Both these mu'fuckas got it real bad, and they don't even know it."

"I want you to love me!" Aria shouted back. She pushed him but did no damage. He barely flinched.

"I do love your little ass!"

She recoiled like the words surprised her. He had never said it. Not straight out. It was always disguised in something else. Always masked behind another phrase that didn't allow him to give her power. A way that didn't make him vulnerable. He had just shouted it out for the world. He wrapped his hands around her face and pressed his body to hers. He was on fire. This display of aggression made his blood race. Aria could feel it, his need, pressing into her as he reached around her body and pulled her into him. Her entire essence dripped for him. She was wet. Mad as hell and soaking wet. Isa sent her emotions on a roller coaster. She wanted to kill him and fuck him all at the same time.

"I just don't want to hurt you, Ali," he whispered. Forehead to hers, he closed his eyes. "The shit I want to do to you . . .

I can't, so I keep one around. She don't mean shit, she can just take it."

"Take what?" Aria asked, confused, squinting, tears forming.

"Pain," he answered simply.

His words shocked her. He looked ashamed, like he was revealing something to her that he hadn't told anyone else.

"If pain is what you like to give women, mission accomplished, Isa. I feel it," she whispered. It broke him when he saw the tear escape from her eye. Only one, but it was enough to let him know he had fucked up. She walked away, and Morgan hurried to her side.

"I need to handle something, Mo. Can you get a ride home?" Aria asked. Her lip quivered. She was barely keeping it together.

"Aria, you don't have to be alone. I'll come. I'll cry with you. We can talk shit about that nigga until you're blue in the face. You don't have to pretend like it doesn't hurt. I'm here," Mo whispered.

"Nah, Mo. That's you. That's not me. A nigga give me hurt, I give it back to his ass. Isa gon' feel me. Can you get a way home?" Aria asked.

Morgan nodded. "Yeah, I'm fine, but, Aria—"

"I'll call you tomorrow, Mo," Aria insisted before climbing into her car and speeding off.

Morgan looked back to the crowd that had lost interest and was dispersing to their vehicles. She noticed White Boy Nick's Audi was still parked, and she crossed the parking lot to see if she could catch him before he left. Ahmeek and Isa stood among a crowd of men; they chopped it up as if the night's events had never happened.

Ahmeek grabbed her fingertips as she passed.

"You good?" he asked.

"I'm fine. I just need a ride," she answered.

"I ain't going back to Flint. I've got business down here, but if you don't mind staying until I'm done, I can run you back afterward," Ahmeek stated.

"I just need to text Alani. Check on the twins," she answered.

Morgan sent a quick text to Alani. It was never a problem. She didn't anticipate one now. She received a response immediately. Ethic and Alani practically wanted the twins with them 24-7, so she was free for the rest of the evening.

"They good?" Ahmeek asked.

She nodded.

He turned to the group of men. "I'm up," he said.

"A'ight, G," Isa replied. They slapped hands, and as Isa hugged Morgan, she poked his chest.

"Fix what you broke, Isa. Like tonight. Don't fuck her over," Morgan warned.

"I hear you, Mo," Isa stated.

Ahmeek led the way to his car.

"Really, Meek? So we not kicking it no more?"

Morgan paused mid-step when she heard the girl call for him. He turned, and his eyes landed on Morgan first before lifting to the pretty redbone with the fat ass that stood yards away.

"I can get another way home, Ahmeek. It's fine," Morgan said, scoffing. She turned, and before she could take one step, his finger was hooked inside her belt loops and he was pulling her back. He pushed her against the passenger door and placed his hands around her, wrapping her in his arms. A temporary box that trapped her. Morgan rolled her eyes.

"You want to find another way home?" he asked.

"Looks like your *business* is pressing," she said.

"That's not important," he answered.

Morgan peered over his shoulder at the girl who was hawking them. "Looks important to me. So let me make sure I got this right. You were going to take me somewhere, drop me off, leave, go handle *her,* then come back and take me home?"

"You got it all figured out, Mo," he stated, a bit perturbed. He had never taken as much back talk as he took from Morgan Atkins.

She folded her arms. "I swear you niggas are a piece of work."

"Don't do that. Don't lump me in with whoever you're comparing me to in your mind."

"All three of y'all! Whole damn crew. That's who I'm comparing you to. The way you just run through women. Make promises, break hearts . . . lie . . ." Morgan shook her head.

"Yeah, you've got me all summed up, Mo."

She didn't miss his sarcasm. "Dismiss her, Ahmeek," Morgan stated. Plain and simple. She wasn't asking, and she was losing patience.

Ahmeek's eyes burned into hers. Morgan lifted a brow. She knew she had no right. It still didn't stop her from asserting her position.

"Yo, Livi!" he shouted.

Oh, so that's Livi? Morgan thought.

He turned his head to the girl, and Morgan grabbed his chin and turned it back to her.

"You're canceled, sweetheart!" he shouted while staring in Morgan's eyes. He licked his lips and then brought them to Morgan's ear. "Get your spoiled ass in the car."

He pulled open the door, and she smirked as she got inside.

Ahmeek walked around the car and got behind the wheel.

Morgan rolled down her window and gave a cute wave to Ms. Livi as Ahmeek drove out of the parking lot.

"You ain't shit." He smirked, chuckling as he hit I-75, headed for downtown Detroit.

"Nah, *you* ain't shit," Morgan countered. "I didn't owe that bitch nothing. You, on the other hand—"

"Owed her nothing," Ahmeek interrupted. He pulled up to a brick building, and a white man opened her door.

"Welcome home, Mr. Harris," the valet greeted.

Ahmeek nodded, and Morgan climbed from the car as she looked up at the building.

"Home?" she asked.

"Just a little low-key spot," he said. "Downtown Detroit is an investment, so I bought a two-bedroom loft."

Ahmeek turned to the man. "Keep it up front. I'm coming right back down."

Morgan turned to him. "You're leaving?"

"I told you. Business," he said as he escorted her inside.

"I thought I just handled that for you," she replied.

"That wasn't business, Mo," he answered.

They stepped into the elevator, and he pressed the letters *PH*. It let out on the top floor, and Morgan walked out into a penthouse apartment. He was being humble by calling it a two-bedroom. The entire top floor of the building was his.

"Wow," she said. Morgan had seen luxury before, but this—coming from him—surprised her. It wasn't the fact that he could afford it, because she knew he was getting money. It was the fact that he had the foresight to purchase it. To invest.

Ahmeek held open the elevator.

"Make yourself comfortable, love," he said. "I might be a while. I'll come back and drive you home as soon as I'm done."

She turned to him. "You're just going to leave me in your crib? I'm nosy, Ahmeek. I'm going through everything."

He smirked. "Be my guest, Mo. You're the only other person who's ever been here. Snoop away."

She smiled as the elevator doors closed and he disappeared.

13

Isa sped down the highway, the winds from the hundred-mile-per-hour speed whipping his jacket as he weaved in and out of traffic, never braking. Aria had his head fucked up.

"If pain is what you like to give women, mission accomplished, Isa. I feel it."

Her words echoed in his mind as his heart pumped. He hated that he had ever laid eyes on Aria. His feelings were convoluted when it came to her. A web of inconsistency. He wanted her for himself. He would kill anyone else who dared look her way, but he wasn't ready to be a one-woman man. He wanted to be, but the idea of that terrified him. Aria played tough, but he knew that he had the potential to hurt her. He already had, and he had been sick for hours at just the notion. His tastes weren't normal, however. Isa had been rough on women since he first discovered them. He ran through them, revolving them, playing with them, picking them up and putting them down at a whim until her. Aria did something to him that he couldn't explain, but he was afraid to relinquish control. He was afraid to show her the sides she couldn't see with the naked eye because she talked big, but she wasn't ready for the shit he liked. His phone rang, the Bluetooth in his helmet going off.

"Answer," he said. "What up?" he greeted.

"We need to talk, Isa."

Aria's voice provided an instant sense of relief. Some of the tension he felt dissipated at just the sound of her voice.

"I want to see you, Ali," he stated.

"Then come see me," she answered. She hung up.

It was that. Her attitude. Her confidence. Like she knew he was on the way just because she had requested his presence. Shit he was. The detour to her place had occurred as soon as the melody of her voice had hit his ears. He had some making up to do. He was at her building within the hour. He would have gotten there sooner, but the stop to his house to shower and switch clothes and hop in his BMW had eaten up a bit of time.

He called her when he was at her door.

"It's open," she said as soon as she answered.

Isa pushed the door open and walked inside.

Candles were lit in the living room, and he pulled off his jacket before locking the door.

"Yo, Ali!" he called out. He noticed the bottle of tequila on the countertop. It was half-empty. "Oh, fuck!"

Isa's brow lifted when he heard her moans coming from the bedroom. He drifted down the hallway and pushed open her bedroom door.

The sight before him both set a blaze in his heart and his loins. His stomach hollowed. He was sick. Aria lay before him on silk sheets, her chocolate legs spread wide as his side bitch, the one she had found him with, devoured her. Aria stared him in the eyes as she fisted the top of the girl's head with one hand and stuck up her middle finger with the other.

He wanted to slap fire from her and fuck her all at the same time.

Imagine us skin to skin, eye to eye
Bodies wet from the sweat, I'm working out with you
Fingertips traveling into places wonderful

The song played slow in the background, and Aria rode the beat, smashing her sex against the girl's face with so much aggression that her mouth fell open in ecstasy.

"You want me to fuck you up," he said. His hand instinctively went to his dick.

"You wanted to fuck her. Me too," Aria groaned. "As a matter of fact, every time I catch you with a bitch, I'm taking her."

Isa's mind was blown. Had she done this before? Was this a onetime thing? The visual of Aria and Mo in the club flashed in his mind. They had done that before. They danced seductively all the time, but he had never thought anything of it. Was it more than a show? Did Aria like women? Prefer them, even? Enjoy them? He knew she could have any man she pleased, but damn if she could have any woman too. His blood coursed, and his dick jumped. It was the sexiest shit he had ever seen, but he couldn't help but be pissed. Man or woman, that pussy was his, and the thought of someone else indulging in her had him thinking about murder.

The girl didn't even stop. It was like Isa wasn't even in the room.

"Sssss," Aria moaned. "Just like fucking that."

Isa crossed the room, stepping out of his jeans and pulling his shirt over his head. He would join now and chastise later.

He placed one knee on the bed.

"No," Aria said, coming up on her elbows. "She's not here for you. Ain't that right?"

The question was for the girl. She lifted her eyes to Aria's, lips still wrapped around Aria's sex as she nodded. "Mmm," the girl moaned.

"Oh my God," Isa groaned. "The *fuck*."

"Niggas don't cheat on me, Isa. It just doesn't happen," she said. Aria couldn't even focus on the lesson she was teaching. Her head fell to the side, and her face scrunched. "Agh!" she cried out.

Isa's heart tensed in anger, in jealousy, in disbelief. His mind was spinning. His stomach was empty, and acid built in his throat.

His eyes burned. *What the fuck?* Aria had him on some bitch shit. On some hurt shit. Why the fuck was she so engaged? Loving this shit. Enjoying this shit. He locked his jaw.

"I don't take pain. You give pain. You hurt me. She's making it feel better," Aria moaned. "God, so much fucking better."

"Yo! Fuck that!" Isa said. He grabbed the girl by her hair and pulled her off Aria.

"Ow! Isa!" the girl shouted as he flung her to the floor. Aria sat up and came up on her knees.

"Get the fuck out!" Aria told him.

"I ain't going no-fucking-where," he countered, pointing a finger in her face. "You on some bullshit right now!"

Aria slapped that finger so hard her hand hurt.

"The same bullshit you were on earlier. You got yours. I'm getting mine," Aria stated. "From every bitch you entertain. That's my bitch now. Your number is already on block in her phone."

Aria was a savage, and Isa's dick was begging him to tame her.

"Ali—"

"That's not my name."

"Ali—"

Aria mushed him and climbed from the bed. "That's not my fucking name!"

She bent down to the girl and helped her from the floor. "Let me handle him, sweetheart. I'll call you, okay?" Aria said, caressing the girl's hair. "And if he calls you . . ."

"Call you and let you know," the girl answered.

Aria kissed her lips. "Good girl," she whispered.

Isa placed both hands on top of his head in dismay.

"Get yo' ass out," he said, charging toward the girl and grabbing her elbow, dragging her toward the door. Aria slipped into her satin kimono and pulled her hair up as she waited patiently for Isa to return. He rushed her, picking her up and forcing her legs around his waist as he put her back to the wall.

He was ready. He was more than ready, and the lines in his forehead told her he was angry.

Aria sneered as she gripped his face with one hand, capturing his chin in the U of her left hand and squeezing hard, making him focus on her.

"I'm not the bitch you play with, Isa," she whispered. The look in her eyes was callous, but her vision was full of tears. "I will kill you. I will gut you, my nigga. Don't fucking play with me. I will leave your heart on the fucking floor."

"You already did, Ali. This shit touched a nigga behind his ribs. You fucking me up, Aria." She knew he was serious because he used her real name. "Fuck I'm supposed to do walking in on some shit like this?" he whispered. "I want to fuck you, baby. I mean I want to fuck the shit out of you, but I want to choke your little ass too. Punish you."

He placed his hands to her neck, and Aria saw fire in his gaze, like he zoned out, like thoughts he couldn't confess had crossed his mind.

"That's what you like," she whispered. "Pain. You said you like pain. That's why you're afraid to touch me. Why you've been going easy?"

He was so close that his shallowed breaths left his lips, and she sucked them in. Her heart raced. Did she want this? Did she want to give permission for something like this? How much pain? How bad would it hurt? Aria had always been up for a challenge.

"Choke me, Isa."

She felt his manhood react, jumping, like an eager animal that was locked behind a cage, waiting to be fed. He was a beast. She was about to feed him.

Aggressive-ass nigga likes to choke women.

The thought both scared and electrified Aria. His hand rested on her chest, then moved up; he traced her collarbone with his finger, then five fingers around her throat. The other hand removed his dick, and before she could gasp at the size of him, he cut off her air.

Aria's mind spun, buzzed, as her body begged her to breathe and he barreled into her fountain, submerging in her, going so deep that Aria's eyes squeezed shut.

He lifted one thumb and suddenly air rushed her brain. She sucked it in.

"Isa, baby!" she whispered.

He carried her to the bed, dick so long and hard it didn't even slip out as he walked across the room. He placed her on her feet and then turned her around, then knocked. Three heavy thuds against the top of her ass made Aria climb onto the bed on all fours. His hand reached around her and wrapped around her neck, then he pulled her back onto him. Aria whimpered. She wasn't experienced enough for this position, so it hurt a bit; an ache filled her as he stroked her deep, kissing her back every time he thrust. His hand tightened, and adrenaline filled her as deep breathing became shallow and shallow became wheezing as he left her with just enough air, just enough space in her throat to not die. It was like riding a roller coaster . . . like being at the highest point of the ride . . . the point that made you question sanity . . . the part that made you ask yourself why you had waited two hours in line just to partake in the near-death experience. It was a thrill, and Aria threw her body back at him because she had never been a punk. There was no bitch in her blood.

"Damn, Ali. Give me that shit!" he gritted as they fucked. Skin to skin, she heard the beat they created, and she danced to it. Her brain tingled from deprivation. She felt high. Her clit was so swollen that she knew one touch would send her river raging. He was squeezing so tight and fucking her so deep. *Beast* was understatement. This nigga was a monster. He was scaring her. Without warning, he wrapped an arm around her body and, still gripping her neck, he picked her up from the bed. He never pulled out as he changed positions, sitting on the bed and her in his lap. Reverse cowgirl. Neck in his hands, he opened his fingers and oxygen flowed. Aria gasped. "Isa!"

"You want me to stop, Ali?" he asked.

"No, go harder," Aria panted. Her hands balanced on his thighs as she bounced on that dick. She did an entire eight count on that thang as he squeezed and lifted his hips, smashing his dick into her with so much aggression she felt like her hips might break. He reached around her body and captured her clit, and Aria collapsed. Her head fell back onto his shoulder, and he released her neck.

"Damn," he groaned. "Ohhhh shit." He squeezed her clit like he was turning on the oven, and she gushed. "Ali, this pussy is the greatest, baby." He pulled out, and she went limp in his arms as she came for the second time. Two for her, one for him. Aria moved to the bed, and they lay face-to-face. He placed one hand to her cheek and moved her hair out of her face.

"I fucked up," he whispered.

She nodded.

"I won't fuck up no more, Ali."

She didn't respond, but she closed the space between them.

"Yo, you took one of my bitches." He snickered.

"That's my bitch now," Aria whispered as she kissed the center of his neck. "You my bitch too."

He snickered. "Yo, that mouth is reckless, Ali."

"I think I need to be punished, Isa," she whispered as she snaked her thigh through his legs and then mounted him. "I need to feel pain, baby. Talking reckless to the god, I think some pain should come with that."

Her voice was dripping in seduction, and his eyes danced with fire. "You don't need nobody else, Isa. I'm not afraid of this." She paused to kiss his lips, and then she reached down to slide him inside her because amazingly, even after orgasm, he was still ready, still able. "I'm not afraid of you. I'll go to fucking war for you. With you, baby, and you let me catch you with another bitch again and I'm going to war against you. You've got me. It's all about me. Not them. I can take this dick, baby, and this mouth is reckless. I'm so disrespectful, so punish me."

•   •   •

> *Baby, don't let me down, got a lot going on right now,*
> *and I need you to hold me.*

The soft voice of Janine oozed throughout the bedroom. Ahmeek came through the door and paused in the threshold. He froze. Morgan lay in his bed, nestled under his Versace duvet like she belonged there. Like she had picked it out herself. She lay on her side, back to the door, one balled fist balancing her head off the pillow because he assumed she didn't want to mess up her hair.

He listened to the lyrics of the song because he knew Mo well enough to know she expressed her mood through music.

He removed his watch and placed it on the dresser along with his keys. Blowing out a deep breath, he shook his head. Morgan in his bed. Even from behind, without even seeing her face yet, the sight jabbed him, hollowing his gut.

He moved through the dark. Only the light that Mo had left on in the bathroom glowed in the room. He peeled out of his jacket, tossing it on the end of the bed. Then he reached down, pulling the cover up over her shoulders. She groaned but didn't open her eyes.

"Sorry. It got late, and I just needed to rest my eyes for a little while," she whispered. Eyes squeezed tight, she yawned. He sat on the edge of the bed.

Ahmeek couldn't even control the hand he used to sweep her hair out of her face. Her eyes opened, and her breath caught in her throat. "I'm rude. I'm intruding. I'm sorry," she whispered as she went to move out of his bed.

"It's fine, Mo. I don't mind," he said, withdrawing his hand.

"What time is it?" she asked.

"Three o'clock," he answered. "You ready? I can drive you to the crib real quick."

"Ahmeek, it's the middle of the night. I'm fine here until morning," she whispered.

"Still lifting semis?" she asked.

"Among other things," he said. His elbows rested on his knees, and he leaned over, head low as his hands swept over his waves.

*Baby, if I open my mouth and let my darkest memories
     come out*

Morgan sat up in his bed, putting her back against the headboard. She could feel his tension. "You want to talk about it?" she asked.

"Not really," he said.

"I'm a really good secret keeper," she pressed.

He glanced back at her, and one side of his mouth lifted into a smirk. He shook his head.

"I could just leave all this shit alone. The street shit. The semis, the drugs . . . I've done good with my money over the years. I've moved real quiet, been real smart. I could leave the rest on the table and get out while I'm free," Ahmeek said.

"Why don't you?" she asked.

"Because Isa's not ready, and we promised each other. We would step into the game together and step out together. We wouldn't leave anybody behind," Ahmeek stated. He grew quiet as his head hung in despair. "We already lost one. If I got out and something happened to bro, I would never be able to live with that. So until he's ready, I'm stuck."

"You're a good friend, Meek," Mo said.

Ahmeek leaned back on the bed. His hands dragged down his face before he focused on the ceiling.

"I'm twenty-seven, Mo. A nigga ready for the next step, but Isa never planned for that, but how old is too old to be doing the same shit? We been running shit for years. Wearing crowns for years. Banging on niggas for years. When is enough, enough?" he asked.

Morgan lifted the covers, and he looked over his head as she climbed across the bed.

"Glad to see you made yourself comfortable," he said, smirking at the fact that she wore one of his shirts.

"I tried to choose something old, but everything had tags on it, so I just chose the ugliest one," she said. He chuckled. Morgan lay beside him, shoulder to shoulder, and then looked up at the ceiling too.

She placed her cheek on his shoulder.

"I like your loft, Meek. It's perfect," she whispered. "Keep planning your exit. Make more investments. Make investments for Isa too, and move smart. Stay out the way. One day, you'll fill this loft with a family, and you'll be able to sleep with both eyes closed. Just be careful so that you make it to see that day."

He rested his head on top of hers and released anxiety in the form of a sigh.

"One day," he said as if pondering the notion in his mind.

Morgan turned into him and lifted one leg over his body as he welcomed her, wrapping an arm around her. Her head rested on his chest.

"You smell like me," he said.

"You have no girl soap," she whispered.

"I don't bring women here," he answered.

"Yet here I am," she countered.

"Here you are," he repeated.

"Who would have thought?" she asked.

"Not a motherfucking soul," he answered.

Morgan nestled closer to him. "I like when you smell like you, love," he whispered. "I'm going to have to get some girl shit up in here." He said it like he planned on bringing her here again.

"Mmm-hmm," she agreed, submitting like she planned on coming here again. Her voice was sleepy. She was tired. "Did you see Isa's face when Aria kicked him off his motorcycle?"

A low rumble erupted from Meek's soul. "Yo, if that nigga had hit the ground . . ."

Morgan and Meek laughed, but she was so tired that she

didn't even open her eyes. She just giggled, half-asleep, half-awake.

"Why doesn't it hurt?" she sighed.

Meek pulled his head back so he could look at her. He frowned. He moved one hand to her chin and lifted her eyes to his. She opened them.

"Why doesn't what hurt?" he asked.

"Your presence," she said.

"It's not supposed to, Mo," he answered. "The day it starts to hurt you, leave it alone, and that's with whatever. Men, friends, whoever. The moment it hurts, you cancel niggas. You hear me?"

She nodded, placing a hand to the side of his face. "I can't breathe around you," she admitted. "I just want to fuck you, Meek. I just want to suck your dick, scream your name, and then roll over in your shirt and go to sleep."

"I swear that mouth is so damn pretty, but it's dirty as fuck, Mo," he said, chuckling.

"You're laughing, but I'm not joking, Ahmeek. I want to wake up and go get my kids and put their cribs in the second bedroom because I don't think you mind having them around."

"They are you, Mo. Why would a nigga mind that?" he whispered. His eyes were closed now too. Hustling was a full-time job, an exhausting shift, especially after a late-night flex at the club. This conversation wouldn't last long. He could barely keep his eyes open. "You making big plans, love."

"Mmm-hmm," she whispered. "I'd make this entire loft my home. I'd get rid of the white furniture because white and babies don't mix, and I'd peel off that hideous fucking wallpaper in the foyer and paint it heather gray. Heather gray with white trim."

They shared another laugh.

"I'm serious. When I'm around you, my heart"—she inhaled a deep breath—"it just aches, but in a good way. It's so exposed. It's almost orgasmic. You make my heart cum, Ahmeek," she whispered. "I don't even know what I was doing before this. Like this feels different. It feels . . ."

"Right," he finished.

Morgan climbed on top of him, mounting him. His shirt rode up her thighs, showing the black boy shorts she wore beneath. She moved her body, grinding slowly as she leaned into his neck.

"Mo, you killing me, love," he groaned.

"I know," she whispered. Her lips to his neck, her tongue to the lobe of his ear. His dick firmed beneath her, and Mo moaned. "God, Ahmeek. This is so wrong, but it feels so good. *You* feel so good." He joined the party when he took a handful of ass.

Baby, if I break down, will you catch my tears before
they hit the ground

He fisted her hair and pulled her inches from his lips. They stared at each other. He was a breath away, eye to eye, as she rolled her hips. This was fucking. Through clothes, Morgan could cum just like this.

"I thought you said no, Mo." Every word came out escorted by a moan.

"Now I'm saying yes," she whispered. Morgan reached down and dipped her finger inside herself before tracing it across his lips.

Ahmeek licked his lips. "Damn."

His eyes scanned every inch of her face, taking his time to process her beauty. Morgan kissed him, and her tongue infiltrated his mouth, bullying, devouring him as she kept riding him. She just wanted the fabric of their clothes to disappear, but she was too afraid to reach for his zipper. Somehow kissing felt acceptable, tasting him, tasting herself on his lips felt okay . . . at least that's what her guilty conscience was screaming. Ahmeek flipped her and laid Morgan on her back, then he took her lips again, but this time his hand slid inside her panties.

"That nigga don't know how to make you nut, do he, Mo?" he asked as he found her clit, thumb pressed to it, and slid three fingers inside her. Morgan tensed, reaching down to grab his hand as her mouth fell open. Before she could close it, his tongue was there, and he kissed her with so much longing that Morgan couldn't breathe.

"Agh!" she cried out as his thumb pressed, then circled right.

"I want to fuck, Mo, but I can't. I just can't, love, but I'ma give you this nut cuz I know that nigga ain't hitting this shit right. Damn, Mo. I just want to bust this shit open," he groaned. "You want me to take care of that for you?"

"Yes!" Morgan shouted. Round and round, in then out, Morgan hadn't been touched like this in a long time. Her clit was so sensitive and swollen that she thought it would burst. Round and round. How were his hands so skilled? In and out. How were his fingers better than dick? He was a mechanic with those hands, screwing the shit out of her body, tuning it up, making it work, fixing what she thought was broken.

"Agh!" she moaned. "Agh!" Spasms. Heavy breathing.

Is that a fucking tear? she thought. She knew it was when she felt his lips meet it. One kiss to her cheek made Morgan's heart explode.

"Mo, you gon' make a nigga go against everything he love. I swear to God, Mo. You got to give a nigga space because shit gon' get ugly. If I hit this shit, it's gon' get real fucking ugly," he whispered in her ear. "Wet ass," he groaned. "So fucking wet, Mo. Pussy don't even get wet like this. Goddamn."

"Oh my God . . . wait . . . stop . . . yes . . . Ahmeeeeek," she moaned. He removed his fingers and flattened his palm against her V and pressed hard, kneading everywhere, her lips, her clit, her pelvis, rubbing all over her, teasing her body so good that she couldn't form a complete thought, let alone speak.

"Ugh!" she groaned as her ass left the mattress, pressing up into his hand, grinding, eyes closed, mouth open. This wasn't even a finger fuck. This was masturbation. He was assisting her self-pleasure because her body didn't even belong to her in this moment. It was his. He touched her like he had been discovering new ways to make her cum for years. How he knew her body better than she knew it herself, she didn't know. Her mind was blown.

"You a good girl, Mo. You don't want shit to get ugly. So just take this nut and let it be, love, because if I fuck you, I'ma love you too, and then you're trapped. Then you're mine, and we both know you ain't mine, love." His words in her ear. His hand on her sex. Morgan gasped, she lost air, her vision went white.

"Ohhh my fucking God. *Ahmeek!*"

She came, and then she covered her face in embarrassment with both hands as her chest quaked and her stomach collapsed.

"Let's see how well you keep that secret, love," he whispered in her ear. She couldn't stop the spasms that took over her body. She felt his lips kiss the side of her head and then felt his body weight rise from the bed.

"Go to sleep, Morgan Atkins."

She didn't lower her hands until she heard the click of the bedroom door as he pulled it shut. Everything was wet. Her eyes, her panties, her soul. He had rained an orgasm over her entire essence, he had stolen a piece of her and warned her to stay away, but Morgan was stubborn. She wanted what she wanted. In this moment, she couldn't foresee the future without him in her life, even if it were only for one purpose ... to make her heart cum.

14

Morgan awoke the next morning to the sound of laughter coming from the living room. She climbed out of bed and walked to the bedroom door, placing her ear close to it. A woman's voice filtered through the wood.

"I don't know who you think you are trying to cancel Sunday breakfast. We've done this every week for years," the voice said. "Whatever little floozy you spent time with last night done kept you up all night, got you canceling on your mama."

"She's not a floozy, Ma," Ahmeek said, chuckling. "And she's still here. She's standing at the bedroom door listening."

Morgan grimaced.

"Come on out, Mo," Ahmeek called.

Morgan's forehead tensed as she pulled open the door and waved in embarrassment. Ahmeek held up the iPad in his hand. "Security cameras, love." He snickered. He winked at her, and Morgan shook her head as a smile broke out on her face.

"Morgan, this is my mother, Marilyn. Ma, this is Morgan Atkins," he said. Morgan pulled at the shirt's hem, wishing she had opted to put on yesterday's clothes, but they were stage clothes—those might have been worse.

Morgan waved politely. "It's very nice to meet you," Morgan said.

Marilyn pulled a carton of eggs from a paper grocery bag. "Nice to meet you," Marilyn answered. She lifted brows of intrigue at Ahmeek as if she were impressed. "Morgan Atkins, huh? You say that like you saying *Queen Elizabeth,* boy. First and last. Like she's important." Marilyn laughed, and Morgan blushed as Ahmeek shook his head.

"Here you go." He chuckled.

"What? I'm just saying. I've never met a girl of yours before. I'm just observing."

"Oh, we're not . . . we're just friends," Morgan said.

"Okay, friend. Are you hungry, baby?" Marilyn asked.

"Yes, ma'am. Starving, actually," Morgan answered.

Marilyn nodded at the seat beside Ahmeek, and Morgan crossed the room. Her bare, pink-painted toes took ten steps before she was at his side. She sat, and he turned her swivel stool toward him, lifting one of her feet into his lap. He rubbed it as he probed her. "You okay?" he asked. She knew what he meant. Last night. Was she okay with what happened last night? She smiled with her eyes, then nodded as she felt her face warm. He was looking at her like she was the sun. Like he had waited up all night just to make sure he didn't miss the sunrise. Marilyn moved around the chef's kitchen a few feet away. Ahmeek leaned into her, hand to her cheek, four fingers behind her neck as he planted a quick kiss to the top of her head.

"I'll take you home after you eat," he said.

"Oh, it's not necessary. I can catch an Uber. Your mom is here. I don't want to interrupt," Morgan stated.

"Never will I fucking ever put Morgan Atkins in an Uber. Did you not hear the threat Ethic gave me? Walk light." Ahmeek smirked. "A nigga like his life." He lifted her foot to his mouth and kissed her big toe. Morgan smiled. The smell of bacon filled the kitchen.

"So tell me, Morgan. How long have you two been . . ." Marilyn paused and smirked at her son. "Friends?"

"A few years now. I've known Ahmeek for a while. Since I was younger. I used to see him around the way." Morgan didn't want to mention Messiah. Hurt would creep into her heart if she said his name, so she left him out of the story. "We lost touch for a while. I went away to school in London."

"Oh, so *that's* why you went to London?" Marilyn asked.

Ahmeek ran a hand down his waves but didn't respond, and Morgan giggled.

"We reconnected a few weeks ago," Morgan finished. "I've seen him a lot since then." She smiled at Ahmeek, a big grin, like they shared a secret. He shook his head and bit his lower lip.

"So, you're in college?" Marilyn asked.

"I graduate soon. I cut down four years' worth of undergrad in two, so I'm walking early. Supposed to go to medical school in the fall," Morgan said.

"She's smart!" Marilyn exclaimed. "Are you sure we can't re-evaluate this just-friends thing?" Marilyn asked as she whipped a bowlful of eggs.

Morgan laughed.

"We're friends, Ma. Morgan's too good for me," he said. He met her eye, and Morgan lowered her gaze, twiddling her fingers.

"I should call and check on the twins," Morgan said.

"You have kids?" Marilyn asked.

Morgan nodded. "I do. Two-year-old twins. A boy and a girl."

"Oh, you're so young!" Marilyn said.

"Yes, ma'am. I went through a lot growing up. It feels like I've lived two lifetimes already, and I'm not even twenty-one yet, but those babies are the best thing that ever happened to me." She lowered her gaze, but Ahmeek's finger was there, beneath her chin, lifting it. She met his eyes, and something unspoken lived there.

Pick your fucking head up, love.

She deciphered the stare with ease, and she gave him a weak smile.

"Kids will do that to you. There's nothing casual about having them. Nothing immature about it. They make you grow up, and anyone around you has to grow up as well. A man has to be ready for a lot of responsibility, a lot of weight on his shoulders when dating a woman with children," Marilyn said, eyes boring into her son.

Morgan's eyes burned him too, marked him. Their gaze was saying something. Exposing that secret that they had created last night. She thought of the way he had been at the zoo. "Ahmeek does okay," Morgan whispered.

"For a friend, right?" Marilyn baited.

Morgan wanted to be respectful and look his mother in the eyes, but she was held prisoner by Ahmeek's stare.

"Not by choice, but I get in where I fit in," he answered. Morgan blushed.

Marilyn chuckled. "Boy, you're in a world of trouble," she said, smiling.

Morgan laughed and turned toward the island. Marilyn had whipped up a full spread in no time, laying it out before them family-style. "Meekie, baby, bless the food," Marilyn directed.

"Meekie?" Morgan teased.

"Since he was running around in diapers," Marilyn said, eyes glowing from the memories. "He was my baby. Still is.

He gives the best kind of love. Always has. I remember he would come into my room when he was about five just to say, 'Mommy, I love you,' 'Mommy, are you okay?' always checking to make sure I was okay. I suppose he's spreading that around a little these days."

Morgan smiled at him.

She could tell he was thoroughly uncomfortable with going down memory lane. He hiked an eyebrow and ran a hand down the back of his head. "Man, we eating or what?" he asked.

"Yeah, Meekie, we're eating," Morgan said. She giggled in delight as his mother joined in the laughter.

"I like her," Marilyn said. "Don't bring none of your little girlfriends around if they not better than her."

"Those little girlfriends have been canceled," Morgan said, smirking. "They won't be around, Ms. Marilyn."

"Mmm-hmm, just friends my ass," Marilyn countered, then held out her hands for Morgan and Ahmeek. They formed a circle and bowed their heads.

"God, thank you for waking us up to see another day. We know that it wasn't guaranteed, and we appreciate the gift of this moment, the gift of those that are present in this moment. We thank you for this meal. May it be nourishing to our bodies, and may the company we keep be nourishing for our souls. Thank you for this company, Big Homie. It's appreciated. In Jesus's name. Amen."

Morgan lifted her eyes, suddenly craving him. Everything about him she wanted. She didn't know how she had missed it before . . . how the distraction of Messiah had made her completely ignore the grandness that sat right beside him. Morgan felt so many things. So much guilt about these feelings that had emerged, but she wasn't guilty enough to deny them, and she suddenly just wanted to touch him. Not sexually, but she craved connection. His fingertips to hers would be enough if it was all she could get in this moment. As if he could read her mind, he closed the space between them. It didn't even matter that his mother was in the room. He wrapped his arms around her waist and lowered his lips to her collarbone. A kiss. So intimate that it made her eyes close and her breath go hollow.

"Let's eat, love, so I can get you home."

She nodded, but this was home. This felt like home. This felt like Benny Atkins had come out of the sky and picked this roof for her himself. Like he had bestowed Ahmeek with the task of taking care of his baby girl because he reminded her so much of her father. Benny Atkins had been stern but kind, powerful yet yielding, and incredibly loving to his three girls. To her sister, Raven. To her mother, Justine. And to Morgan. He had been the perfect mixture of a gentleman and a gangster. Ahmeek was that. Where Messiah reminded her of Ethic, Ahmeek reminded her of her father. She loved them both, would never be able to choose between them. Just like Benny and Ethic. Life had made the choice for her because Benny had been taken away, and she had been left in Ethic's care. Her heart was much like that. She had been robbed of Messiah, and Ahmeek was there, left to clean up the mess the tragedy had made of her. Her eyes watered as she made the comparisons in her mind. A daddy versus a father. Ethic versus Benny. A zaddy versus a partner. Messiah versus Ahmeek. The thought haunted her. He released her and rounded the island to begin to fix her a plate.

"Ahmeek?" her voice was small—injured, even—and he lifted eyes of concern in her direction. "Can we go now? I should get back."

Thoughts of her father always unnerved her. Her lips quivered as he looked at her. Even the way his forehead creased when he was serious and the way his chest swelled with tension reminded her of her father. "Now, please. I need to leave now," she whispered.

Marilyn turned and looked at Morgan. "Ahmeek, go get her things, son," she whispered.

Morgan drew in a sharp breath. "I'm sorry. My kids . . . I just . . ." Morgan stopped talking. "It was really nice to meet you."

"Morgan, there is no right or wrong way to move on," Marilyn said. "No one can tell you how to process your grief but you. No one can tell you what makes it better but you. I know you loved Messiah. I know how conflicted you must feel being here now with Ahmeek."

Morgan's eyes widened in shock.

"You didn't think I knew you were with Messiah? I knew that boy a long time. Fed him at my dinner table plenty of nights when no one else would. I know exactly who you are, Morgan. To him and to Ahmeek. You take your time deciding what you want your life to look like, and don't let anybody make you feel bad about the way you choose to live after someone you gave your all died. You hear me?"

Morgan swiped the tear that fell from her eyes away and nodded while clearing her throat.

"Now sit down and get you some food, baby. You don't let a nigga fuck you without feeding you either." Marilyn giggled.

Morgan's mouth fell open. "We didn't . . . we're just . . ."

"Friends, mmm-hmm." Marilyn cackled. "I hear you, but I don't think either of you really believe that. If you did, you wouldn't be here in his shirt with wild hair and eyes that control every beat of my son's heart. There would be no breakfast in the morning because Ahmeek doesn't bring women home, especially here. No, neither of you believe that at all."

By the time Morgan made it to her place, it was midafternoon. After Ethic had requested another night with the twins, Marilyn had insisted Morgan stay. Breakfast had turned to lunch, and lunch had somehow turned to hustling to old-school music in the middle of Ahmeek's living room, right in front of the big-screen television where Ahmeek sat trying to see around them because he had money on Sunday's big football game. It had been such a lighthearted time, and the laughs Morgan shared with Marilyn felt natural. Morgan could love a woman like that. Marilyn was even easier to love on than Ahmeek, and Morgan realized where he'd inherited the trait from. He had been raised on love. Ahmeek's loving nature, no matter how deeply hidden behind the guns and the money and the street pedigree, was innate. All it took was the right woman to pull it out of him. Morgan had no idea how their wrong infatuation was somehow the right key to unlock those chambers in his heart. When he pulled up to her apartment, he placed his BMW in Park.

"No more fighting in nightclubs, love," Meek said as he placed a hand on the headrest behind her.

"You caught me on a bad day," Morgan replied, smirking.

He gave up a lazy smile.

"About last night, Ahmeek," she whispered. She lowered her eyes to her lap and twirled the rings that rested on her fingers. One on her thumb, two on her pointer, and one for her pinkie. Her engagement ring was missing, tucked away in her jewelry box in her panty drawer.

Ahmeek lifted her chin with one finger. "In my eyes, Morgan Atkins. FaceTime remember?"

Morgan could barely hold his stare. "I don't think it's wise to see each other," she stammered. The finality of her words hit her heart like a sledgehammer. "We have no business being friends. I can't just be friends. Not after last night," she whispered. She was ashamed of herself for not being ashamed. She was so unapologetic about what she had done with him last night that it scared her. She had to nip this in the bud . . . end it before it got out of control. She had an entire family to consider.

"Want to know the fucked-up part, Mo?" Ahmeek asked. He moved his hand from the headrest to the back of her neck and massaged the tension building there. He felt it, and just his touch caused her eyes to prickle. Morgan was spoiled. She had never been denied anything a day of her life, but here she was putting the brakes on this. Depriving herself of something she desperately wanted. "I knew last night that it was the end. The end before it even fucking started." Ahmeek scoffed. "Shit's wild."

Morgan felt the tears on her face before she even realized she was crying. She was so attached . . . too attached. It wasn't even normal because it was too new to be this potent, but raw dope was raw dope, and Ahmeek was uncut. She was high.

"This is so stupid!" she exclaimed as she tilted her head to the sky and chased her tears with the backs of her thumbs. "I hate this. Let's just forget all of this even happened, Ahmeek. Everything since London. Let's just go back to the people we were two years ago."

"Whatever you want me to do, I'ma do," Ahmeek stated. "Is that what you want?"

He ran his hand down his waves, and Morgan's heart plummeted. His brows were hiked, and a mixture of distress and annoyance played on his face. He was a man who was used to having his way with women. *No* wasn't a word he knew well, and hearing it from Morgan had put him in a mood.

"I'm getting married, Ahmeek," she whispered.

"I know," he answered.

"So whatever this is. Whatever it was. We can't. It just can't happen."

"Only it has happened, love. It is happening," he stated.

She shook her head. "Not anymore," she answered.

She pulled on the handle of her door and rushed out of the car, slamming the door. She took heavy steps all the way to her door, hurrying some, because she needed the safety of her apartment, the privacy of its four walls . . . she couldn't expose how affected she was. Morgan closed her door and placed both hands against it, leaning over, because she was sick to her stomach. Ahmeek had infiltrated every crevice of her brain, and she might be able to keep him away, but she couldn't erase the impression he had left behind.

Morgan did the only thing she could think to keep herself from caving for Ahmeek, to keep herself from submitting to the pull he had on her. She picked up the phone and called Bash. She lured him home because she needed him in her face, reminding her that she was a taken woman.

15

Morgan was sick to her stomach as she waited at the airport. The longer she stood near baggage claim, the more she began to regret calling Bash to town. When they were apart, she had freedom. She could be herself. As soon as she saw his smiling face, she felt it being rescinded, like he was repossessing her ability to make her own decisions. With every step he took in her direction, Morgan's insides screamed, "*Run!*"

"My girl!" he groaned as he bent down to wrap her in a hug, lifting her. Her feet left the ground for a split second. He placed her down, and Morgan felt guilty because he had missed her, she could tell—and while he was missing her, Morgan had been in the throes of something so passionate it made her blush just thinking about it.

"Where are the twins?" he asked.

"At Alani and Ethic's," she informed. "Do you have bags?" she asked.

"Nah, I didn't pack much. I have an entire Michigan wardrobe at the house here. I'm good. I just brought work," he said. "Are you ready for commencement?"

"I am. Two years of nonstop work and sleepless nights are finally paying off," she said. "I'm right out front."

She led the way to her car, and she couldn't help but notice that the giddiness she felt with Ahmeek was missing. She had been away from Bash for an extended period of time, and it was like she didn't even care. It hadn't even been twenty-four hours of being without Ahmeek, and Morgan's heart was bleeding. He hadn't called or texted. He did what he was told. He fell back.

"Hey, you good, Mo?" Bash asked.

She shook the thoughts of another man from her mind and nodded, putting on the fake smile she had mastered around him before heading to her place. She should have taken him home to his family's estate, but she needed him to play interference. She needed him to stop her from losing control of her emotions. Morgan had to be rational. She had invested the past two years of her life into being with Bash. She allowed him to play Daddy to her children, and things had been good . . . well, maybe not good . . . tolerable . . . Things had been uncomplicated for two whole years. When Aria had brought Ahmeek to London, her entire world had been shaken up.

"Yeah, of course, I'm fine," she lied. Always lying. Always concealing how she felt around him. Always forcing a smile while thoughts of despair swirled in her head, but she feigned normalcy. She faked it because if she told anyone her true thoughts, they would think she was crazy. They would think she was depressed and suicidal. They would overanalyze and control. Ethic would worry, and her family would look at her with skeptical eyes. So instead, she pretended she was happy. A lot of women had a lot less, so certainly Morgan should be grateful for Bash.

They arrived at her place, and as soon as they were through

the door, Bash's hands were on her, pulling her into him, kissing her, and Morgan cringed.

"Bash, stop," she whispered as she shimmied out of his grasp.

"I know, I know. You got your rules, Mo," he conceded, lifting his hands. He had no idea the ways in which she had broken those rules. Sex after Messiah scared her until Ahmeek. Now the thought of him touching her body sent a flood through her panties. She had cum three times just thinking about him the night before, but Bash saw no action. It was like her body didn't even respond the same. Like her sexual language was French and he was speaking Mandarin. Together, they just weren't fluent.

Her phone buzzed, and she felt like she had been saved by the bell. She made her way to the living room. "Why don't you go shower? This is Aria; I need to take this," she said. She answered, "Hey, girl."

"Not too long. It's not often that I get you all to myself. I don't want to share you with anyone else," Bash mumbled in her ear as he passed.

"Boy, shut yo' ass up!" Aria shouted, expressing her frustration with Bash. "Guess your warden is in town, huh?"

"Yeah, he got in not too long ago," Morgan informed.

"Why did this man show up a day before the show? He probably smelled the fun that was about to go down," Aria fussed.

"What show?" Morgan asked.

"Vegas! Morgan! What do you mean what show? We talked about this! You said you'd perform," Aria reminded.

"I can't, Aria," Mo said. "Bash is back. We have the twins to think about. I can't just pick up and go away for the weekend."

"And why the hell not? Bash want to play Daddy, so let

that nigga play Daddy. He can watch the twins while you come to Vegas and do the show," Aria stated. "Aren't the twins still at Ethic's anyway?"

Morgan knew Alani and Ethic would care for her babies. She was looking for excuses not to go. Bash's presence was already changing the way she made decisions. She wanted to go; he wouldn't want her to go, however, so to avoid conflict, she would just sit this one out.

"Mo, you said you would perform," Aria stated. "You owe me. I came all the way to London for your ass."

"When the hell did I say that?" she protested.

"In London that night at the dance studio. You agreed. The promoter already has your name on the bill. You haven't hit the stage in two years."

"Bitch, I danced with you the other night," Mo argued.

"A club gig is not a show! You can do that shit in your sleep. Come on, Mo! People are hype to see you again; plus, he's paying. A hundred thousand, Mo. Split four ways, we walk away with a nice little bag."

Morgan rolled her eyes. It was good money, but money didn't move Morgan Atkins. Between Raven's life insurance and the money Ethic had put up for her over the years, she was set. She didn't have to lift a finger if she didn't want to, but the fact that she was good enough to command that large of a fee after two years of disappearing from the scene made her consider it. "He's going to hate this. His family doesn't like the look. It doesn't fit their image."

"Who cares about what they like, Mo? Do you like it? Bash knew you were gang when he met you. Now he has you serving tea and biscuits and shit. It's like you're not even the same person with him," Aria said. Morgan could hear the irritation in Aria's voice, and she couldn't blame her because it reflected in her soul. "Fuck these niggas, Mo. You don't have to change with every relationship you get into. Who are you when you're alone? When you look in the mirror? The Mo I know ain't the one I saw in London!"

Morgan knew Aria was right. She had been stifling herself. She loved to dance, but she always hid that part of her while in London. The urge to dance. The urge to be loud, the urge to be herself. She was a muted version of Morgan Atkins with Bash—one his parents would accept, a version Christiana had taught her to be. She was already the girl with two babies out of wedlock. Bash was already accepting children that weren't his. She felt obligated to be what he needed, what he preferred.

"Go on IG and look at how many people have commented on my flyer. If I show up without you, they're going to boo us off the set, no matter how fire it is," Aria said.

"I'll think about it," Mo answered.

"Look, I'll forward you the flight reservation. I leave tonight. Your flight is for tomorrow morning. Be on it, Morgan."

"I said I'll think about it, nigga! Don't Morgan me!" Mo fussed. She hung up the phone and opened her Instagram. The first thing she saw was a notification for a direct message. She opened it.

MURDERKING810

You look unhappy and I ain't happy about that. You vibrate too high for your smile not to match. Fix that.

Mo frowned. She normally ignored messages from men, but she found herself typing back.

SHORTYDOOWOP

You get all that from an IG post, huh? Does this introspective, I-pay-attention-I-can-see-past-your-smile thing normally work for you?

To Morgan's surprise, instant dots danced on the screen.

MURDERKING810

I've only ever tried it on you. It works because I know for a fact
you're smiling right now.

Morgan felt her face turn red and her mouth opened in
shock.

SHORTYDOOWOP

Boy, you don't know shit and you don't know me. Have a nice day,
sir. And stop sliding in DMs. It makes you seem thirsty.

MURDERKING810

A nigga could use a sip of that.

Morgan snickered, and her fingers were lightning on the
screen.

SHORTYDOOWOP

Never happening, bruh. Move around.

MURDERKING810

I've tried. I'm stuck on you.

SHORTYDOOWOP

Good luck with that. Oh, and change the name. I hate it. It's corny.

Morgan clicked out of the message and went to Aria's page.
Stiletto Gang fans were swarming the comments under Morgan's picture. Her thumb slid down the screen as Bash entered
the room, wearing a towel around his waist, his wet body dripping onto her floor. His toned abdomen, Ritz cracker–colored

skin, and full beard was more than attractive. Bash was a man who attracted women daily, but somehow Morgan didn't feel it. No spark, no butterflies. Oh, how she wished for those butterflies with him; maybe then she could keep herself away from Ahmeek.

"What time do we have to pick up the twins?" Bash asked.

"Ethic said he would call, which means never." Morgan snickered.

"Damn, I miss them. Should we go pick them up?" Bash asked. He walked to her and took her chin in his hand, then leaned down to kiss her. A quick peck, never more, never passion filled, but Morgan still felt his appreciation. She knew he was giving all he knew how to give. His family had bred up a gentleman.

"They haven't seen them in months. No way is Alani letting them go today," she said, smiling. "It's crazy how she loves on them. I fought her for a long time, but nobody loves like Alani. I'm glad that they have her and Ethic."

"She's good people. Ethic doesn't care for me too much, but what father does, right? I'd like to talk to him about the engagement. I'd like to be the one to let him know, if that's okay with you. I didn't get the chance to ask his permission, and I'd still like to," Bash said.

"I don't know, Bash. I think I should be the one to tell him. He's my father. He raised me. That news should come from me," Morgan said.

"You make it sound like you're delivering bad news, Mo," he said, worry filling his forehead as lines creased his face.

Morgan took a deep breath. "That's not what I mean."

"Do I not give you everything? Do I not do everything for you? I got you into the medical program at Cambridge next year. I help with the twins so you can go full-time. Taking them to class with me daily. My students know them, they're there so much. You've finished four years of undergrad in two years because of me. I believe in you. I'm here every step of the way. My mother has you on the fast track at the finest hospital in London after you finish medical school. A surgeon in the family goes a long way. We've all invested in you, Mo."

"I know. I didn't mean to make it seem like I'm ungrateful. That's not what I meant. I'd just like to tell him. I'm twenty years old."

"You'll be twenty-one soon," Bash stated. "And I'm hoping to throw my fiancée a party. I can't do that if no one in your family knows you're engaged. You're not even wearing your ring."

Morgan glanced down at her bare finger. "I wear it, Bash," she said defensively.

"Do you even want me here, Mo?" he asked.

"Of course!" Morgan shouted.

"I missed you," he said, pulling her into his arms, bending so that his lips were on her ear. Kissing there. "Did you miss me?"

"I did, I did," she said. She closed her eyes, frowning. She didn't know who she was trying to convince, him or herself. She knew what it was like to miss someone. Messiah used to leave her for mere hours and she counted every second until his return. Being away from him used to give her anxiety. She would be sick until his return. Hell, Ahmeek had been out of her sights for three days, and it felt like months. It had been two weeks since she'd seen Bash, and she had felt nothing. In fact, she had been relieved to have some separation . . . some distance because she had been able to be herself. It wasn't that she didn't love him. She did. He was a great friend to her, but that all-consuming love that had seized her heart with Messiah didn't exist with Bash. She wouldn't allow it to. That type of love left you broken . . . it led to dark places, and Morgan wanted to be in control of her heart this time around. She held back and re-sisted Bash every step of the way. She was lucky he was around at all. His patience was a show of his infatuation for her. His hand flirted with the hem of her dress, and Morgan cuffed his wrists, stopping him.

"Bash," she whispered.

"I know. Celibacy. I know. I take it that ends when I make an honest woman out of you?" he asked.

"It ends when it ends, Bash," she answered.

"Damn, Morgan. It's been two years," he said in frustra-tion. "You act like I can't touch you."

"You can't. I don't like the shit, okay? I was raped, Bash. Raped by two niggas, and I couldn't even say no. I can say no now, and it's going to continue to be no until I feel like fucking saying yes!" she shouted. She closed her eyes and drew in a deep breath because she hadn't meant to divulge so much. She had wanted to scream it since the very first time he had tried his hand at her two years ago.

Shock wore him. "I didn't know, Mo," he said, reaching for her. She snatched her arm out of his grasp. "I'm sorry. I'm dead wrong. You're just beautiful. I love you, and it seems like you're holding that back from me. I just want to know you . . . experience every part of you. Make love to my future wife."

The speech didn't move her even a little because even if she were game, making love was the last thing she wanted to do. What Morgan Atkins had been introduced to was sexual liberation. It was wild and free and passionate . . . Messiah had pulled an orgasm out of her a dozen different ways, and every single time, Morgan was left weak. She doubted that Bash could follow that act, and she wasn't in a rush to find out. She had no clue how she was supposed to be his wife if she couldn't stomach the thought of him inside her. Guilt weighed on her because she knew he wasn't the man she was supposed to marry.

Bash was a great man. His kindness was remarkable. His ability to accept her children as his own. His ability to accept her with all her flaws, but Morgan struggled with love. She loved him, yes, but to fall in love with someone again . . . to give her mind, body, and soul to a man and trust him to keep it safe . . . it felt foolish . . . it felt risky because she knew what was at stake. Her sanity. She was wrong, and she knew it. Dangling intimacy in front of Bash like he were chasing a carrot, stringing him along, when she knew he deserved more. *Maybe I should just get it over with. Maybe after the first time with someone else, it'll get easier. Meek was easier. I let him touch me without thinking twice.*

"I'm sorry," she whispered.

"Don't apologize," Bash said. "I didn't know that sex was associated with pain for you. I didn't know, Mo."

Now she felt like an even bigger piece of shit because Bash was being understanding. He was being the good guy. He was being the perfect guy. He was the perfect guy. In every way since the day they had met, he had treated her like she was golden. He was everything a woman could ask for in a man, but her first love had been a gangster. He had been a menace and had helped her develop a taste that a good guy couldn't satisfy. Morgan craved a bad boy, and Bash didn't even have a teaspoon's worth of street in his makeup.

I'm an asshole.

"Stop," she whispered. She walked up to him and placed her hands around his neck as she looked up at him. "You're right. It's been two years. I've been unfair to you," she admitted. "Maybe we can take a trip this weekend. Aria wants me to dance with Stiletto Gang in Vegas—"

"Stiletto Gang," Bash interrupted. The disdain that dripped off those two words put Morgan on the defensive.

Tension filled his shoulders, and his brow dipped. "I don't know if that's the most tasteful look, Mo. I thought you'd decided to take a step back from that."

"No," Mo shot back. "Your mother decided that I should take a step back for a while, and I never agreed. I've just been busy. With the twins, with MAM, and school, but I'm not as busy now. Graduation is in a few weeks. Classes are over. Ethic and Alani will keep the twins. I have no excuse not to do what I love."

"Morgan, my family's name—"

"Is not my name yet, Bash, and if you ever want it to be, I have to have freedom," Morgan argued.

"I don't like it, Morgan," Bash pressed.

Morgan pulled back, frowning as a hand went to her hip. "You act like I'm stripping, Bash. When we met, I was gang. You knew that I danced."

"You're headed to medical school, Mo, and you want to taint your image? You want to have your face all over social media, dancing onstage with hardly any clothes on and then walk into a hospital to apply for an internship? You really think that's wise?"

He was making sense . . . too much sense, and Morgan hated it. "Fine. I won't do it, but we could still go. We could go to Vegas and support Aria and spend some time together. We could try to . . ." She paused and shrugged. "We can do it there. Get a dope suite, order some room service, have a few drinks, and let things go where they go."

His brow softened, and she could see him considering it.

"Yeah, Mo, we can go support your friend," Bash said.

"Yay!" she screamed in excitement. "I'm so excited!" She jumped up and down like a little girl, clapping her hands together before planting a kiss to his cheek. "But first, I need to go spend time with my babies. I've never been without them for that long. Going four days will feel like torture."

"So bring them," Bash said.

"To Las Vegas?" she asked, frowning. "I don't know. I mean, I've never been, but that just doesn't seem like a good place for kids, and the flight is four hours. I don't think that's the best idea."

"They've been flying back and forth to London since they were born. I think they can handle a quick four hours," Bash said. "We've been apart for two weeks. It'll be nice for the four of us to spend a few days together. We can find something appropriate for them to do. As long as we're all together, that's all that matters to me."

Morgan softened. He really was such a good guy. "Okay," she agreed. "They can come."

Bash kissed the side of her head. "And promise me you won't dance. I'm cool with you supporting your friend and all, but you onstage is a no go."

A tightlipped smile was all the agreement she could muster. At least she was going. At least she wouldn't miss the experience completely. She would be there rooting Aria on. That would just have to be good enough.

Her phone buzzed, and Morgan opened her notifications. She unlocked her phone, and a snicker of amusement fell from her lips at first glance.

MORGANSKING810

Better?

She smirked, shaking her head. Men were so good at flirting behind the veil of anonymity. She would bet her bottom dollar that this man wasn't so confident in person.

SHORTYDOOWOP
Cute. Real cute. You're still corny.

Morgan smiled and shook her head, surprised that she felt the unsettling in her gut that told her she was flattered.

A stranger online makes me feel more excited than the man I'm about to marry.

She had no idea that the stranger wasn't so strange at all. He was better acquainted with her than anyone else had ever been before.

16

The hustle and bustle of the ARIA hotel and casino was pure chaos as Morgan stood holding on to her twins' hands. She sat off to the side, waiting for Bash to check in to their room, but after a long flight, the twins were bursting with energy.

"Ssari, come here, baby," she said while simultaneously fumbling with Yara in her arms. Yara was crying; her snotty nose and watery eyes had made a handkerchief of Morgan's Versace silk shirt.

"Yara, baby," she said to herself as Yara twisted and turned in her arm, throwing a temper tantrum. Morgan looked around for a place to sit. "Messari, come, baby." She headed for the seating area and sat Yara down. She got on her knees in front of her daughter as Messari slid next to his sister.

"Yolly Pop, what's wrong?" she signed. "Is it your ears? Do they hurt?"

"What's wrong, Yolly Pop?" Messari signed too. Messari leaned in and kissed Yara's ear, and Morgan smiled. She loved how he loved on his sister.

Yara continued to cry, yelling so loud that people stopped to stare as they passed by.

"Yolly," Morgan moaned. She knew the pressure from flying was worse for Yara, and she hoped this didn't last all day. Morgan turned for a split second, checking Bash's place in line. There were still ten or so people in front of him. When she turned back to her twins, only one sat there. "Yara!" she shouted as she turned, her heart dropping. She panicked instantly. "Yolly Pop!" She was calling out of instinct because it would do no good. Yara couldn't hear her. When she saw Ahmeek stroll through the crowd, carrying her daughter, Morgan breathed a sigh of relief, but a different type of anxiety settled into her heart.

"I think I have something that belongs to you," he said. Isa and Aria came through the door next, and they all huddled in a small crowd. "What's up, homie?" Meek greeted, bending down to extend his hand to Messari.

"Sup!" Messari shouted back. Isa scooped him. Her babies in the arms of the crew made her stress lessen some. She now had eight arms. Help. She now had help to manage them while Bash checked in.

Morgan tried to retrieve Yara from Ahmeek's arms, but Yara pulled away and rested her head against Ahmeek's chest. His shirt became the next victim to her runny nose.

"Ahmeek, she's ruining your shirt," Morgan said.

"A little snot never hurt nobody," he said. He leaned back and swiped her nose with his thumb. "Or a lot of snot." He chuckled. Yara shook her head, protesting as he tried to clean her face, rubbing the snot across his chest as she turned to the other side. "Yup. Yolly Pop, fuck it all up," he said. Morgan smiled and then leaned to grab baby wipes from her bag. She gripped the sides of Yolly's cheeks with one hand, then cleared her nose with the other. She grabbed another wipe and lifted his free hand to clean that as well. The coarseness of his skin, the way he gave her fingers a discreet squeeze, Morgan's insides liquefied. Her entire face turned red.

"I'm sorry," she said.

"Don't worry about it," he answered. They took a few steps away from Aria and Isa.

"What are you doing here, Ahmeek?" she asked.

"I've got business. Isa and I . . . out here. Aria said you weren't coming, Mo. I heard you. I'll keep my distance," he said.

She nodded. "Thank you." It came out in a whisper because it was the most ridiculous thing she had ever shown gratitude for. Distance from him was torture. Even standing here with him holding her daughter, at his side with bags at their feet like they had traveled here together, made her knees go weak. She was wound so tightly that Ahmeek could see it.

"Hey," he said. "Relax, love. We're good. I understand your position, Mo. I hold no resentments."

Bash's timing couldn't have been worse. He walked up carrying their room key.

"Meek, right?" he asked. He held out his hand. "Good to see you again, man."

Morgan tensed because Ahmeek's eyes held some animosity. His entire body stiffened, and Yara popped her little head up because Morgan was sure his chest had turned to steel. He was staring at the man who had the girl he wanted. His eyes said so much.

Clown-ass nigga.

The audacity that it was Bash stopping him from having her. He pulled his bottom lip into his mouth, biting hard, before meeting Morgan's worried stare. To act anything but cordial would raise questions. He didn't give a fuck, but it was clear that Morgan did. For a second time, he took the high road. No handshakes this time, however, just a nod of acknowledgment. Barely a greeting at all.

"You ready?" Bash asked, slapping the key card against the palm of his hand.

Morgan nodded and then forced a protesting Yara from Ahmeek's hands. Her skin touched his briefly, and Morgan's mind went numb. He felt it too. She knew he did because he looked at her like he was in shock as he passed Yara off to her. A look of envy creased his brow when she passed Yara to Bash before grabbing Messari from Isa.

"I'll see you later," she said to Aria.

"Don't be late. We go on at ten," Aria said.

"About that," Mo said. "I can't perform. I'm just coming to support."

"Mo!" Aria protested.

"Aria, I can't," she whispered. Quick feet carried her to Bash's side as they headed for the elevator bank. She glanced over her shoulder because she couldn't help but to look back, but Ahmeek was gone, and Morgan felt a churning in her soul that told her she was walking next to the wrong man.

Morgan walked into the arena carrying Messari on one hip. Bash trailed her with Yara.

"We're late," she said. "Aria's going to kill me. First, I bail on her, now I'm not even here on time."

"You didn't bail on her, Mo. You're in a different place in your life than she is. Dancing isn't your priority," Bash said, trying to soothe the guilt Morgan had been expressing all day about backing out of the show. "The twins shouldn't even be out this late."

"They wouldn't have to be if you didn't insist on coming. You don't have to babysit me. I told you I wouldn't go onstage," Morgan said as they maneuvered through the back entrance with the passes Aria had left at the front desk.

"I'm not babysitting. I'm just showing love," he said.

Morgan rolled her eyes as she made her way toward Stiletto Gang's dressing room. As soon as she pushed through the metal doors, she heard Aria yelling.

"I don't care what the contract says! You can't make someone perform!" Aria shouted. "She didn't sign it. I did!"

"We only paid top dollar because we thought we would have both principal dancers of Stiletto Gang. We need you both. Our crowd is expecting Mo Money onstage tonight," the promoter said.

Morgan frowned as she stepped up to the conversation.

"What's going on?" she asked White Boy Nick, who leaned against the wall.

"Your ass is what's going on," he shot back.

"Is this about me?" Morgan stepped up next to Aria.

"We booked you both; we need you both. The rest of Stiletto Gang is good, but they're just backup."

"Who's backup, baby? Your mama's backup. I'm a motherfucking star," White Boy Nick interjected.

The promoter swiped a hand of frustration over his face. "Look, no shade, but I need the two of you onstage. The artist paid for the both of you, and on top of that, we promised the fans an encore performance with just Gang," the promoter explained.

"I have my kids with me. I can't go onstage. Do you see what I have on?" Morgan defended.

"I'll let y'all work it out, but either honor the contract or don't perform at all. You've got about a half hour to decide."

An exasperated Aria turned to Morgan. "Mo, I know you aren't going to make me beg. Shit like this gets out. I signed a contract. If I don't fulfill my end of this, we won't be able to secure a show for months. My name is all I have. I promised them you."

"They can't make you dance, Mo," Bash said over her shoulder.

"And you can't tell her not to dance. Only reason she even canceling is because of you, Bash!" Aria snapped.

"I don't have clothes, Aria," Morgan said.

"Bitch, it's a dressing room full of shit to choose from," Aria countered.

Morgan handed Messari to Bash.

"I thought we talked about this, Mo."

"Do I really have a choice at this point?" she asked, shrugging. "It's just one performance."

She followed Aria into the dressing room, and before Bash could follow, Aria stopped him, putting her arm across the door to stop him from entering. "You and the twins can wait backstage to watch the show," she said, pointing down the hallway. "She's performing. Live with it."

She slammed the door, and Morgan smiled at her through the reflection of the mirror she stood in front of.

"Gang, gang, bitch." Aria smirked.

"Gang, gang," Mo replied.

"Kumbaya, motherfuckers. Hurry up, Power Puff Girls. We get it, you defeated the lame-ass, overbearing, insecure fiancé." Nick clapped his hands together. "Chop! Chop! We've got a stage to burn down."

"Gang! Gang! Gang! Gang!"

Morgan's heart was like a drum. She heard it in her ears, beating, creating a cadence, building an anxiety inside her as she looked out over the crowd in front of her. There were so many people ... too many people ... never had it been this many people ... watching her. She felt like she would pass out. Two years ago, she would have eaten this stage alive. She would have anticipated the beat drop and waited arrogantly for the music to feed her soul. Two years ago, she had Messiah in the crowd watching, and whenever he was there, no one else existed. She danced for him, pictured him, only him, and her nerves faded. Now all she saw was a roomful of strangers . . . and they terrified her. The lights above the stage blinded her, and the crowd was cloaked in darkness. Flashes from cell phone cameras went off one after another. Morgan stood, frozen, paralyzed, unarmed as her insecurities ate away at her. She slipped a finger in the nude one-piece bodysuit, snapping it against her thighs. She might as well have been naked. The color of the bodysuit matched her skin perfectly, and the cut was so seductive she was serving side boob and high thigh. She wished she had shorts to cover her weight gain. Her thighs were thick and busting through the nude fabric of her fishnet stockings. She wasn't little Morgan anymore. Twin babies had put twenty-five pounds on her frame. A dancer's frame was now a stripper's dream. Shorty Doo Wop was stacked, but she was so insecure, she didn't even feel like she belonged on a stage anymore. She hadn't stepped into Mo Money's dancing stilettos in two years. The little club performances didn't count. That was for fun. This was big business, and if she missed one count, she would ruin Stiletto Gang's reputation. Most days, she wore sneakers and leggings with toddler puke accenting a matching sweatshirt. No way did she belong on this stage. She had her hands full. How Aria had talked her into this performance, she had no idea. *A moment of temporary insanity.*

"Ayo!"

Morgan heard the call through the crowd. Her neck snapped to the side, and her eyes found him instantly. Ahmeek stood backstage, next to Isa, and when their eyes met, he put two fingers to his forehead in salute. It was like he could read her body language . . . like he knew that she was nervous, despite her most valiant efforts to pretend otherwise. His acknowledgment erased her insecurities. That hollow feeling in her belly hardened some. Ahmeek, behind her, watching, encouraging put a bit of moxie in her spine. She hadn't known he would be there, but she was glad he had decided to come. She put her hands on her hips.

The beat dropped, and Morgan turned the fuck on.

Broke up with that nigga he had me stressing, I was taught to turn my losses into lessons

Morgan's sixteen count was so dope that Aria went crazy beside her. She jumped up and down, waving the Moschino scarf in her hand like a helicopter above her head. Morgan Atkins was gone. Mo Money was in the building.

"Bitch!" Aria yelled. Aria grabbed a mic from the DJ. "Ayeeeee," she said. The entire crowd joined her in hyping Mo up. Morgan took off like Aria was Phil Jackson and she was Kobe in the fourth quarter. Mo forgot about all insecurities; those nude-colored shorts might as well have been invisible because the way her ass was moving had everyone in the crowd bothered. Morgan was dancing so hard that sweat dripped everywhere. Her mouth curled up in an arrogant sneer. She felt these words . . . felt this beat.

Fucked up for a minute, now I'm back to flexin'

Morgan smiled and lifted her head to the sky as she lifted her hands, opening them wide like energy was entering her body. This felt amazing. It felt like her identity was back. Like she had forgotten who she was for two years and this stage, this crowd, was reminding her.

I run up my haters going ghost, I hope God don't let me do the most

Morgan brought praying hands to her chin and bounced them there before one hand went to her hip and the other in the sky like she held that Moschino scarf. Roll. Mo turned to the back, and the crowd roared because they knew what was next. *Twerk!*

Out of nowhere, her babies bolted onto the stage, and Morgan smiled as Messari began dancing. The crowd turned up higher. It was the cutest thing anyone had ever seen. Aria laughed and joined Messari as Morgan picked up Yara. She took her daughter to the speakers. She knew that Yara couldn't join in until she felt the subwoofers. She placed Yara's hand on the speaker and then did a bop to the beat while her daughter smiled. Morgan took her back-center stage and put her down, and Yara took off, dancing with her brother under the bright lights.

"Mo Money, everybody! Stiletto Gang in this bitch!"

White Boy Nick skipped back out onto the stage along with the other dancers, and they all formed a circle around Ssari and Yara, clapping, dancing, and encouraging them as they danced. Morgan had never received love like this. The crowd was on another level, and she picked up Yara as Aria grabbed her son. They waved.

"Say hi!" Mo signed to Yara. Yara waved shyly, then hugged her mother's neck, overwhelmed. Messari, on the other hand, ate up the spotlight, waving and blowing kisses to the crowd. Such a charmer.

Morgan retreated backstage to their dressing room where Isa and Ahmeek sat waiting.

"The fuck! Them babies murdered everything," Isa said, laughing as he lifted a Styrofoam cup to his lips. He grabbed Aria, pulling her into him roughly. "We need to go make a couple of them. I want two like yesterday. Fucking dancing-ass twins. Cute-ass mu'fucking kids." He snickered.

Morgan hollered, "Where is Bash? How did they even end up onstage?" she asked.

"Corny-ass nigga left," Isa said.

"He left my babies backstage and walked out?" Morgan asked, eyes narrowing into slits. Morgan rushed to her bag and dug through it until she found her phone. She held Yara on one hip and put the phone to her ear.

"Have you lost your mind? Why would you leave them backstage alone? What the fuck were you thinking?" Morgan screamed the words as her heart raged. Her eyes burned. She was a crier. Whenever she was angry, she cried, and she hated it in this moment. "I didn't plan to go onstage! It just happened! And that doesn't fucking excuse the fact that you left my kids alone, backstage, around motherfuckers they don't even know!"

She paused as Bash responded. All eyes were on her, but she didn't care. She closed her eyes and took a deep breath.

"Oh, now you want to come back to get them? Don't bother!" Morgan ended the call and tossed her phone on the vanity in front of her. She rushed into the bathroom.

Yara's hands on her face, then her little lips on her cheek reminded Morgan to breathe. She hugged her daughter. She knew that Yara processed everything. She soaked up other people's energy, and Mo didn't want her to feel anything other than peace.

She sat her on the sink and signed, "Mommy is okay. You did so good, Yolly Pop! You danced so beautifully!"

"Thank you, Mommy," Yara signed.

Morgan smiled. Yara was so intelligent. So sharp. She was learning her signs at record pace, and Morgan was so proud to be her mother.

A knock at the door interrupted them, and Morgan pulled a paper towel from the dispenser, wetting it.

"One second!" she called out.

She blotted her face. It was still red from crying, but she couldn't hide in the bathroom forever. She lifted Yara and snatched open the door.

Ahmeek stood there, brow knitted in concern, eyes locked in on hers.

"You good?" he asked.

She nodded.

"Words, Mo. If you're good, tell me you're good. If you ain't, all it takes is a word and it's handled," he whispered. "You know that."

Morgan sighed in relief. "How could he leave them?"

"They were fine, Mo. They were safe," Meek stated. "Eyes on them at all times."

They were standing in the threshold that separated the bathroom from the dressing room. He was keeping her there until he saw her worry dissipate. "Fuck that nigga, Mo. To-night's about you. You're a fucking star, love, and you shined. The twins too." He snickered. He pulled out his phone and held it up for Mo to see. "You're everywhere, love. Niggas is spreading love. Don't let anybody dim that light." A popular gossip account had reposted a clip of Mo's performance. She was going viral.

She smiled.

Yara leaned lazily against Morgan's cheek and groaned as a big yawn left her mouth. "I've got to get them to bed," she whispered. "Can you drop me at the hotel?"

"Yeah, whatever you need, Mo," he said as he stepped aside.

"You okay?" Aria asked.

Morgan nodded. "I'm fine. I'm going to get the kids back. I'll catch up with you when we get back, okay?"

"Do you want to stay in my suite tonight?" Aria asked.

Morgan shook her head. "I'm fine," she said.

Aria stood removing a key card from her purse. She

handed it to Mo. "Just in case he's on some bullshit and you don't feel like arguing."

"Won't be no arguing," Ahmeek stated.

Aria jerked her neck back. "Mmkay, Ahmeek! Step, then!" she instigated. Morgan took the room key anyway and gave Aria a departing hug. She hugged Isa too, then walked out with Ahmeek, who carried Messari.

His hand to the small of her back acted as a guide until they were outside. He didn't speak, neither did she, but Messari was full of conversation.

"Hey, you! Wook!" Messari pointed to the fountains across the street. The Bellagio was beautiful at night, and Messari was fully invested in the waterworks going off in the distance.

"His name is Meek, Ssari. Can you say *Meek?*"

Messari nodded. "Wook, Meek!"

"I'm wooking, homie," Ahmeek answered, chuckling.

"Go see!" Messari said, turning Meek's head in the direction of the show.

"I guess we're going to see the fountains," Meek said.

Morgan sighed. "It's late, and I'm barely dressed. I'm wearing stage clothes."

"Yeah, we need to talk about that too, Mo. You really fucking showing out. Got me ready to put the burner to a nigga out here," he said. "You know what you do."

Morgan snickered as she watched him put Messari down and remove his jacket. He placed it around her shoulders, then he leaned to grab Messari's hand.

"Come on, Mommy!" Messari said.

"Yeah, Mommy, come on," Meek instigated.

Morgan looked at Yara. "You want to see the fountains?" Morgan signed.

Yara nodded, sleepy, but Mo knew she would last. She sighed, adjusted the jacket, and walked beside Meek.

They took the bridge across Las Vegas Boulevard, and Messari took off running as fast as his little legs would carry him. Meek took off after him, scooping him, then tossing him so high into the air that Morgan's heart tensed in worry. Meek caught him effortlessly, then placed Messari on his shoulders. He held on to Messari's legs to keep him secure. Morgan smiled as she caught up.

"Don't do that," Meek said.

"Do what?" she asked.

"Fake smile," he stated as they found a spot in the center to watch the show. Morgan turned her eyes to the man-made lake in front of the hotel.

"I just don't want to fight with him," she whispered. "But I want to dance too. I want to dance with Stiletto Gang."

"So dance, Mo," he said. "Medical school will be there if you choose to pursue it later. No offense, but I don't want a doctor working on me that don't love medicine. You're supposed to be passionate about saving lives like you are about being onstage."

"I guess," she said, shrugging. She hoisted Yara up on her hip. "She's not going to make it until the next show." Yara's little eyes were closing, and he took her from Mo's hands.

"They run every few minutes or so," he said. "I've got her."

"Come on, Mommy's Ssari," Morgan said, pulling Messari off Meek's shoulders and placing him on his feet.

"He was fine. I can handle your babies, Mo," he said.

"I can see that," she answered, amazed at how good with them he truly was. A smile melted on her face.

"Don't do that either," he said.

"What now?" she asked.

"The real smile stops my heart, Morgan Atkins. Bring the fake shit back."

Morgan's entire body warmed. She leaned her head on his shoulder. "You make me feel . . ." She stopped speaking and sighed. She couldn't finish that sentence, and she was grateful when he didn't push.

"Wook, Mommy!" Messari shouted.

The fountains erupted, and Morgan reached for her daughter, who was sleeping against Meek's chest. "Look, Yolly Pop!" Yara turned to the lights, then turned her head in the opposite direction, going right back to sleep.

Ahmeek laughed with Mo as she picked up Messari to give him a better view.

"Wooooowwwww!"

Morgan loved his excitement. Meek did too. He smiled more than Morgan had ever witnessed before as he watched Messari's reactions. When it was over, Messari reached for Mo and nestled on her shoulder.

"Do you feel like walking back? I know your car is in valet at the club, but—"

"It's cool, Mo. We can walk," he interrupted. "It's whatever you want to do."

They strolled down the lively street, laughing and talking. Mo wasn't in a rush to get to the drama. She stopped to stroll through the different hotels along the way. It took them two hours to walk a half mile. She didn't even care that her feet were aching; her soul was glowing.

"You're staying here, right?" she asked.

He nodded. "I'm in 2514," he stated. "I'll walk you to your suite. Make sure you and the twins are good."

Morgan shook her head. "That's not necessary, Meek."

"You're going to carry two sleeping toddlers upstairs by

yourself?" he asked. He headed toward the elevators before she could even respond.

Yara stirred in his arms as they stepped inside, and he placed a comforting hand on her back, rubbing gently, then patting as he bounced a little. Morgan swooned.

"You're going to make some girl very happy one day, Ahmeek. You're a beautiful man." Morgan sighed, shaking her head.

Ahmeek's brows lifted, and amusement played in his eyes. "I've been called a lot of shit before, Mo. An *ain't-shit nigga, that nigga, Daddy,* but never that . . . never *beautiful.*" He chuckled. "I don't know if I like that too much."

One of those real smiles that he hated blessed her face. He stood next to her, leaning against the back of the elevator. "Now that," he said, looking at her lips. "That smile. That's beautiful." She blushed. "Me. I'm a real nigga."

"Yup," she agreed. "A real, beautiful-ass nigga."

He hollered, and she shared in the laughter. Two sleeping babies didn't stop them from gravitating to each other. Morgan turned to him, and he leaned down. A moth to a flame. Morgan knew she was flying toward danger, and still her eyes closed.

"I can't breathe, Meek," she whispered. Their lips. So close. His breath. So sweet. She waited, waited for the kiss. Her body was going haywire. Her insides malfunctioning, screaming.

"Can I kiss you, Mo?" Ahmeek whispered. He was so close that he was already kissing her. The movement of his lips as he spoke the words caused their lips to grace in the slightest way. A match that set her soul on fire.

"Everywhere." The word was so airy he barely heard it.

One hand was occupied by a toddler, and he wished it were free because he wanted to do things with it. He had plans for that hand. One would have to do. A fist to her hair and a slight pull craned her neck back.

Morgan withered under his command. He was so aggressive. So rough. She loved it. His lips barely graced hers as Yara stirred, crying, and on cue, the slightest whimper from his sister awakened Messari every time. Two toddlers, tired and screaming, interrupted them. Morgan pulled back, and the doors opened.

Morgan stepped out. When Ahmeek went to follow, she stopped him. "No. You—" Morgan stumbled, panicking as she maneuvered out of his hold and held out a hand to keep him at arm's distance. "No, Meek. No," she whispered. She put Yara on her feet and took Messari from Meek's arms.

"Morgan—"

"Ahmeek, if we keep playing . . . if we keep pretending like this is just friendly just to make ourselves feel better, we're going to go too far," she whispered.

He held the elevator door open. "Too far for who?" he asked.

"For everyone!" She shouted that part.

Her twins were whining, pulling at her, crying.

"Mo, let me help you," he said, reaching for her son.

Morgan snatched his hand. "Ahmeek. I can't take it there. I just can't, and you're literally everything I want, but I can't, and if I keep pretending like we're just friends, if you keep coming around with Isa or if I keep coming with Aria, I'm going to . . ." She paused as she shook her head. She didn't even know what Meek saw in her. She came with hella baggage. She was holding on to her baggage at this very moment, and that was only the baggage that could be seen. The emotional baggage was heavier. It was impossible for someone else to carry. She could barely handle it herself.

"You're gonna what?" he pushed.

"Fuck you! I'm going to fuck you, Ahmeek. You're going to turn me into a whole hoe, and I don't want to be a *hoe!* I'm already a little hoe-ish for the shit you did to me at your loft. I don't want to be a whole hoe. Right now, I'm half a hoe, and I need to keep some self-respect."

Meek couldn't hide his amusement as he finessed his chin. She was throwing a fit, and he found it completely fucking adorable. If she was trying to convince him not to pass go, she was failing miserably.

Morgan slapped his chest. "It's not funny!" she whined.

He snickered. "It kind of is, Mo. Shit's fucking hilarious."

She laughed too, shaking her head. The elevator began to ding repeatedly from being held up.

"Good night," Mo said, pleading with him with just her eyes to walk away.

"Night, love," he answered. He pressed the button, and the elevator closed. Morgan breathed a sigh of relief before leading her babies to her room.

"Where you been, Mo?" Bash's voice was like nails on a chalkboard.

"Let me put the twins down," she said.

He was on her heels as she took them to the bedroom. "Your phone don't work?" he pressed.

Morgan turned abruptly. "I'm not talking about anything until my kids are asleep, Bash."

"I just want to know where you were."

Morgan could see that waiting wasn't an option. "I was with Ahmeek. After you left, the kids ran out onstage—"

"Oh, I know. It's all over the internet. My mother called. Do you know how ridiculous this looks for my family? My fiancée half-naked onstage! My family's name is prestigious, Morgan. You have to think about everything you do before you do it."

"You act like I'm a stripper!" Morgan shouted.

He motioned to her clothes. "Look at you, Morgan! You might as well be."

Morgan recoiled, jerking her neck back so hard that it hurt. She scoffed in disgust, shaking her head. "I'm not staying here tonight," she said. "I might not be staying with you at all." She reached for her suitcase and scooped Yara in her arms. "Come on, Messari." Messari shimmied down off the bed, following Mo without question. Bash scooped him up.

"Put my fucking son down!" Morgan shouted. "You left them backstage with strangers!"

"Don't be dramatic. Your friends were there," Bash said.

"You don't even know them! I know them! You don't! But you can get to know them real well if you keep trying me!" Morgan had snapped.

"I'm not afraid of your little thugs from Flint. You've always been real easy to impress. I've given you access to the whole world, Mo, and you want to shake your ass onstage like you're for sale!" Bash screamed. "I wasn't watching that."

"So, you left my children unattended? They're two years old! You left them because you were pissed that I chose to dance with Stiletto Gang? Nah, this is because I made a decision of my own for the first time in two years! I didn't do what you or your mother wanted me to. I did what I wanted to, and you left me hanging! And now I'm a stripper? When you met me, I was dancing! You used to act real cool, real chill, Bash, like you was a good kid from around the way. Now I embarrass your family? Fuck you, and fuck your family!"

Morgan released the bag and grabbed Messari from Bash's arms.

"Where are you going, Mo? I apologize. I should have—"

Morgan seated Messari on the top of the suitcase. "Hold

on for Mommy, okay? I'm going to take you on a ride. It'll be fun, but you have to hold tight."

She kissed his head and then leaned the suitcase forward onto two wheels.

"Mo!"

With one kid on her hip and dragging one on the piece of luggage behind her, she stormed out the room.

Morgan was so angry she couldn't even cry. She struggled with Yara and Messari and the luggage all the way down to Aria's room. She wondered if this was what it would be like if she left Bash. If she would struggle balancing it all . . . if she would drop the ball with her twins because they would be fatherless. How much easier things would be if they had a father. Morgan's lip trembled. When she opened the door to the suite, she flicked on the light.

"Shit! Mo!" Aria screamed, scrambling as she jumped off Isa. She was in the middle of a ride.

"Oh! Sorry!" Morgan sang as she dropped the luggage.

"Fuck you stop for? Mo know what dick look like. Keep going, Ali," Isa groaned.

Morgan hurried her babies to the adjoining room as the soundtrack to Aria and Isa's escapade filled the entire suite.

"Mommy, what's that noise?" Messari asked.

"Auntie Aria is being a . . ." Mo turned away from her son to open her luggage. "Hoe," she whispered to herself, chuckling.

"Her being a what, Mommy?" Messari asked. His little voice was so innocent, so curious. Morgan loved him. She looked at Yara, who, through all the fuss, was protected from the chaos because she couldn't hear it.

"Nothing, baby." She put headphones over his ears and changed them into pajamas as they watched their favorite cartoons. She took a special moment with Yara. "I love you, Yara

Rae. You are always enough. You are loved. No more, no less than Ssari. You are equal, and I cherish you, Yolly Pop. Do you love Mommy too?" Morgan signed, tears accumulating in her eyes. It was all she had wanted to hear as a child, and she made sure that Yara heard it every day.

Yara signed, "Yes, Mommy. I love you."

They were asleep in minutes.

Morgan's mind was all over the place. She tossed and turned because she was unable to turn off her thoughts. Thoughts of Bash filled her mind. Fantasies of Ahmeek snuck in behind those. Then her fears. Fears of being alone. Fears of never finding love again. Fears of her children growing up the way she had, without a father to call their own. It was the number-one reason why she'd let things with Bash go on this long. He loved her children, and for a long time, that was enough. Her happiness didn't matter. Then Ahmeek had come to London and messed everything up. He had made her feel those goddamn butterflies that her mother had told her about so long ago. Morgan had always been a hardheaded girl. She didn't run from them. She chased them because, to her, the butterflies weren't a warning sign—they signified love, and more than all else, Morgan Atkins wanted love. Morgan envied the rise and fall of her children's tiny chests. She envied their peace. She promised herself she would always keep them that way. At peace. Morgan showered, hoping that the steam would entice her to sleep, but it only awakened her more. She dressed, throwing on jeans and a white V-neck T-shirt. The pair of heels she'd danced in were all she had with her. They would have to do.

I just need some air and some food, she thought.

She crept out of the room and saw the glow from a laptop from the couch.

"Hey?" Aria greeted. "I didn't know you were still up. Are you okay?"

Morgan nodded.

"I'm fine. Just a bad argument with Bash. I'm sorry for interrupting," Morgan said. "Hey, I need to clear my head. Do you mind watching the twins? They're asleep. They won't wake up. They normally sleep through the night."

"Yeah, no problem," Aria said. "I'm in for the night."

Mo nodded. "Thanks." She grabbed her handbag and one of the room keys off the table before walking out the door.

The casino floor was alive, even at the late hour. She waltzed through the rows and rows of machines, headed for the door. Out of the thousands of people in the building, she saw the one she wanted to avoid. Ahmeek, standing at the craps table near the exit. She thought of turning around, of just going up to her room and calling it a night, but when his eyes glanced up, it was like he had sensed her. It was like someone had whispered in his ear and said, "Yo, bruh, there's Morgan."

Morgan sucked in a deep breath, and her feet carried her to his side.

"Hey," she greeted with a soft smile as she slid into the space next to him at the craps table. "You look like you're getting lucky tonight." She nodded at the girl beside him, and Meek smirked.

"Nah, I don't pay to play," he responded.

Morgan squinted and peeked over at the beautiful woman in the fire-red dress. She was nestled in tight beside Meek, who had a rackful of black chips in front of him. She was laughing, touching him lightly, whispering in his ear. Nothing about her screamed *professional*.

"Really?" Morgan whispered.

"Really." Meek snickered. "She the type to get a nigga hemmed up out here. It's a price tag on that." Meek motioned toward the game. "You want to shoot something?"

Morgan shook her head. "I don't know how," she said. "Not in the mood. I'm just going to get some air."

"Mo, it's one in the morning. You don't walk the strip by yourself this late," he said. Meek turned to the dealers standing over the colorful table. "Color me up."

Meek collected his chips and then led her to the cage of cashiers to retrieve his money.

"Risking fifty thousand on a dice game like it's nothing, huh?" Mo asked as they walked away.

"It is nothing," Meek answered.

Morgan scoffed. Ahmeek had come a long way. She remembered back in the day when she used to bend corners with Nish, she used to see him and the crew out on the block, trapping small dollars. Back then, she was sure every twenty-dollar bill counted. He had bossed up, and she could tell. Demeanor, pockets, crown . . . all three were heavy. Ahmeek was a king.

They stepped out into the desert air.

"Now, why are you awake? It's like four a.m. back home," Meek said.

She folded her arms across her chest, shrugging. "I had a fight with Bash," she admitted. "He doesn't like when I'm onstage."

"When he met you, weren't you dancing already?" Meek asked.

"My point exactly," she stated. "I don't want to talk about him, though."

She leaned her head on his arm as they strolled down Las Vegas Boulevard. Even in the middle of the night, it was alive.

"I know that's your man and all, but if he ever do anything out of order, he can get his tape pulled back real proper. Shit can get ugly over you. Anything, Morgan, and I'm dead fucking serious," Meek stated.

Morgan lifted one side of her mouth in a halfhearted smile. "He wouldn't. He's not that guy, but thank you," she said.

A drunk girl stumbled into her, and Morgan grimaced as beer spilled all over her shirt.

"I'm soooo sorry," the girl said, an octave too loud and slurring. She reached for Mo's breasts, trying to drunkenly wipe the wetness away with her bare hands.

"It's okay," Morgan said, lips pulled tight and forehead bent as she stepped toward the row of souvenir shops that lined the boulevard.

Meek grabbed a tourist shirt, and Morgan shook her head. "I guess that's what happens when you're the only sad and sober person on the strip. Can we go somewhere else? Somewhere quiet?"

She turned toward the counter where Meek was paying for his items. Her eyes fell on a swimsuit hanging behind the cashier. "We'll take those too," she said, pointing at the cheap, matching, two-piece bikini and swim trunks. "A large and an XL." She grabbed six mini shots of Patrón. "These too."

"Who's swimming?" Meek asked, brows lifted in wonder. "And tequila ain't good for a nigga, Mo. I get on another level off that shit." He smirked and shook his head.

"We're swimming—and good," she said. Meek peeled off a hundred-dollar bill and grabbed the bag as Morgan led him back to their hotel.

They bypassed the action in the casino and went to the back of the popular resort.

"Yo, Mo, it's closed. Pools in Vegas close at like six," he said.

"That's why we're going to sneak in," she answered. She grabbed the steel bars of the security fence. "Help me up."

"You're a real thug, huh?" he asked, smirking.

"You can smack a nigga, but you're afraid to bypass a tiny sign and a locked gate?" she challenged. He shook his head and finessed the side of his face before bending down to create a bridge for her to put her foot in. He hoisted her up and over the gate before jumping it himself.

Morgan peeled out of her clothes instantly, stripping down to her bra and panties. Meek's brow lifted, and he glanced away, being polite as Morgan changed into the two-piece swimsuit.

She tucked her clothes inside the plastic bag and grabbed a towel from the towel stand. She opened one of the mini bottles of tequila and tilted her head back as she drank it all. She grimaced as it heated her entire body. She reached for another and tossed it to Meek. "Your turn. Get changed. I'll be in the hot tub," she said, walking into the darkness with a second shot in her hand. Palm trees lined the pool area, and dim lights cast a small glow over the dark area. She pressed the button on the side of the massive hot tub and then slid her body inside. Her tension melted instantly. Morgan tilted her head back and wet her hair, then waited patiently for Meek to join her. Strong thighs and ugly feet are what she saw first as he approached. His body was incredible. His strong physique explained why he was able to break a nigga's jaw with one punch. He was disciplined, always had been. While Messiah and Isa ran around terrorizing the city, Meek was a strategist; he was a thinker. He plotted his moves from A to Z. He was the one the opposition never saw coming. Smooth-ass Ahmeek. He slid into the hot tub.

"This feels amazing," she groaned. He threw his arms over the side of the hot tub and peered at her as bubbles filled the space between them.

"Yo, the twins onstage tonight was legendary," Meek said, snickering. "The crowd went crazy. I still can't believe they belong to you."

She beamed and shrugged. "Yep, all mine."

He shook his head. "That body don't look like a body that housed twins, Mo," he returned.

She smirked, blushing, before shrinking farther into the

water, up to her neck. He didn't know the insecurities she carried over the weight she'd gained . . . over the weight Christiana constantly encouraged her to lose.

"It felt great. They loved it. Yara's a little shy, but Messari . . ." She snickered, shaking her head. "That boy is a whole trip. He'll do anything. He's fearless."

She knew where he'd gotten that spirit from. It was in his DNA to be kingly, to not fear anything or anyone walking on two legs. He was his father's child. Mo saddened because things should have turned out so differently. Things could have been so beautiful. Once upon a time, they had been; now it was just lonely. She wasn't living. She was just floating . . . being steered through life at someone else's direction. Morgan had never been so unhappy. Even years ago, when she was a little girl, things had been better because at least then she had her sister to confide in. Morgan felt alone. She was drowning in a sea of unfulfillment. Except with Ahmeek . . . he was like a life raft. He was like a breath of fresh air. Ahmeek was like going home after being away and smelling your mama's favorite dish as soon as you walked through the door. He gave her a nostalgic feeling she would never forget, bringing out a side of her that had only existed for a short moment in time before she had suppressed it. He made her feel beautiful and strong and wild and free. Like a butterfly.

"What you looking at, Mo? You looking but not talking. What's in your head?" he asked.

She shrugged. "Just thinking. I go inside my head sometimes because I know if I spoke my thoughts, I'd seem ungrateful."

"You won't, so speak," he ordered.

"I mean, I have everything. Every single luxury with Bash. I damn near live in a castle. His family's name will be my name soon, and it's powerful. Money, influence. I'm about to graduate and start med school. My babies are beautiful and healthy, Ethic and Alani are happy, they support me through everything. Bella and Eazy love on me, and I still feel like something's missing. Like none of it is good enough. I'm not in love with him, Meek, and I'm about to marry him. I'm terrified."

"So do something about it," Meek shot back.

"I can't," she said, scoffing. She knew he wouldn't understand. No one understood. Hell, Morgan didn't even understand. She was simply a girl who had always needed a man to love her. First her father, then Ethic, then Messiah, on to Bash. She needed to pull strength from men. Needed them to hold her up. Bash believed in her so much that it made her believe in herself. He was in a lot of ways her best friend. *God, he's the perfect friend.* But her husband, he was never meant to be. How he had snuck out of the friend zone and trapped her in his world, she didn't know, but Morgan felt like she were living behind the constraints of a glass wall. Like that royal palace was a prison. Like she was a pretty picture on display at a museum and Bash wanted all his family and friends to come see his new art piece.

"You can, Mo. He's your kids' father, not your master. When you ready to step, you let me know," Meek answered.

"What you gon' do, Ahmeek? If I step?" she asked.

"You ain't gon' step, so it don't matter." He snickered.

Morgan bent her brows at him in offense. "I'm about that life. Don't act like you've never seen me act up," she said, rolling her eyes.

He laughed at that. He remembered. He remembered every single tantrum she'd ever thrown. He licked his lips and leaned his head back as he looked up into the night sky.

He felt something hit his chest, and he lifted to see her coming across the hot tub.

"Sorry." She laughed, fishing the mini Patrón bottle she'd thrown at him out of the water. She twisted the top and held it to her lips, only taking half before lifting it to his mouth. "Open up."

"You're trouble as fuck, Mo," he said.

"I'm not. I'm a good girl, Ahmeek," she answered. She sat beside him and turned to face him.

"No lies told there," he said.

"You love me, don't you?" she said playfully.

"No lies told there either," he repeated.

Morgan steeled. Her heart. Her words. Her eyes. On his. She couldn't breathe. "Meek, you're on the outside looking in. You don't know me enough to love me. You just see a pretty girl."

"Everybody sees a pretty girl, Mo. That's the obvious. They probably even see the weak girl. I see the strong girl. I see the bitch in you, Mo. The part you keep tucked, but the fire that's trying to start that lives in the deepest part of you. It's flickering, and it just can't catch because you won't let it, but I see it. Little Morgan got the power to burn the whole damn kingdom down. There's a fire in you. You're a fighter, Mo."

Morgan's eyes prickled. No one had ever described her that way. She didn't even see herself that way. How could he? How could he think she was strong?

"You were in my life every day, Mo. Couldn't touch you, couldn't have you, but you were there. You walked by me every day. I don't even know if you noticed how you stopped a nigga heart. I saw you smile every day. Every fucking single day . . . the most beautiful girl I'd ever seen. That's hard on a nigga. Being in your presence but not being present. Putting all that in a box so I wouldn't do no disrespectful shit. You weren't mine. Any other nigga and I would have snatched you, but Messiah was my brother, and he needed you more. It just wasn't shit to be done. No moves to be made. You were with my nigga, so the shit I felt couldn't exist. I shut the shit down, but some of the shit that has run through my mind about you . . ." Meek paused, shaking his head. "I have no business thinking about you like that."

Morgan was speechless. She hadn't known that he felt like that back then. Even if she had, it wouldn't have mattered because at the time she only saw one man, but hearing the words from Meek now made her feel sick to her stomach. Morgan lifted out of the hot tub and sat on the edge. She gripped the lip of the cement and shook her head.

"I'm not perfect, Meek. You only feel that way because you don't know the fucked-up shit about me. I'm spoiled and selfish. I'm a handful."

"Handful or not, you're love, Morgan Atkins. Just looking at you right fucking now is love. You and love . . . the same . . . it's just who you are. I feel the shit every time you place those fucking eyes on me. You just drive a nigga crazy. Have a nigga ready to air shit out if your smile dip even a little bit. Your smile dips around him, Mo, and my trigger finger starts itching. So like I said, when you ready to step, you let me know."

Morgan sucked in air, holding her breath at the conviction she heard in his voice. Morgan leaned back to get the bag that was within arm's reach. Another shot. She needed another shot. She tilted it to her lips, and then Meek stood and walked between her thighs as she poured the rest into his mouth.

She placed both hands on the sides of his face, and her heart fluttered as he captured her in that gaze, in that dark place behind his eyes.

"You got to stop touching me, Mo." The way he said it, like he was struggling, like there was yearning in him, like the pads of her fingertips were unbearable torture against his skin.

His toned body lifted out of the water slightly, biceps flexed, abs tensed, as he fisted her wet hair with one hand. He kept her there, trapped in his gaze, a breath away as he took in every inch of her face. Neither spoke; the tension in the air labored her breaths. She could hear her heart racing in her ear, and then he kissed her. He kissed her like he didn't need permission, like he knew she would consent. The tension between them had been building since London, and they both wanted to cross a line that a dead man had drawn in the sand.

Morgan's body exploded. TNT. A fucking demolition erupted in her as her heart raced and their lips danced. She could feel years of wanting in this kiss. Fireworks, a full display, erupting, one after another each time his full lips enveloped hers. They were soft and thick, and his tongue was skilled and sweet. Morgan moaned it as her forehead collapsed in wrinkles, and her back arched. Guilt, lust, desperation filled her as she opened her mouth, accepting it all, again and again because damn, Ahmeek tasted sooooo good. He was dominant and strong and a whole fucking goon, and Morgan felt dizzy. His touch made her light-headed. She was high, and it felt familiar. She hadn't realized how much she had missed being with a man in position until now. Different dog, same breed. Aggressive. The type of man that had some bite behind his bark, and Morgan knew just how to tame him. He traveled down the interstate of her body, lips everywhere, tongue everywhere. Her neck. She gasped, her collarbone . . . a kiss . . . her sternum . . . who the fuck kissed there? Ahmeek. Ahmeek kissed there before sliding a finger along the seam of her bikini top, peeling it back to reveal her taut nipple. Her breath caught as he tasted there, pulling it into his mouth, circling once with his tongue before dipping farther. He was unafraid of her depths, unafraid of her wet as he slid her bikini bottom to the side. Morgan's mind went to the tattoo that used to be there. Messiah's name. She had branded it because she had thought it would always belong to him. Tiny butterflies covered it now, but Morgan still felt like Meek could see behind them. Like the butterflies were mad with invisible ink and Messiah's name was staring back at Meek. Morgan tensed. He paused, kissing the face of her intimacy and then placing steepled hands in front of him.

"What are you doing?" she whispered.

"A nigga like to bless his meal."

Smooth ass.

He looked up at her over his furrowed brow, eyes never leaving hers as he tasted her. His first sample, a long, flat tongue to her clit, pressed firmly and then circles.

"*Ahmeek!*" she screamed. His tongue on her body melted her. He wrapped his hands around her ass and pulled her off the edge of the hot tub, surrounding his head with her thighs as he held the tiny fabric out of the way.

"Mmm." He moaned like she was the best thing he'd ever tasted. She exploded instantly. His lips around her clit, pulling, flicking, as three fingers worked her middle, made stars glow behind her pinched eyes. *Slurp.* One long pull of her clit, finessing it out of the hood with just his tongue alone. Morgan's eyes popped open in ecstasy.

All Morgan saw were the waves on the top of his head as it bobbed between her legs. She was seasick. She palmed his head with one hand as she placed the other behind her body for balance, and then she rolled her hips in his face, adding pressure, riding his tongue like she rode a dope beat. Morgan on the fucking off beat . . . Mo Money on the tongue. Slip and slide, down to ride on it for the one time.

"Feed it to me, Mo," he whispered, pausing to kiss her inner thigh. Morgan had that pussy on a spoon for that nigga, and he was overindulging. He pressed a thumb to her clit and rotated clockwise. Morgan bucked as her legs opened wider.

"Mmm," he groaned. *Lick.* "You got it."

Morgan felt her entire body prickle, and she tensed.

The phrase. It was too similar. *"Yo, shorty, you got it."*

Common enough, but as soon as she heard it fall off Meek's lips, she thought of Messiah.

"No, Meek, no," she whispered. She scrambled to her feet, dripping water and seduction all at the same time.

Meek exited the hot tub.

"Mo . . ."

"No, this is a mistake," she whispered, wrapping the towel around her body. "What am I doing? God." Her face contorted, her lips trembled, and shame filled her.

"Mo, whoa, talk to me," he said. "I thought we were on the same page. I didn't mean to offend, love." He pinched his lips, the taste of her lingering there, simmering on his tongue like a concoction that needed time for the flavor to settle in. She was steeping on his tongue, and he licked his lips just to get another taste because it was the best he'd ever had.

Morgan felt like she was falling apart. Her eyes burned so badly, and her vision blurred with tears. She couldn't look at him, so she snatched her arm away and grabbed her clothes before rushing, damn near running, away. She was terrified of what she was feeling. It wasn't right. How could she feel this? For Meek. Morgan rushed into the hotel, putting as much distance as she could between herself and temptation because she wasn't sure what giving in would mean.

17

Morgan's tears fell down her face as she stumbled into the hotel suite. She needed to lay eyes on Bash. She needed to try to trick her heart . . . convince it that he was the one, that he could produce the same feeling . . . that he was capable of making it skip beats . . . of making her soak. Morgan didn't even think about what she would say about being soaking wet and in a bikini. She rushed through the large room, seeking him, needing him to make her feel. She opened the door to the bedroom and stopped when she saw that he was asleep. Her feet were at the threshold of the room. All she had to do was step across it and climb in the bed with her fiancé. She could do this. She could find her place in his world. She had done a good job of faking these past two years. She had gotten quite skilled at pretending to be happy, but Christiana chose everything in her life. From what she majored in to what she wore. Morgan had lost her identity, and as she stood there, she realized she might not have ever known who she was to begin with. She had been reacting to life for a long time instead of creating the life she wanted.

The last time she remembered living, truly living, and knowing who she was . . .

The night at the club . . . two years ago. The day I found out I was pregnant.

Things had fallen apart after that day. Everything that she had thought was real had been exposed as fake, and confusion settled into her life . . . it had taken permanent residence in her soul. With Meek, she didn't feel unsure. Afraid, yes. Ashamed, maybe. Uncertain, no. She knew exactly who she could be with him, and he saw her for who she was, not who she was pretending to be. He saw through her, and the cracked mirror that no one else could see still held value to him. Morgan turned and walked out of the suite. Her heart was racing, and she was crying because she knew it was a possibility that she was about to ruin her life. She was about to risk it all on a man that she had never even considered until now. A man that she should have never considered . . . even now. Nerves filled her as she headed to the elevator. She got inside and pressed the button for the twenty-fifth floor. She had fifteen stories to change her mind. She wished that she would. She prayed for someone or something to stop this from happening because once she did this one thing, there was no taking it back. She knew all the reasons why she shouldn't, but when the doors opened, she stepped off anyway.

Room 2514.

She spun in circles, trying to figure out which way to go, and then hurried feet carried her to Meek's door. She lifted her hand to knock, and before the anxiety eating away at her stomach stopped her, she connected her knuckles with the wood. Meek pulled open the door, dressed in a Versace robe and nothing else, holding his phone in his hand. He stopped speaking midsentence, caught up in her rapture. He froze, stunned.

"Yo, bro, I'ma get with you in the a.m." He hung up the phone without waiting for a response.

"I need it, Meek," she whispered. Lust and desperation clung to every word. She stepped closer to him, shivering because now the towel covering the wet swimsuit was soaked and the air-conditioning was on blast. Or at least that's what she told herself. The chills were from the cold, not from Meek . . . but she knew better. He made her quiver. He hadn't even touched her yet, and her toes were already curling.

"Nah, Mo."

His rejection shocked her. She wore her surprise on her pretty face and recoiled, jerking her neck back. "I'm that easy to dismiss," she scoffed. "That easy to move on from. Fuck Mo . . . forget her like that," she said, snapping her fingers. She saw Messiah in her mind, cursing her out and deserting her on Bleu's lawn all over again. Feelings on the floor. Self-esteem beneath his heels. Self-worth dug into the dirt. Meek's rejection was the moral thing to do, but damn, Morgan just wanted to be bad. She shook her head as droplets of emotion threatened to spill from her eyes. She turned, and Meek grabbed her fingertips, pulling her into the room. He closed and locked the door and then trapped her against it.

"I'm not curving you, Morgan. You're just not ready," Meek said. He looked down at her. She looked up at him. Then his hands cupped her face, swiping away at her tears. "Let's press Pause. Wait. If it's supposed to happen, it'll happen. If it ain't, it won't." He said it like he wasn't stressing over pussy, like he had it on speed dial, like he could order the shit up. Pussy, extra wet with a side of head. She knew he could. She knew he had options, and suddenly the idea of that burned her.

"I need it, Meek," she repeated. "I can't wait."

She placed both hands on his chest, then slid one south

until she found his gangster. He was solid in her palm, wide and long. The motherfucking trifecta. Her breath caught in her throat, and he stood there, staring, waiting, letting her probe his manhood with one hand, then two. She could feel him pulsing. His desire for her was palpable, but still there was hesitation in those eyes. They were as dark as midnight and held some remorse.

"Mo," he whispered. "Stop, love. We both know this is wrong."

"But what if it's not?" she asked.

Ahmeek blew out air. He was frustrated. She could see his conflict. She could feel hers.

"The shit I want to do to you," he admitted. There was pain behind that statement. Shame. Morgan didn't care.

"Show me," she gasped, her hands moving up and down his length as he grew in her grasp.

He gripped her shoulders, leaning forward, placing his forehead against hers, eyes closed, restraint wavering. She brought her hands back to an appropriate place, to his face.

"Never knew Murder Meek to hesitate." She could barely whisper the words. Her emotions were all over the place, choking her. A storm destroyed her insides, uprooting every single principle she thought she stood for. What was right and wrong anyway? "Shoot first, ask questions later, remember?"

"Mo, I ain't the nigga to hit something and give the shit back. You hear me?" he asked. "If it's what I think it is, I'ma be possessive over that shit, and I'ma want it when I want it. That nigga can't touch you if I'm touching you, because I'ma kill him. I get real ig'nant over mine."

"Ahmeek," she whispered, almost whining. "It took everything in me to come to your room . . . all that I had. Every piece of courage I could find. Can we work out the details later?"

He reached around her and helped himself to a helping of

her ass, a handful, then two, then her feet left the ground as
he scooped her. She climbed him, wrapping her hands behind
his neck as he kissed her. Morgan's heart bled out. It oozed
emotion, her angst spilling across the floor, leaving invisible
remnants of her need in a trail at his feet. She was filled with
unbelievable need as he carried her across the room. He placed
her on her feet, then turned her around.

She turned to him, but he spun her around, placing a delicate kiss to the back of her neck before bending her over the
bed. "Hold your ankles, love," he said, planting teeth in one ass
cheek. Morgan's arch was like the heel on a six-inch red bottom.
That weight gain looked like a platter to a nigga like Meek. He
placed his hands on her behind and gripped her flesh, rotating
before planting a light smack. The blow didn't injure. It was in-
stigating, like he wanted to see how all that ass would react to
his touch. "Yooo," he groaned in appreciation as it moved for
him. He took a knee, like Morgan deserved a little respect, like
an injustice had been committed, like this was NFL Sunday
and he was suited up on the field, then he peeled that bikini
bottom off her body.

Morgan's knees planted into the bed and she reached for
her ankles, head cocked to the side, pretty yellow ass tooted
high, as her chest pressed into the bed.

"Sssssss, boy, stop. Oh my fucking God." She was open, on
full display, and he arrested her clit from behind. A face full of
real nigga explored her depths, finessing her swollen sex with
expertise. She wouldn't last long in this position. She wouldn't
last long at all, in fact. She was already creaming. Morgan was
in trouble. She knew it. Head like this would drive her crazy.
Meek was submerged in her, hands on the sides of her ass, opening her wider so he could go deeper.

"Meek?" she whimpered.

"Yeah, love?" he whispered. A peck to her most sensitive

place, then three fingers, not two, never two because two wouldn't prep her for what he was about to deliver.

"This is bad . . . this is so bad," she whined.

"Nah, love. This is good . . . all good, Ms. Atkins," he whispered. He sucked on her again. "Mmm," he groaned. "So fucking good, Mo." He started at her seed and licked backward all the way until he reached the end and then ate her there too. Morgan came back on her thighs and stretched her arms forward. "Feed a nigga, Mo," he groaned.

"I'm dying," she moaned. "My God, Meek, stop. It feels sooooo . . ."

Before she could finish her sentence, he was inside her. "Ahmeek!" No condom, and she didn't even care because she didn't want a barrier between them. For two years, an entire ocean had been between them; now he was swimming in one, in her waters, no life jacket.

Morgan hadn't been touched in so long. Two years of emptiness to being filled in an instant had her climbing the walls. Meek pulled her wrists, reining her in so she couldn't run as he tagged her from the back. It was a mixture between love making and fucking . . . not rough, not gentle, but appreciative, like he had sexed her before in his dreams and it was finally coming true.

"Ohhh, fuck," he groaned. Two hands to her hips for guidance, and then he pulled.

Slap! Slap! Slap! Slap! Slap!

Skin to skin, he beat it, and the music their bodies made echoed off the walls accompanied by the soundtrack of Mo's falsetto as she screamed his name. He had knocked down two orgasms like they were bowling pins. He was trying to pick up the spare as he pulled the rest out of her all in one round.

She gripped the sheets, clasping them, her fingers curling in delirium from the stroke he was gifting her with. A tender ache filled her every time he went deep, never too deep, never with the intention to assault, but to bring pleasure. He was walking a tightrope between pleasure and pain, using all his ability to keep the balance that kept her soaked for him, that made her open wider for him. Morgan wasn't running. She was taking all of him, every single inch, as he thugged on her . . . beasting on her . . . the kiss to the middle of her back left tingles in the place of acknowledgment. She wondered why he'd chosen that spot . . . what was he appreciating about the crease down the center of her back. His next stroke snatched the thought from her mind, and Morgan threw her body back onto him.

"Damn, love." He gritted his teeth, and then she felt him lose restraint as he entered her with aggression, splitting her in half with one volatile stroke before pulling out and releasing onto the bed.

Morgan rolled onto her back, moving wet hair out of her face and staring at the ceiling in disbelief. He was fucking phenomenal. Her womanhood throbbed. It had taken a licking, and she could feel it ticking in response from all it had endured. He came up her body and hovered over her.

"You okay?"

So thoughtful. Kind. No voids in his ability to show emotion, but far from soft . . . only behaving this way because it was her. His dream girl.

She nodded.

"You sure?"

The consideration. The double-checking to make sure that she spoke truth and nothing less. It melted her heart. She nodded again as a tear ran out of the crease of her eye. He used his thumb to clear it.

"What now?" she asked, the frog in her throat capturing her voice. It was barely audible. She was afraid. He could see it. He could feel it. Her hesitation.

"We take it one step at a time, love," he said. He lowered, kissing her lips. The way his skin stuck to hers and then peeled away slowly as he pulled back made Morgan's eyes close. She relished there because the feeling was glorious. It wasn't the act of being coveted. It was being coveted by someone who didn't like to, who didn't know how to, who only did it because his heart wouldn't allow him to do anything else. Meek didn't love women. He fucked many, but loved none . . . until now . . . now he loved one and it wasn't new. Morgan didn't know how she had ever missed it before. She had been in love with another, and Meek had watched from afar. Now that he had her beneath him, connected through her essence, to his life source, she felt every single inch of his affection.

My God, every inch.

Morgan gasped as he reached down, gripping his strength before guiding it back into her depths. "I'ma take it real slow," he whispered.

A night of passion, full of pleasure, and Morgan endured it all as Meek helped himself to her body over every inch of his suite. Even when she thought he was done, when they thought the moment had passed, he hit Rewind and pressed Play all over again. Morgan was exhausted. After hours of this marathon, her inner thighs were so weak she could barely walk. She lay under him, the white sheets covering their bodies, as he reached for the room service they had ordered.

"Give me some," she said, opening her mouth as she leaned into his plate.

He placed his fork in her mouth. "My plate is your plate too. That's the type of girl you are, huh?" He chuckled as she nodded, closing her eyes to savor the buttermilk pancakes.

"That's the exact type of girl I am," she answered, smiling. She stood from the bed, and her bare body arrested his attention. Morgan was thick. A man's dream. Two babies had done her well. She had more ass than she preferred, and her hips had spread something vicious. Meek's favorite part was the one roll right where her bra rested. It only appeared at certain angles, and it had driven him crazy all night as he'd hit her from the back.

"Gorgeous as fuck." He reached for her and pulled her back to the bed.

She giggled. Such a carefree sound, like she'd loved him all her life. She didn't know if this was love or infatuation, but it brought out her inner being . . . it brought out the girl who loved to dance, the girl who kicked ass at spades and collected the books while talking cash shit, the girl who wanted to open a dance studio for deaf kids, not pursue medicine. He turned her into the girl she was brave enough to be two years ago.

"You can have the food," he said. "Let me just get this, one more time." He pulled her to his face and sat her down right on top of it.

"I can't," she moaned. "The twins wake up at seven religiously."

He glanced over at the clock. It was already 6:04 in the morning.

"This is fast food, love."

"Meek, nooooo." She laughed, trying to resist.

Meek reached for his phone as Morgan sat on his chest. "I tell you what," he said, thumbing through his screen. "Give me one song."

She smirked. "One song, Ahmeek."

He pressed Play.

Ain't never been a man wanting anythang much as I
want you
Sun doesn't come up 'til morning, so tonight there's no
excuse

Marques Houston filled the room. An old song, but new to Mo because she hadn't been able to hear when it had come out. It was the longest song on his playlist. Four minutes. Twenty-seven seconds. Mealtime. He smirked, lifting her right onto his lips.

Morgan's head fell forward as his tongue made a quick meal of her womanhood. She rolled her body slowly, riding both his face and the beat. She lifted a dainty finger, snapping, and she closed her eyes as she got lost in the lyrics.

Come on, baby, turn the lights off, let's get naked

The music vibrated through her body, lifting her, making her heart flutter, and she forgot that this was sex . . . it felt like art . . . like she was expressing sensuality, dancing to the slow beat, and riding his tongue so viciously that he groaned. He held her backside and attacked her clit.

"*Fuck!*" she screamed. She lifted her hands and kept grinding, slow, like they were two-stepping instead of fucking, and those fingers snapped. Her forehead wrinkled as she trailed one hand down the opposite arm, then down her neck, then across her breasts, tweaking her nipples in satisfaction.

Morgan lifted on her tiptoes and worked her middle, making him lift his head to reach her pussy. She bounced, eyes still closed. She was in a groove, a beautiful groove as Meek captured her swollen clit and pulled it into his mouth, between those sexy lips, then sucked with just the right pressure. A finger finessed her other hole, and Morgan exploded. He was nasty. The nastiest—and Morgan loved it.

"I'm cumming," she whispered. She had lost count. The night had been so long she didn't know anymore. He had her in a sexual fog. After a drought of two years and some change, this was too much. One body wasn't supposed to experience this much pleasure. How did he even know how to give this much pleasure? How the fuck did this much pleasure even exist? Morgan had only been with one man before, and he had been the best, but something about the way Meek touched her ... the way he used it ... the way he didn't care to let his enjoyment leave his lips in moans. Calling her name ... praising her sex ... worshipping her wet ... he was a fucking beast, and she understood why he had his pick of every woman in every room he'd ever entered.

The song faded, and Morgan gripped the top of the headboard, breathing so heavy that her breasts rose, then fell.

She lifted from him, and he pulled her to his face, kissing her forehead.

"Thank you, Ms. Atkins, for blessing a nigga," he said. "Made a young nigga from Flint dreams come true like a mu'fucka."

She blushed and pulled back before rushing into the bathroom. Not even the steaming-hot shower could wash away her sins. She had been kissed everywhere, and his lips had left a stain. Messiah's best friend had taken her places that he shouldn't even know the way to. She had handed him the road map to her body, and he had explored every route. She didn't know how to feel. A mixture of shame and contentment swirled inside her because she knew what it looked like. She knew what people would say. When she emerged, he stood there phone in hand.

"Yo, I don't give a fuck about none of that shit, nigga. The schedule don't change. Who set the schedule. I set it, or you set it? I work for you now?" he barked. He was back to gangster. Back to business. Morgan pulled her hair into a quick ponytail as she scrambled around the room.

"Oh shit ... my clothes," she whispered. She had left the plastic bag in her hotel suite the night before.

Meek snapped his fingers at her, trying not to break up

his phone conversation and get her attention all at once. He pointed to the bags that sat by the front door of the suite.

Morgan frowned, walking over to them and opening them. An Adidas women's jogging suit and new Yeezy sneakers in her exact size lay inside. She opened the La Perla bag to find undergarments, down to the socks. She lifted stunned eyes to him. He had measured her by eye. He was so well versed with pussy that he could guess her sizes without asking. She didn't know if she should be flattered by the thought or offended that he hadn't gotten anything wrong.

How many women has he been with?

The way he worked her body over, she suspected more than a few. He was a connoisseur.

She slipped into the clothes, and he walked over to her, slightly distracted by the transaction taking place in his ear.

"Hold on," he said. He lowered the phone to his side and wrapped one hand around her waist, jerking her toward him. He helped himself to her lips, and just like that, Morgan's worries eased. She didn't care who he was with besides her. She had a situation too. Who was she to judge?

"I'll call you when we get back," he said. "If that's okay?"

She stalled as she looked at him. "Are we sure about this? People will talk. They'll think—"

"What they want to think. As long as you know what it is, I'm good," he stated.

Morgan felt a pull in her chest. Did she know? What did this mean? "I don't like being judged, Meek. I don't like being whispered about or stared at," Morgan said.

He could hear the insecurities in her. "They do that anyway. Every time you enter a room. They talk, and they stare. You have no clue what you do, love," Meek said. "No fucking clue."

"I'm afraid of this with you," she admitted.

"No bullshit, love. Me too," he answered. She smiled at that. "I can press Pause. I can act like none of this ever happened if you want me to, Mo. Ball's in your court."

"How will it happen again if I pretend it never happened the first time?" she asked.

She headed for the door, and as she pulled it open, his baritone made her take pause.

"Yo!"

She turned to him with curious eyes.

"London is a wrap . . . I need you around for a while," he said. No inflection in his tone because it wasn't a question. He wasn't requesting her presence. She knew an order when she heard one, and as much as she wanted to buck, she didn't, because she liked that shit. She smirked, and her heart raced because he was a motherfucking man—all dominance, no waver. She didn't answer because she was a woman, with covert manipulation that turned his dominance into her own. She walked out of the room feeling her power as a woman, as Morgan Atkins, as Benny Atkins's seed, as Ethic Okafor's daughter. For the first time in a long time, Morgan felt like she was in control of her life.

18

Morgan crept back into Aria's suite and rushed to the second bedroom, where her babies were still sleeping. She pulled Messari up and cradled him in her arms.

"Wake up, my handsome boy," she whispered. She kissed the top of his head, and the sound of his whines melted her. "Mommy's Ssari," she sang as she rocked him in her arms. She loved both her babies, but Messari reminded her of his father so much. The very best parts. She closed her eyes. She placed him on the bed and then reached for their luggage. She removed clothes and pull-ups and quickly dressed Messari. "Did you have fun with Auntie Aria?" she asked.

Messari nodded.

"Of course he did."

Morgan turned to the door to find Aria at the door.

"Isn't that right, boyfriend?" Aria asked. Messari struggled to jump from the high bed, not caring that he wasn't big enough to do it on his own. He was fearless, and Morgan shook her head as he hit the floor hard and then quickly recovered to run full speed to Aria. "Are you hungry?" Aria asked.

Messari made kissy noises as he gave Aria a big kiss and wrapped his arms around her neck.

"Aww, you make me feel so special, Ssari," Aria sang. Morgan smiled and then reached for Yara. "So, you want to tell me where you snuck off to last night? I know you weren't with Bash because he called here looking for you."

"What did you tell him?" Morgan asked, her heart sinking. The thought of having to explain where she was terrified her for some reason. Morgan wasn't instinctively dishonest, and having to conceal last night's escapades gave her anxiety.

"I told him you were asleep," Aria answered. "I'm down for the alibi, but where the hell were you?"

"I just sat in the casino all night. I just needed to think," Morgan lied.

The sound of the suite's doorbell rang out, and Morgan sighed in relief as Aria turned. "I'm ordering food. You want anything? What the kids like?"

"Anything you order is fine," Mo said. "I'll be out after I dress Yara."

Aria nodded and pulled the door closed, taking Messari with her.

Yara whined and hugged Morgan's neck tightly. She was fussy in the morning; it never failed.

Morgan rubbed her hair and rocked her. She pulled back and signed to her daughter. "Mommy loves her Yolly Pop."

Yara pouted and rested her sleepy head on Morgan's chest. She wasn't in the mood to reply. A true meanie in the morning, Yara wasn't ready to interact with anyone but the sandman. Morgan sat her down and changed her into fresh clothes. A Burberry check dress and cardigan because it was cool inside the hotel. She brushed her hair up into a pretty puff and placed a headband around her head. She carried her on her hip and walked out of the room.

She stopped mid-step when she saw Ahmeek sitting at the long rectangular table.

Her heart lurched inside her chest, and she forgot to breathe. Yara lit up when she saw him and scrambled to get down. Morgan placed her on her feet, and she ran to the table to Ahmeek's side.

"What up, smart girl?" Ahmeek asked as he reached down to lift her onto the table in front of him.

Morgan was stuck. She just stood there looking stupid as Aria, Ahmeek, and her kids ate breakfast.

Aria's brow pinched as she looked from Mo to Ahmeek and back to Mo. "Hmm," she said. "Casino all night, huh?" Aria snickered.

Morgan blew out a flustered breath and made her way to the table. She felt exposed like everyone in the room could see through her.

"Hey, Meek. What are you doing here?" she asked.

"Good morning, Mo," he greeted, playing it much cooler than she was capable of doing. He fisted his beard and smiled, then focused his attention on Yara. "How's my favorite girl?"

"His favorite girl," Aria repeated and stared a hole through Morgan. Morgan refused to look at Aria. She felt the accusing stare, but she simply reached for a plate and began to help herself to the spread. Yara was giving her away. No way should she be this familiar with Ahmeek.

Stop feeding that nigga Cheerios! Yolly Pop, no!

She made a mental note to never commit a murder with Yara . . . she would for sure get them caught.

"So, what you do last night, Murder Meek?" Aria asked.

"I was cooling," Ahmeek answered, his eyes never leaving Yara as she pulled on his beard.

Aria pinched off a piece of pancake and placed it in Messari's mouth. "Hmm . . ." She rolled suspicious eyes back to

Morgan. "You might want to put some makeup on that hickey before you go back to Bash," she stated bluntly.

Morgan's hand shot to her neck. The side Ahmeek had devoured just hours ago.

"Something must have bitten me," she said as she rushed to the mirror on the wall. Sure enough, there was a hickey on her neck.

"Probably," Aria said, giving Morgan a knowing look. Isa emerged from the master bedroom.

"Yo, bruh, you ready to mob?" Ahmeek asked, standing with Yara in his arms.

"Yeah, we up," Isa said. "Rebook that flight, Ali. I want you in my bed when I get back."

Aria glanced at Mo. "You want to stay a few more days?" Aria asked.

"I can't," Mo declined.

"She didn't ask if you could. She asked if you wanted to," Ahmeek said, eyes on his phone screen as he struggled to text with one hand while holding Yara with the other.

Morgan's insides twisted as she wondered who was on the other end of that message.

"Mo?" Aria pushed.

"I, umm . . . I can't . . ."

Ahmeek's brow knitted, and he walked over to her, standing directly in front of her. Morgan reached for Yara, but Yara pulled against her, wanting to stay in Ahmeek's arms. Morgan felt that. She hadn't wanted to let him go either.

"Come on, Yolly Pop," she signed. "He has to go." She forced Yara to let go and put her down. Yara instantly clung to her leg.

"Hey." The word came with a finger beneath her chin as he lifted her face to his, forcing her to meet his eyes. "If you want to stay, stay. The twins ain't a problem. I've got business out here, but afterward—"

"I know you fucking lying," Aria whispered in disbelief.

"Mind yours," Isa stated, not bothering to look up from his phone.

"Why, when hers is so much juicier?" Aria stated.

Morgan turned red. "Ahmeek . . ."

"Right. You can't," Ahmeek stated, nodding.

Morgan had never felt so nervous. Ahmeek was standing too close, looking too hard. He was worse than Yolly Pop! The nigga was a snitch! He was letting it be known that he was invested, and he didn't seem fazed that Isa or Aria was witnessing this public display. He pinched her chin and then rubbed his thumb over her lips.

Morgan couldn't breathe, let alone speak. He pulled his bottom lip into his mouth like he was restraining himself. A part of Morgan wished he wouldn't.

"Travel safe, Mo."

Morgan held her breath until Isa and Ahmeek walked out the door.

"Bitch! You fucking Meek?" Aria shouted.

"Aria, my babies—"

"Girl, fuck these kids! Your ass is fucking Ahmeek!" Aria stood from the table as Morgan scooped Yara and retreated to the bedroom where her babies had slept. "Oh my God! When did this happen? How did it happen? Bitch, was it good? I bet he's good!"

"Aria!" Morgan shouted. "What if I asked if you were fucking Isa?"

"You saw us last night! You want details? The nigga dick is big as fuck and he eat that shit from the back! There you go. You got all my tea! Now fucking spill!" Aria shouted.

"He's amazing," Morgan moaned as she collapsed onto her bed. She sat Yara down beside her and then buried her head in her hands. "How did I let this happen?"

"Fuck all the guilt trips, Mo. I need the play-by-play," Aria said, clapping with every word. She sat in the chair across the room.

"I'm engaged," Morgan said.

"And you shouldn't be," Aria said.

"Ahmeek makes me feel . . ." Morgan paused. "I don't know." She shrugged.

"He makes you feel what?" Aria pushed.

"The last time I felt like this was with Messiah. He makes me feel like I'm all he sees. I know that I can't have him . . . can't love him . . ."

"Love him, Mo? How long has this been going on?" Aria asked.

"Since London. He's the reason I came home. I knew I couldn't stay there. As soon as he left London, I wanted to leave too. I just wanted the possibility to run into him. My heart aches around him. And it was friendly at first. We talked, we chilled, but the time together feels natural. It feels good, and then last night . . ." Morgan's eyes closed. "It felt like love, Aria. Every touch, the places he kissed, the things he said . . . my heart just craves him. Even right now, I just want to be around him. I want to be under him, watching Netflix. I want to go grocery shopping with him because he occupies the twins so well. I just want him, and he's Messiah's friend. It's wrong."

"First of all, you don't owe Messiah anything. Yeah, it's a little fucked up, but he's dead, Mo, and before he was dead, he tore you apart. You tried to kill yourself behind that boy, Mo. He sucked the life out of you. If you think this thing with you and Meek is real, you deserve to see where it leads. You deserve to be happy, and that's not with Bash."

"I can't leave Bash," Mo whispered.

"Well, if you think Meek is going to be your side nigga and keep it on the low, you're highly mistaken. Men like Meek don't stay in the shadows. You see what he just pulled in here. He's fucking you, and from the looks of it, he's in his feelings. He sniffed it one time, and now he wants more. He's got Yara feeding him Cheerios, and he's caressing your lips and shit like you've got a ring on your finger. He won't care who's watching. If he fucks with you, he's going to fuck with you all the time. You won't be able to keep it a secret. Be careful, Mo. You're going to have to make a choice. Let Bash go or leave Meek alone. They're both really good guys, and you deserve a good guy. You don't have to feel guilty about it either, because it ain't shit a ghost can do but haunt you. You shouldn't feel bad about finding happiness with Meek. Messiah left you with a lot of pain. I say you're entitled to heal what he broke any way you see fit as long as it's healthy."

"So, you want to tell me about little Morgan, G?" Isa asked as they stepped out of the elevator and headed toward the exit.

"What's to tell?" Ahmeek asked, eyes on his phone screen as they stepped out into the scorching sun. Isa pulled a valet ticket from his pocket and handed it to the attendant.

"So, you finally doing what Messiah asked you to do?" Isa asked.

"It ain't about Messiah," Ahmeek answered. "I don't know what it's about, but it ain't for play, and I ain't looking for permission."

"Be careful with her, bro. We all know how it ended last time. Mo's family. We all fucked up when it came to her. She don't deserve that twice."

"She didn't deserve it the first time. I don't intend on fucking up," Ahmeek stated. The S-Class Mercedes they had rented pulled up, and Ahmeek climbed into the passenger seat. Isa hopped behind the wheel. "Now, you ready to talk about this money, or you still worried about where I'm sticking my dick, bitch-ass nigga?"

"Yo, on some real shit, though, bruh, I just got one more question, then we can move on. Messiah was secretive as fuck about the shit, but I got to know . . . little Morgan? What that shit hitting for? I know shorty sitting on that medicine. Heal-a-nigga type of pussy."

"Nigga," Ahmeek said, shooting a warning glare at Isa.

"You've got it bad, G," Isa said, snickering as he put the car in drive.

Ahmeek's jaw tensed as they took the highway away from the tourist trap. It was hard to keep his mind on business. Morgan had put something on him last night that had left a stain. He would never confirm for Isa, but the type of pussy she was serving was the type to heal a nigga. It was the type with the potential to hurt a nigga too. From the moment she had walked out of his suite, he had been in his feelings. It had taken everything in him not to go to her room and pack up her and her twins and buck on her fiancé. The thought of her going from his bed to Bash's made him feel raw on the inside. Morgan had a pull on him something serious, and he knew she was a problem. A big fucking problem.

The city gave way to golden sand and a two-way highway, and Isa hit 90 mph.

"Who you say these mu'fuckas were again?" Ahmeek asked.

"Some tribal investors want to open a casino about an hour and a half north of Flint. They'll have armored trucks running up and down the highway. I'm talking big money, nigga. This is different than the semis. One armored truck is enough to live for life. They want to guarantee that their loads make it to their destinations safe. It's a tax for that. They got to pay the toll," Isa said. "Otherwise, I'm lifting that bitch."

"Armored trucks are a different game, G," Ahmeek answered. "Dye packs on the cash, armed drivers, an armed man in the bed of the truck, GPS under the hood, marked bills. The shit's risky."

"You scared, nigga?" Isa asked.

"I'm smart, mu'fucka," Meek answered. "I know you be on your adrenaline shit, bro, but this shit ain't the move. Popping the back of the fucking truck alone would be a task. That shit is military-grade steel."

"Well, let's hope it doesn't come to that. They pay the toll to pass those trucks through the city and we can get the easy bag," Isa stated.

They saw a bar in the middle of nowhere. A little wooden shack on the side of the road. Three cars sat parked out front.

"This the spot?" Ahmeek asked. Ahmeek reached under the seat and retrieved a 9 mm pistol. The price of the private jet was worth the ability to stay strapped. He didn't go anywhere unprotected. If you saw Ahmeek, he was strapped. At the doctor's office, in church, at funerals—any door he graced, he carried a gun through it.

"Yeah, I think so. Shit is two hours outside of Vegas; it better be it," Isa added. They stepped out the car, tucked their pistols, then swaggered to the front door. Ahmeek pulled it open and walked inside.

A man with skin so rich it appeared red stood behind the bar. Long raven-hued hair hung down his shoulders, center parted. Wrinkles filled his face as if they told a story; like the aged leather on a good bag, his every mark was representative of a journey he had taken.

"Long way from where you're welcome," the man gruffed. He reached beneath the counter and came up with a shotgun.

"We were invited," Isa said.

"Might want to lower that gun, old man, before I lose my patience. By the time you cock that bitch back, I'll serve that ass the daily special," Ahmeek stated in a cool baritone. Not an ounce of fear lived in either of them because they knew if it came down to them walking out of the building or the men in this bar, they were going to step.

The Native American man looked at the other patrons at the bar and lifted his hand off the shotgun.

"We're here for Hakani," Isa stated.

The man pulled out a cell phone and kept skeptical eyes on the duo before placing the phone to his ear.

"Hak expecting someone?" the man gruffed. Ahmeek's hands rested in front of him. One fist over the opposite wrists, on the ready.

"Stay cool, bruh," Isa said under his breath. "This is just an introduction."

"Two of 'em," the man reported to the other end of the phone. "I'm sure they're holding." Another pause. "Mmm-hmm. I'll send 'em back."

"Jasper, take 'em to the reservation. Hak says let them keep their weapons. Apparently, this is a friendly visit," the man gruffed.

A stout man stood from the bar. His long hair was snow white, his skin bronzed and aged by the sun. When he turned to them, a long scar permanently sealed one eye.

"He will take you to Hak," the bartender said.

Ahmeek gave Isa a skeptical look, and as Isa followed the man out of the bar, Ahmeek backpedaled, keeping eyes on the men remaining inside. They walked over to an open-air Jeep, and Ahmeek took the back seat as Isa hopped into the passenger side. The man drove behind the bar, taking them off-road through the sand, leaving a cloud of dust behind them as they ventured two miles deep into the desert. They stopped in front of a large brick building—a compound of sorts—and Ahmeek climbed out. Armed men stood like soldiers outside; warrior paint covered their faces.

What the fuck? Ahmeek thought as he followed the man inside.

They passed twenty people working on laptops as they made their way to the back and entered an office door.

A man in tailored designer slacks, Ferragamo shoes, and an Oxford shirt stood speaking on the phone. One hand was in his pants pocket, and he removed it to hold up a finger for them.

"I'll need the permits immediately. We have a schedule to keep. Sounds like a plan. Speak soon."

He ended the phone call, and a smile accompanied the hand he extended to them.

"I'm Hak. You must be Isa and Ahmeek," he stated. Ahmeek shook the man's hand, followed by Isa. "Please sit."

They all took a seat on the relaxed side of the luxurious office. This space didn't seem like it belonged in the middle of the desert, more like in a high-rise building in New York City. It was like a mirage; it almost didn't exist.

"I'm a man who does my homework. I own Hakani Enterprises, and I'm building a casino on tribal land in Saginaw. That's in your backyard. I hear there are pretty strict laws of the land that I need to respect if my business is going to be successful. The thirty-mile stretch of highway between Flint and Saginaw is yours. I'd like free access to it. I need to insure my investments. I'd like my trucks to be able to pass through without interference. I'd even like for them to be escorted by your team to make sure they aren't disturbed by others as well. I'm willing to pay for this insurance."

"How many trucks a week?" Ahmeek asked.

"Fourteen. One at the start of business, one at the end of business each day," Hak said.

"That's a lot of insurance," Isa stated.

"I understand," Hak said. "How does a hundred thousand a month sound?"

"Sounds like you think we're still working corners. That's less than two grand a truck. We can't even pay our people with that," Ahmeek said. "We can just take the fucking trucks."

"The art of business is in the negotiation, Ahmeek. You tell me a more appropriate number," Hak said.

"I'll know it when I hear it," Ahmeek stated.

Isa knew to let Ahmeek work. They had very distinct roles, and Ahmeek's was in the gift of gab. He already had a number in his head, but he would never undercut the team by speaking first. He needed to see how high Hak was willing to go first.

"You're a smart man," Hak complimented, wagging a finger at Ahmeek.

"What's your number?" Isa added.

"Fifty thousand a truck," Hak said.

"Each," Ahmeek interjected. "Small price to pay to make sure those trucks go untouched."

Hak sat back in his chair and steepled his hands under his chin. He took his time before nodding. He reached into his desk drawer and removed two iPads. He slid them across the desk.

"Swiss accounts have been set up on these devices for you. The money for the first month's runs will be deposited within the hour. You can log into your accounts and check them anytime. Nice doing business with you, gentlemen. It's time to get rich."

"Smile, Morgan. I swear, the way you sulk sometimes, I'd think you don't know what family you're marrying into," Christiana said as she sipped the glass of champagne in her left hand while flipping the page of the picture book she was reading to Messari with the other. Messari rested comfortably in her arms. She was his nana, and suddenly Morgan hated that she had created the attachment for her children.

"Ease up, Ma," Bash said. He reached across the divider that separated their seats and grabbed her hand, but she pulled away, tucking her hands between her crossed legs. Yara sat on his lap, and Morgan's eyes bounced back and forth between her twins. They were so comfortable with the Fredricks. They were family. From the day they were born, they had been accepted by the prestigious family. Morgan knew she should be grateful, and she was, but it wasn't like they had pulled her out of the gutter. They acted like she came from a third-world country. Like she was missing meals and lacking shelter when they'd met her. She knew they didn't mean to offend her, but she'd held her tongue for so long that it was growing tiresome.

"Sometimes, I think you forget the family I come from," Morgan muttered.

Christiana and Bash both lifted eyes of shock to her. Ahmeek had fucked some courage into her, apparently, because Morgan had never enforced an opinion of her own on Bash or Christiana. They were used to her going with the flow, but after Meek, after feeling the way he made her heart skip beats, the way he made her body ride beats, the way he made her back arch to catch his beat, Mo just wanted to go against the current, to swim upstream. She wanted to hop off the plane, run across the tarmac, and catch one of the black cars back to him immediately.

"Morgan, really, we already have so much to repair after your little striptease last night. I flew all the way stateside just to check on you. The last thing I need is attitude," Christiana said. "What has gotten into you lately?"

Good dick.

Morgan sighed and stood from her seat. "I'm just kind of tired and not in the mood to be scolded," Morgan answered.

"I'm not scolding, dear, just advising. You're in position to take over the world one day, Morgan. With Bash and these beautiful babies, you could run high society of London. After medical school, you'll open your practice and . . ."

Why did Morgan need to listen? Christiana already had her entire life plotted out anyway.

Morgan tuned Christiana out as her thumb slid across her phone screen.

She tapped on Ahmeek's name. He hadn't texted her in hours. It wasn't like they communicated all the time anyway, but she expected something, anything . . . after the night before, Morgan craved connection. Even the thought of him made her pulse raise, and she felt it most between her thighs.

MORGAN

Is it bad that I miss you?

Anxiety tightened her belly, and she glanced up at Bash— who was occupied with Yara—before tilting to the side so he couldn't see her messages. She didn't have to wait long. Within seconds, bubbles danced on her screen.

AHMEEK

Nah, love, that ain't bad at all.

Morgan smiled. Then her fingers tapped away.

MORGAN

That thing you did last night? With your tongue? I'ma need you to do that again ASAP.

AHMEEK
Love, no nasty talk. Shit's going to kill a nigga.

Morgan snickered, then stood. She needed to see his face. She yearned to hear his voice. Texting was no longer enough.

"I'm gonna lie down for a bit. I'm kind of tired. Are the twins okay out here?"

"Of course, Morgan," Christiana answered. "We should be taking off soon. Get some rest. We can handle them during the flight."

Morgan stood and retreated to the private sleeping quarters on the private jet. She still couldn't believe Christiana had come swooping in from London just to meet them at the airport. "To keep things in order," she had said, but Morgan couldn't lie. She didn't mind the luxury of flying back to Michigan on the private jet. It beat commercial flying every day of the week. A perk of being engaged to Bash. She hit FaceTime before she could even lock the door. She smiled when his face popped up on her screen. He was walking. Busy. She could tell from the pinched brow he sported, but still he answered.

"I'm sorry if I'm interrupting. I know you said you have business to handle," Morgan said.

"Business is interrupting you, Mo. How can I be of service, love?" Ahmeek asked.

Morgan smiled. "Just like that, huh? Stop everything for little ol' me?"

"Every time," he answered while looking around, checking his surroundings and not focusing on the screen.

"I just wanted to see you," she answered, speaking in hushed tones.

"So stay," he countered.

"I'm on the jet right now," Morgan said. "I can't."

"Yeah, I'm already not liking this," Meek stated.

"Not liking what?" Morgan asked, frowning.

"You telling me no," he answered.

"So ask me something I can say yes to," she shot back.

"You miss me, Mo?" he asked.

"Like crazy," she whispered. "God, what have you done to me?"

"Nah, Mo. A nigga chest been mad tender since you walked out my room this morning. What the fuck have you done to me, love?"

Morgan smiled. "I just loved on you a little bit, that's all. I know you're not lacking for female attention, but all you get from women is physical. It's all about sex. I gave you a little bit more. Nothing major," she said, smirking.

"So, you loving on me, Mo? You loving a nigga?" he asked.

She paused. Did she? Could she? Whatever she was feeling, it was very familiar. It was blissful and hopeful and light. "Only questions you can say yes to, remember?" he reminded with a wink.

Her heart felt giddy, and it raced as her lips pulled tighter and she smiled wider. "You want me to love you, Ahmeek?" she shot back.

"Very much so, Morgan Atkins, but let a nigga earn it first. I ain't afraid to earn it," he stated. "I can make some plans to do that."

She swooned. Ahmeek Harris was such a gangster, but he had the gentleman thing down to a science.

Morgan felt the plane begin to move. "I've got to go. We're about to take off."

"Call me when you land?" he suggested.

"I'll text you," she said.

"We ain't doing easy, remember. Texting is easy. I need to look in your eyes to see if you're bullshitting me," Ahmeek said.

"That only applies to me, Meek," she said.

"Nah, love, in this equation, you the only one with the potential to break hearts around here. I'ma carry you proper, Morgan Atkins, but I got a feeling you gon' drop a nigga shit on the floor, walk all over it, ding my shit up," he stated.

"Never." She smiled. "I'm going to love you real good, Ahmeek. I want to be the one you remember."

"You can't be that," Meek shot back.

She jerked her neck backward. "And why the hell not?"

"To remember you means I'll have to lose you. I ain't doing that," he said. "I'ma do my part, Mo, and eventually that corny nigga gon' be the one reminiscing."

Morgan blushed. "I've got to go."

"Then hang up, because right now you got me on some real sucka shit. I don't like to disconnect from you, Mo. I swear to God, I been fucked up since you climbed out my bed earlier."

"Yeah, I know what you mean," she whispered. There were stars in her eyes, flutters in her heart. She just wanted to run to him, to stay behind with him, but she couldn't. "I want to go skating," Morgan said.

"Skating?" he asked.

"Yes. Roller-skating. I want to go when you get back, and I want to skate. I don't want you to be too cool and watch me from the sidelines either. I want you to hold my hand and skate with me," she said.

Ahmeek chuckled. "We'll see, love. Now hang up."

"Do I have to?" she whined.

He gifted her a full-blown smile as he stopped walking and focused on the camera, finessing his beard. "Yeah, you do. You got me out here caking in broad daylight," he said.

Morgan stifled her laughter, smiling so bright that her cheeks hurt. She couldn't ever remember smiling like that. A knock at the door caused her to look away.

"Mo! We're about to take off. Make sure you're buckled in," Bash called through the door.

"I will!" she called back. She turned back to the phone. "I'll FaceTime you when I'm home."

"Okay," he answered.

Morgan went to hang up but hesitated. Just hanging up didn't feel right. It was like she was supposed to say something. Do something more. Express more. Be more to him. Say more to him. Act as if she'd never see him again just to get a bit of glee off her chest. "Ahmeek?"

"Yeah, love?"

"I think this might be something." She paused. She was afraid to say it. A bit ashamed to admit it because it was way too soon to be feeling like this . . . it was way too wrong to feel it at all . . . it had to be the dick. Morgan was still reeling from the way he'd handled her. Had to be. It couldn't be emotional. "Something good."

"You think right," he said.

Morgan hung up the phone before she told him she loved him. She could feel the words bubbling inside her chest. He made her feel like a fifteen-year-old girl with a crush . . . like she wanted to write his name next to hers and plan their wedding during third period. Morgan stood and hurried back to her seat. She sighed and leaned her head back onto the headrest, closing her eyes in appreciation. Two hands over her heart to stop it from beating out of her chest.

She shook her head in disbelief. She didn't care that Bash was sitting right next to her. It made her no never mind that Christiana was across from her staring with inquisitive eyes. Morgan was covered in the remnants of Ahmeek's love, and she couldn't hide it. She was glowing. She felt it. For too long, she had thought she'd die without ever feeling something so potent again. She had seen Ahmeek a hundred times, but she was seeing him through new eyes, and she was smitten. She never wanted to come down from this high. Morgan didn't care how risky it was, she was willing to jeopardize her entire world to keep Ahmeek in her life. Fuck a friend. She wanted him as her own, and now that he'd given her a sample, she wanted the whole thing.

19

Messiah rode through the derelict city blocks with his neck on a swivel. One hand wrapped around the leather steering wheel of his BMW while the other wrapped tightly around the .45-caliber chrome pistol in his lap. It was his first time in the city in over two years, but he wasn't naïve enough to think things had changed. It was still the Wild, Wild West, and he would never be caught slipping. He nodded to Jeezy as he took the streets by memory. There was something about being home, in the hood, that made Messiah come alive. He had run through these blocks like a renegade as a kid. They were his. They used to be his, at least, but he could see at first sight that the empire he had built with Isa and Ahmeek was still standing. The graffiti that marked the abandoned houses he passed on the way signified that niggas still saluted his crew. He was an urban legend in the city, and it was nostalgic to cruise through the hood. He knew what people believed. He was dead. He was supposed to be, at least. For a long time, he hadn't thought he would survive. For two years, he couldn't see past the pain to even fathom the notion of living, but he had been convinced to try. He had nothing to lose, so why not? He had walked away from the love of his life, from the kingdom he'd built, to die, but he hadn't, and now that he had years in front of him, he couldn't see himself enjoying them without her.

Messiah pulled up to the elementary school and hopped out of his car. He didn't have much to his name, but the house he'd left with Bleu and the car he'd taken with him were paid in full. He didn't worry about the rest. Messiah was a man of means. He would make the rest back in no time, but none of it was worth anything if he didn't have Morgan. He had to get to her. Had to talk to her. To lay eyes on her in person would be a blessing. The school bell rang, and Messiah posted up on the hood of his car as he watched the kids filter outside. When he spotted the one he was looking, for he shouted, "Ayo, homie!"

Time away had matured little Saviour. His locks were shoulder length and bleached blond at the bottom, he had gotten tall, and he had two big front teeth that were larger than the others.

"Uncle Messiah!"

Saviour took off, running full speed into him, never slowing and throwing his arms around Messiah.

"Ma said you were gone! She said you were in a better place!" Saviour exclaimed.

Messiah pulled back, feeling tender as he pinched his nose. Bleu Montgomery, his best friend and Saviour's mother, was one of few people he cared for. Saviour had a special place in his heart. He could only imagine the confusion he felt.

"Nah, nephew. Nothing's better than home. I had to go away for a while. I was real sick, homie. Your mom didn't think I would get better, but I'm feeling real good now. I'm doing good."

"So you can stay this time?" Saviour asked, excitement playing in his tone.

"Yeah, nephew. I'm staying," Messiah said. He gripped the top of Saviour's head and ruffled his locks. "Come on. Let's get you home so your mama can kill me."

Saviour snickered and hopped in Messiah's passenger side.

The five-minute drive to Bleu's house filled Messiah with tension. He was anxious to see her. Besides Morgan, Bleu had been the only other woman Messiah had ever loved, but their bond was different. Mo drove him mad, his emotions for her were so intense that he had a hard time staying sane when in her presence. He lived in a heightened reality with Morgan. Their love made him feel so raw that he hated it at the same time. The vulnerability. With Bleu, he was different. Bleu kept him sane ... balanced ... she grounded him, and he couldn't wait to see her. If anyone could help piece together fragments of his old life, she could.

He pulled in front of the white house, and his gut tightened. The last time he had been there had been catastrophic. He could almost see the scene playing back in his mind. He and Mo on the front lawn, screaming at each other. He had hurt her that day. Everyone saw it. He saw it. Hanging off her shoulders, leaking from her eyes, vibrating in her voice. Only her pain was acknowledged that day, but his hurt had been present too. His had been overwhelming because it was the day he learned that her love for him had no limits. She had been willing to forgive the unforgiveable, and it had angered him ... enraged him ... that she would be so selfless for him, that she would be so loyal to him, that she could love him so, that love didn't flee when in the face of adversity because everyone before her abandoned him. Not Morgan, not even Ethic. The disappointment he had seen in their eyes that fated day could only be an offspring of one emotion ... of love, and it angered him.

He hated them that day because although no one else knew, he knew that he couldn't stay. Because his fate was already decided. He had been sick, and he was dying, and they didn't know. They had no idea the resentments they caused in Messiah, because before Morgan, he had been okay with dying. He had been cool with having his life snatched from him. Before her, he was getting money, fucking bitches, living fast, and taking risks, going hard to make sure his name lived after he was gone—but after her, after drowning in her depths, after exploring her soul, after hearing his name on her lips, and standing on the pedestal she placed him on, Messiah had wanted to live. He thought for sure she would leave like everyone else when she found out he was Mizan's brother, but he had witnessed her love double after finding out. She had run to him, and he had turned her away because he was pissed that he was dying, and he could never, would never let her watch him fade to black.

He exited the car and placed a hand on top of Saviour's head as he guided him to the front door. He heard Bleu's voice through the open screen door before he even knocked.

"What do you mean he didn't get on the bus? Where the hell is my son?" she shouted.

"I'm right here, Ma," Saviour said.

Bleu turned, and when she saw Messiah, the phone slipped from her grasp, hitting the floor.

"Uncle Messiah picked me up," Saviour said.

"What up, Shorty Doo Wop?" Messiah greeted with a mischievous grin.

Bleu's lip trembled, and her eyes misted. She choked a bit on her own damn breath as she reached for the kitchen counter to steady herself because her legs had gone weak. A ghost had snatched the strength right out of her.

"Messiah?" Bleu rushed him. "I don't even know how you're in front of me right now. If I wasn't so happy to see you,

I would kill you!" she cried, her tears falling with ease as her heartbeat threatened to tear through her chest. He squeezed her tight, strong arms trapping her. He kissed the side of her head, getting emotional himself but fighting the burning of his eyes by closing them. This woman was his best damn friend. He owed her everything. She had let him use her in ways that he knew had stained her soul. She had stuck by him, giving him everything, setting no limits in ways that would have eased his transition. She had loved him, and in return, he would always love her. He would never love her the most, but on a list where only one other had ever gotten to his heart, Bleu had been added. Their friendship was potent, and he could never give her back all that she had given him.

"I missed your shit-talking, B," Messiah said, chuckling before letting her go. Bleu pulled back to look at him and couldn't help but to throw her arms around him again.

Bleu placed both hands on his shoulders and looked at him in disbelief. She touched him, moving her hands to his face. She couldn't believe he was in front of her, alive, breathing. She struggled to control her emotions as her face twitched, lip quivering, eyes prickling with tears. She shook her head.

"We've got a lot to talk about. You have some explaining to do, boy. Have a seat. I'm almost done with dinner. You're staying. Iman's in Cali, so it's just me and Saviour. We just got you back. No way is this going to be a quick visit, so I hope you didn't make plans."

"No plans, just you," he replied. "I hope you making Flint tacos. I need 'bout five of those ASAP."

"Taco Tuesday ain't changed, boy, you already know," she replied, laughing through tears. "Now, start at the beginning and leave nothing out. It's been two years, Messiah. Where the hell have you been?"

After four hours, twelve tacos, and a game of Monopoly

with Saviour, Bleu and Messiah sat at her kitchen table. She was crying and holding his hand so tightly that her knuckles lightened.

"Why would you let everyone think you were dead? Messiah! I would have been there for you! You went through chemo and surgeries and rehab alone!" Bleu cried. She was distraught.

"I thought I was dead, B. They gave a nigga a five percent chance of surviving. The shit was everywhere. Cancer was everywhere, they cut me into so many pieces just to try to get it all out. I never thought I would live through that. I still question how I did. The pain. B . . ." Messiah shook his head and lowered it, clearing his throat. "It was worse than death. It was like the devil had me and I was in hell. I was just waiting to die. No need for everybody to go through that. A nigga know how to die. I didn't require company for that."

"I called the hospital. I came to the hospital. They told me your file had been archived. That it was with the patients that had been terminated. I threw a fit at that hospital when they refused to show me a body. They just kept saying I wasn't family, so they wouldn't divulge any information, and this whole time you're alive! What about Morgan? Messiah! What about her? I tried to call her after I found out. Even went to her place, but she was gone. She moved to London. I heard she has kids now."

"Shorty Doo Wop got shorties." Messiah snickered. He already knew, but hearing it again was mind-numbing. There was no masking his somberness. He tried to be lighthearted about it, but he was heartbroken. He had imagined her with babies before, but they had been his babies, children they would share. Ones that looked like him and loved like her. It injured him something serious to know she had received that gift from another man. "Shit's wild."

"Messiah . . . ," Bleu whispered. He never was good at concealing his emotions from her.

"She did what she was supposed to do, B. She moved on. She lived, but I got to see her. I got to put eyes on her because that's my baby. That's my baby girl. She said my name first, Bleu, and she said it like nobody had ever said it before, like she loved saying it. Like she loved me and I just got to see her. I got to see her, so I can ask her to let me come home, B. Shorty got to let me come home, and I know she changed the locks and all'at, but it's still my house. I built it. She's still mine," Messiah ranted, moving his hands in front of him like he was trying to grasp the notion of someone else taking his spot. "What I'ma do without Mo? How a nigga supposed to appreciate this new air without her? I know I should stay away. I should just watch Shorty from across the street and let her grow and be beautiful, but a nigga like to pick his flowers and put 'em in my pocket. I got to have her with me. I just got to. I can't fucking breathe when she's not around. For two years, doctors been saving me, but living without her has been killing me."

"Ethic told you to stay away. If you want Morgan, you'll have to get past him first, and I'm not talking about the way you're used to handling things. He isn't an enemy. He's your family. He's like her father, so getting rid of him hurts her. The only way to her is through love. You have to tap into the love he has for you and get his forgiveness before you can even get to her. A lot of people never get a second chance. This is yours. You handled their entire family wrong the first time. This is your chance to fix it."

"Ain't no talking to Ethic after what I did. He see my face, he busting first," Messiah said. "Won't be no questions asked."

Bleu shrugged. "You better make him listen, Messiah, or watch Morgan love someone else from afar."

20

Morgan sat at the dining room table. Twelve seats and formal place settings separated her from Christiana. The six-thousand-square foot home was a mile from Michigan State and was the residence the Fredricks family owned in Michigan.

"I'm glad you've decided to stay here, Morgan. Clear your head a bit and focus on what's important," Christiana said. "You don't have time to waste."

"I didn't say I was staying, Christiana. I'm going to my place," Morgan said as she picked at the plate of food before her. Kale salad, balsamic vinaigrette. "What is this? This isn't what I ordered from the chef." Mo's face turned in irritation as she lifted eyes to Bash's mom.

"Pre-wedding food. We've got to get that waistline down if Vera Wang is going to work with you," Christiana said.

Morgan set her fork down, and it took everything in her to trap her thoughts inside her head.

Her phone buzzed against the table.

"Not during meal service, Morgan," Christiana said.

Morgan's fingertips were on the edge of her phone. Her heart fluttered because the notification let her know it was Ahmeek. It had been four days since she'd landed in Michigan. He had FaceTimed, not called, because they needed the eye-to-eye contact, but Morgan hadn't answered. Once call for each day that had passed. Mo hadn't answered once. Morgan didn't even know what to say or how to feel. It all felt like it was happening so fast, and her heart was so exposed that she was afraid. She didn't want to talk on the phone. She needed Face-Time. She needed to see his deep-set eyes and dark skin. She needed to rest her head on his chest to hear the way his heart beat because when it beat too slow, it meant he was trying to maintain his composure. It meant he was lying. Whenever he was calm around her, it meant he was fighting his emotions, trying not to love her. It was when his pulse raced that he was telling the truth. Morgan knew that a phone call or text wouldn't suffice, but Christiana had her under lock and key. Escorted everywhere, days planned out like she were the Queen of England. Wedding planners, preschool appointment for the twins even though they were only two years old, looking at venues, and homes for after the wedding because Bash would be buying her one as a gift. Not even a piece of time over the past four days had been left unaccounted for. Morgan had been put on a schedule so that she couldn't make any more decisions that would tarnish the formal announcement of their engagement.

"Where are the twins?" she asked.

"They're out back with Bash," Christiana answered. "They'll be spending the day with him while we try on dresses."

"Who decided that?" Morgan asked. "I'd prefer if they were with me. And why are we trying on dresses already? How do you know I don't have plans today, Christiana?"

"Whatever's planned can wait. I have someone from *The*

Detroit Free Press coming to cover you for the society and style section of their website," Christiana said.

"What?" Morgan called out.

"Relax, Morgan. Your dress will be custom. Off rack is mostly size twos and fours. We both know you aren't either of those. It'll just let people know that a new Fredricks woman is on the horizon. It's good for you. Your brand as a woman, emerging on London's elite . . . Michigan's elite. A young medical student marrying into our family. If we make the right moves and establish a strong social circle, when you finally finish medical school, your practice will flourish! The money is in private practice."

"Christiana, I haven't even told my family yet—"

"And why not?" Christiana's tone was intolerant. Like she couldn't fathom why Morgan wouldn't have bragged about the news. "Morgan, the ways you have benefited with this family holds value. The same way I pulled strings for you at Cambridge, I can tie them back. I can knot them. No one likes knots, dear. It's best for you to stay on board."

"That sounds like a threat," Morgan said.

"Come on, dear, you can't think you've gotten this far at Cambridge on your own merit. Every class, every grade, every milestone was paid for, Morgan. How devastating would a public scandal be if that news came out? You would be back at square one. Your career would be over before it even began," Christiana said. "Now eat the kale and like it."

Morgan stood in front of the mirror. Here she was, not even twenty-one years old, and she was about to get married. She had promised herself to a man for forever, and she was sick to her stomach. This felt like a trap. Like she was a butterfly trapped in a jar, and no matter how hard she flapped her wings, the glass she was encompassed in stopped her from freedom. The white wedding gown was beautiful. She felt just like the princesses in the stories she'd read coming up. Like the one stuck in the tower. The bitch with the long hair that let people pull on it hurt her just to climb to the top. Yup. Morgan felt just like that.

Morgan pressed flat hands to the bodice of the ball gown and sighed.

"Can we get a smile, Morgan?" Christiana said.

Morgan looked at her reflection and then at her future mother-in-law, who sat behind her, legs crossed at the ankles, and wearing vintage Chanel.

She gave up a tight-lipped smile, a disingenuous leer, and the cameras flashed. This wasn't what this moment was supposed to feel like. She was almost sure of it. Her eyes watered.

"The bride is crying," the journalist cooed. "Aww, this will be amazing for the viewers."

"Morgan?"

Aria's voice was so soft that it almost got lost in the excitement of the others in the room.

Morgan's eyes met Aria's in the reflection of the mirror.

"Uh-uh, she needs a minute," Aria said, standing.

"Well, unfortunately, she doesn't have a minute. *The Free Press* opened up their entire schedule to be here," Christiana stated as she sipped champagne from the crystal flute.

"It's cute that you think I was asking," Aria stated. She stood. "Everybody get the fuck out. Out, out!" Aria said.

"How about we just take a beat?" the photographer suggested. The staff from the newspapers exited the room, heading back to the main floor as Christiana stayed seated.

The dead stare Aria placed on Bash's mom was enough to make her rise from her seat.

"I suppose I should go smooth things over with them," Christiana said.

"Mmm-hmm," Aria said.

When they were alone, Morgan caved.

"I need him!" Morgan cried.

"Okay, Mo, I'll call Ethic," Aria whispered. "I don't even know why you're here trying on dresses. You haven't even told yo' fine-ass daddy."

"Ewww, Aria!" Morgan protested.

"I'm just saying." Aria snickered. "If you're afraid to tell him, it isn't right."

"I'm not talking about Ethic," Morgan whispered.

"Who are you—"

"Ahmeek," Morgan whispered. "I need Ahmeek."

Aria's eyes widened.

"Please call him," Morgan whispered.

"Morgan!" Aria exclaimed. "What is happening between you and Ahmeek? He hit that one time! You think he's going to come running up in here after one time? What you sitting on, girl? Is your whole damn vagina dipped in gold?"

"It's dipped in Ahmeek, bitch. Get him here now," Morgan answered.

A knock at the door interrupted them. "We really need to continue," Christiana said, peeking in.

Aria looked at Morgan. "I will chase these motherfuckers out of here right now," Aria said. "Just say the word, sis, and I'm stepping."

"I'm locked in this goddamn castle," Morgan whispered. "Just take my phone and drop my location. He'll come."

"Nigga, open your mouth," Isa said as he gripped the collar of the man on the floor before him.

"Bro, please, man," the man sniveled.

"Now you begging, nigga? Now you showing respect?" Isa asked. He bit into his bottom lip as his fist crashed into the man's face.

"Meek, man, please!" The call was desperate like he needed someone to intervene.

Ahmeek stood behind Isa, one leg propped against the wall as he held his cell phone in one hand. He held out his other hand. The word *Flint* was spelled out in ink on his fingers. He balled his fist, flexing it, casually, calmly. Without looking in the man's direction, he said, "Nigga, you know the rules. They're clear. We putting whole loaves of bread on your table, and you thieving, nigga? You still running around the kitchen scrounging for more. Stealing crumbs. Like a fucking rat, just getting what the fuck you can," Ahmeek stated. "Beg God, nigga; don't beg me. I don't save lives, I end 'em, homie."

Isa stuffed a handful of Xanis in the man's mouth. "Swallow that shit, nigga, before I blow your head off," Isa stated.

The next step should have been death. They were an unforgiving crew, but when Morgan's name appeared on Ahmeek's phone screen and he viewed the pin she had sent, revealing her location, Ahmeek's plans changed instantly. He could get to her, or he could finish this business. Cleaning up a body would take all day. He only had a small window of opportunity to see Mo, and his gut told him that she couldn't wait. His intuition urged him to drop everything. There had been no message behind the location. No words, just coordinates.

"Yo, Isa, we out. Let the nigga breathe," Ahmeek stated. "Looks like your prayers were answered, G. Tighten up."

Isa asked no questions. He pushed the man to the ground, and they stepped over him as they walked out of the warehouse.

"Since when you giving niggas second chances?" Isa asked.

"I got other business," Ahmeek answered. "I'ma get with you."

He climbed onto his bike, wishing he had time to stop and switch to his car. If Morgan wanted to leave with him, he preferred the safety of four wheels. Walking light and such meant he had to think of all possibility of danger. Caring for someone like Morgan meant taking no risks with her at all, but there was no time. He hit the highway as his mind did circles, thinking of the reasons why she had ignored all his efforts to reach out since Vegas. He had called and sent texts, only one a day, because anything more would give her proof that he was pressed. It would show her that he hadn't slept, that she lived in the back of his mind, and that he had replayed the vision of her sitting on his tongue in his mind on repeat. He had turned down women for three days just because they weren't her. He had it fucking bad for her, and it bothered him because the fact that she could go three days without calling him meant she had the power. All the cards were in her pretty little hands. When he pulled up to the address on his screen, he frowned. The wedding dress boutique threw him for a loop. He parked his motorcycle directly in front and removed his helmet before climbing down.

When he entered, he spotted her instantly. White dress, veil hanging from the crown of her head, standing on her tiptoes.

"Hi, can I help you?" a woman asked as she eyed him curiously.

"Nah, baby, you can't. She can help me. Only her," he answered, voice a ghost of his normal baritone as he stood there, enchanted by the fucking blessing that was Morgan in a white dress. His heart ached, and he took steps in her direction until her eyes lifted in the mirror, discovering his presence. The only thing missing from her face was happiness. She had the dress and the tiara and all the makings of a bride, but that smile was missing. As soon as she saw him, it appeared. Morgan startled him as she came down off the pedestal she was standing on. She ran barefoot across the store and into his arms.

"Get me out of here," she whispered.

"Morgan!" Christiana called after her. Aria stepped in her path, blocking her as Morgan ran out the door in the white wedding dress.

Morgan lifted the dress, balling the mountains of fabric around her waist as she hopped onto the back of his bike. He placed the helmet on her head.

"Morgan!" Christiana shouted as she emerged from the shop.

"Go, go!" Morgan urged. Ahmeek kicked off the stand and rotated his throttle before taking off.

Morgan laughed in his ear as she held on to him. "I can't believe I just did that!" she shouted.

Ahmeek chuckled as he carried her all the way to Detroit. To his loft. The one she wanted to redecorate and make her own.

Morgan climbed down, and Ahmeek reached for the tips of her fingers, catching his pinkie to hers and then pulling her into him. Morgan beamed as one hand caught her chin and he tipped her neck back, forcing her eyes to meet his. He held her prisoner there for a beat before kissing her.

"Are the twins with him?" he asked.

"Not anymore. Aria sent a text to Alani and Ethic to pick them up from him. When she texted you, she texted them too," Morgan answered.

He nodded. "Come on," he said, leading her into the building.

They stood on separate sides of the elevator. Him basking in all his cool and her letting her nerves eat her alive. She was questioning everything in this moment. If she left Bash, her life would be ruined. Everything she had worked hard for would be gone in the blink of an eye, but she would have Ahmeek. Or would she? Would he stick around, or was this just something fun for him to do in the moment? Morgan was unsure of so many things, and her bond with Ahmeek was too new to question his intent. She didn't want to scare him away.

"You're beautiful, Mo," Meek complimented. "Like for real. Not on no bad-bitch shit, not on no face-full-of-makeup shit. Just fucking stunning, yo. I lose time looking at you, love. You just take niggas hearts and eat 'em for breakfast, Morgan Atkins. Fucking playing games with me, yo." He scoffed and shook his head like he was her latest victim, like he didn't even know how he had let it happen.

Morgan's entire body warmed. It was statements like that . . . the way he looked at her . . . the way he spoke to her . . . any thought she had about making a mistake with him was erased.

"How long do I have you?" Ahmeek asked.

She shrugged. "How long do you want me?" she countered.

He finessed his beard and crossed the elevator. "You don't want me to answer that, love," he whispered. "I answer that and you're never going back."

He placed his hands on the wall behind her and leaned into her. Morgan didn't even wait for him to ask this time. She gave up her lips without protest. No permission needed. They were his, so why ask? Who asked to ride their own bike anyway?

The elevator opened to Ahmeek's penthouse, and Morgan stepped out first.

To her surprise, the wallpaper in the foyer was gone and replaced with gray paint and white trim. She looked at him in shock, but he pushed forward into the loft like it was no big deal.

The frill of the huge gown was cumbersome as she followed behind him. "I think I just stole a ten-thousand-dollar gown." She laughed.

"Call the boutique and put it on my card," Ahmeek said.

He reached into his back pocket and removed his wallet, removing his credit card. He held it out for her.

"Just like that, huh?" she asked.

"Just like that," he answered.

"Aria has my phone," she said.

He tossed her his without a second thought. "Code's the same—1128," he said, just in case she'd forgotten.

Morgan didn't even feel the need to snoop as she unlocked his phone. He gave up pertinent information without falter. It made her not want to look. She placed the call, paid the boutique, and then tossed his phone back to him. He spent the ten bands like it was ten dollars, without a second thought.

"Now can you help me out of this?"

She turned her back to him and moved her hair out of the way. Ahmeek arose from the couch and placed hands on her hips before placing his lips to the back of her neck.

"Nah, keep it on for a little bit," he said.

Ahmeek pulled out his phone, and he pressed Play.

The sound of guitar strings played throughout the loft. She turned to him, and he stood in front of her. Towering over her. Taking her fingertips and lacing them with one hand. The slightest touch from him made Morgan quiver.

> *Never thought that we would ever be more than friends*
> *Now I'm all confused cuz for you I have deeper feelings*

"Halfcrazy." Musiq was singing her emotions, except she was more like full crazy. She was too invested in Ahmeek. All in. So involved.

> *Cuz my mind's gone halfcrazy cuz I can't leave you alone*

They didn't even dance. They just stood there, his hand on her face, her eyes locked on his as the words to the song did all the work. She could see the confusion in his eyes. The turmoil.

"I missed you," she whispered.

"That's what your mouth says, Morgan Atkins, but you ain't hit a nigga line," he said.

"I couldn't, but I thought about you. God, I thought about you every second. I'm here now. Can we just be here right now? In the present? Just me and you?"

Their kiss lasted forever. The song played five times and they never tired. It was like she had him back in middle school where somehow kisses were enough.

"Can I see your phone?" she asked out of the blue. He frowned but handed it over. No checking it first, no clearing things she couldn't see from it. Just transparency. She typed for a few seconds, and then the song changed.

I see your face when I close my eyes

She tossed the phone to the table and lifted mischievous eyes to him.

"Ro James," Ahmeek said.

She nodded.

"You want to dance to Ro James," he assumed.

Morgan shook her head. "I want to fuck to Ro James," she whispered.

"Pretty-ass mouth . . . dirty-ass lips," Ahmeek whispered.

"Got to shake shit up sometimes. Give people what they don't expect." She smiled. She turned her back to him and held up her hair.

All day I dream about sexing you

"Get this off me."

This time, he complied. He kissed her neck and then slid the zipper south, his lips following, kissing every inch of her back that was revealed on the way down. By the time the dress fell to the floor, Ahmeek was on his knees, hands steepled because he wasn't a liar. He prayed before he ate. He followed Morgan as she swayed her hips from side to side, riding that beat like only she could. She felt the sting of his hand. A smack. He couldn't help it. She had so much to appreciate.

He placed a hand on the small of her back and then pressed down, bending her over. Morgan placed her knees on the couch and Ahmeek devoured her from behind.

"You're going to spoil me, Ahmeek," she groaned.

"Every fucking time I see you." He had to mumble the words because he had a mouthful. The delicacy between her thighs marinated on his tongue. She was like wine. You had to let it sit for a few seconds, let it breathe on your taste buds, taste the notes behind the initial flavor before you swallowed. Morgan reached for him. She had indulged in him twice, and neither time had she tasted him. That couldn't happen a third time. She turned and sat on the couch, destroying his cushions with her wet, staining them, but neither cared as she reached for his jeans. When he was in her hands, she couldn't help but lick there. Morgan didn't repel at the taste of him; the anticipation of her had him coated in need. A little pre-cum on the tip of him that Morgan took her time cleaning up.

"Ohh shit." Ahmeek wrapped four fingers around her neck. He lifted one leg onto the couch and tensed into her. He was a head connoisseur, but he didn't know if he had ever had better. Sight alone. His strength between her pouted lips, that tongue going to work, her face tensing as she tried her hardest to slay Goliath, gagging on that thang, spitting on it, as those pretty fucking short, French-manicured tips Hula-Hooped on his length. She was the fucking best. The fact that she was never supposed to be on her knees for any man but was here before him, submitting to him, made Ahmeek's prowess heighten.

"Mmm, so good, boy," Morgan moaned. She moaned like she was receiving instead of giving, and it made him want to give . . . made him want to be benevolent.

"Lie down, love," he whispered as he moved her hair out of her face. Morgan had a mouthful, and she didn't stop. "Morgan." She looked up. Her name on his tongue barely even existed. It was always *love,* sometimes *Ms. Atkins,* sometimes first then last, but never just *Morgan.* It caught her attention, and he stared at her for a beat before lowering to his knees. She sat on the couch and he pulled her to the edge before one thumb exposed the source of her pleasure. "Tell me what you want, Mo."

"Eat my fucking pussy, boy, and stop playing!" she cried. He snickered and lowered his head. Morgan saw God. He pushed her legs to her ears, exposing everything, folding her thick ass up in a pretzel as he mopped her up. Tongue everywhere, he plugged her leak, eating her with a hunger she didn't even realize he had for her.

"Mmm, damn, love," Ahmeek groaned.

Morgan loved how vocal he was. If he liked it, he said it. If he couldn't stand it much longer, he announced that shit like he were the captain flying high and he was warning his passenger about turbulence. Morgan felt his tongue in places where tongues didn't belong, and her eyes closed.

This nasty-ass fucking . . . shiiit!

Then she felt her body stretch because no way was she built to take a dick so long and wide. He dug fingers into the cushion of her ass and pulled her cheeks apart, went deep, then pushed them together, smothering his dick as he pulled out. It seemed like he was withdrawing forever, all the way to the head, fucking inch after inch, then . . .

"Agh!" Morgan screamed as he pulled her hair with one hand and gripped one hip. Bracing for impact, Morgan tensed. He felt her apprehension, and he pulled out. His lips touched her back. Then her ass.

"Relax, love. It'll never hurt with me," he whispered.

Morgan exhaled her tension, and then he kissed her clit. One time. A quick peck like he was coming back to it again soon, then he split her pink again. Morgan's sex pushed out air, farting, because he was so big he had left her vacant. Now he was moving in, now he was knocking down walls, and Morgan shouted as she reached for her clit. He could press the accelerator and she would steer. Morgan's fingers were soaked as she rubbed and he stroked.

Her brow crashed, her mouth fell open, and she reached behind her body, grabbing his neck as she trembled.

"Let that shit go," he whispered. Her sex throbbed around him, massaging him.

"Damn, baby. Throw that shit at a nigga," he groaned. Morgan's body was making all types of noise. Pussy farting, ass clapping, throat-trapping grunts of pleasure, and then whines of delirium sneaking out. He pulled her up onto his lap, and Morgan reached both hands behind her body, pulling his head to her ear. "Talk to me, Ahmeek," she whispered.

"You want me to talk to you, love?" he whispered. He reached around her body and found her clit.

"Yes!" she shouted.

I found true love in you. Ohh-ohh

"Cum for me. Be a good girl and wet that shit, love," he whispered, lips pressed to the back of her neck.

Morgan was in heat. Bouncing on him, matching his stroke.

"This is your dick, love. Shit ain't for nobody else. Just you," he groaned. "Goddamn, just you, Mo."

"Promise me, Ahmeek," she whimpered. "Promise me, it's mine."

"Property of Queen Atkins, love," he whispered the words in her ear. "Wet ass. Ain't nobody wetting dick like you, love. Shit is yours, Mo. Take it with you when you leave, baby."

"Agh!" she screamed. "Meek!"

He licked the nape of her neck, and Morgan exploded. He bent her over, then grabbed one of her feet as he increased the intensity of his stroke. Hard. Fast.

"Meeeeeeeeeek . . . Meeee . . ."

She felt him pulsing, and a part of her wanted to get pregnant. Sex this good could only result in a baby. Fuck it. She'd be his baby mama. She'd wear that badge with fucking honor, but he pulled out, using better judgment than what Morgan possessed currently. "Shit," he groaned.

He stood and pulled her hand, forcing her to rise with him. She followed him to the bathroom. A shower, a quick round two because Morgan couldn't endure anything else. He had her cumming from touch alone, so she wasn't worth much more than a quick one. When they climbed out, Morgan was all smiles.

"So, skating," he said as he dried her hair with the plush white towel in his hands. "You want to go skating. I need you available tomorrow."

"Okay," she said. "Just tell me when to be ready."

"I'll pick you up at three? That sound good?" he asked.

She nodded as he kissed the tip of her nose. "Don't be late."

"A nigga gon' always pull up right on time. Never late. I ain't missing no shots with you, love."

21

Messiah stood off in the distance, watching Ethic. He had been there for hours, witnessing the remnants of love as Ethic sat on the grass, his head leaned back on the headstone of Raven Atkins. He could see Ethic interacting, talking and laughing, as if Raven were speaking back to him. Messiah wondered if Mo had ever done the same for him. Had she visited his grave just to get a little piece of him? Had they had conversations that transcended life and death?

He hoped so. He prayed she had at least thought of him from time to time, because he had thought of her every single day.

"Are you going to say something? We've been sitting her for hours," Bleu said. "Go talk to him, Messiah."

"The nigga might fucking shoot me." Messiah scoffed. "He really might, and I'd deserve it."

"This is crazy. Messiah, the man is sitting at his dead love's grave. He's not carrying a gun," Bleu reasoned.

"Ethic is always carrying," Messiah shot back. He walked

over to Ethic, and when he was within voice's reach, he said, "OG."

Ethic lifted his head, and shock wore away like a flash of lightning as confusion, then rage took over. Ethic stood, hand dipped to his waist from instinct alone . . . add in the mistrust that existed between them and Messiah couldn't guarantee he would walk out the cemetery alive.

"I'm not on no bullshit," Messiah said, lifting his shirt and turning around to show he wasn't strapped.

"Niggas like you are always on bullshit, Messiah," Ethic stated, voice deep and unforgiving. "I thought you were dead."

"I was close to it," Messiah revealed.

"You left my fucking . . ." Ethic stopped himself and cleared his throat. "I picked up a lot of broken pieces after you disappeared, Messiah. You broke Mo down. Even before she thought you died, and now you come back like it's nothing. Like the shit you do don't affect her!"

The longer he spoke, the louder he got. Anger spilled from him; it poured out of him.

"Shorty said I could come home," Messiah whispered. "She said she'd always be home." His face contorted. "I ain't never had nobody, man, until her."

"Then you should have taken better care of her. I told you *not to fuck with her,* and you did it anyway, knowing you would hurt her. I told you no, little nigga!"

"I know. I want to say I would do it different if I could go back, but I wouldn't, OG. I love her," Messiah said. "I'd risk it all every time just to feel that with her."

"Where the fuck you been, Messiah? You don't leave somebody you love for two years. I'm trying real hard to control myself. You have no idea what you left behind."

"I have cancer, big homie. I didn't come back because I couldn't, and I left because I didn't want her to see me die. I sent her every dime I ever saved in the game. A million-dollar check. Sold my businesses, my houses, all the cars, and cleared the safe so I could leave her with something. I thought I was dead. God had other plans," Messiah said.

"Cancer." Ethic said the word like he was pondering it. "What stage?"

"Four," Messiah revealed. Ethic closed his eyes and rubbed a hand over his head. Messiah had stressed him many times over the years, but this time had to be the most weighted. "It was everywhere, man—probably still is, but the doctors say it's chilling for now. Remission. I've got a little time. Whatever time I got, I want to spend it with her. I want to see her face, man, because some days that face was the only thing that got me through. I've had a hard time, man." His voice cracked, and his lip trembled.

Ethic's defenses lowered.

"And you went through it by yourself? Chemo? Radiation?" Ethic asked.

"I ain't got nobody, man," Messiah said. He was broken as he dropped his head and tears fell from his eyes. He sniffed loudly, pinching the bridge of his nose. Ethic advanced on him, giving him a strong pat on the back followed by a strong embrace.

"Pick your head up, boy," Ethic said, clenching his jaw because he was fighting through rage to feel empathy for someone he had looked at as a brother . . . at times he had thought of him as a son.

"I need her, man. I went through all that. So much pain just to get back to her. I can't not have her. I need her back." Messiah broke down.

He sniffed away his emotion only for it to flood him again. It took him a minute to gain his composure.

"Morgan is delicate, Messiah. This isn't something you can just drop on her. She's been through a lot. The timing has to be right."

Ethic thought about the suicide attempt and the birthing of twins that Messiah didn't even know belonged to him. He wanted to tell him, but neither secret was his to share. Morgan had to reveal those things, and he feared that Messiah's sudden return may be detrimental to Morgan's health.

"I'll do whatever it takes, whatever you say. I need you to help me, OG. I need you to help me come home to her. Help me, man. Nobody ever helped me. I was little as fuck, man, and nobody did shit!" Messiah cried. "Don't leave me stuck, man. Just help me get her back. She the only one that ever loved me, man. I got to get her back."

Messiah's head landed in the center of Ethic's chest as he sobbed, and Ethic tightened his face as he placed his hands on Messiah's head. He knew Messiah wasn't talking about Morgan anymore. He was talking about his childhood, about surviving molestation, about abuse confusing him, making him angry. He was talking about every single adult in his life that was supposed to protect him inflicting harm or disregard. Ethic couldn't be another. Somebody had to step up. "I got you," Ethic said. "I got you."

Relief flooded Messiah as Ethic held him. Another man had never touched him without inflicting harm. Another man had never fathered him, and the void Ethic was filling in this moment was healing. Messiah was in desperate need of forgiveness, and Ethic was willing to offer absolution. Messiah was back in the city, but he wasn't home. Home was with Morgan Atkins, and he was determined to earn her back, what he didn't know was that he was starting late in the race for her heart. There were two other contenders, and Messiah was already losing. Winning her wouldn't be easy because now that she had been loved correctly, he wouldn't be able to come to her with anything less than his best . . .

TO BE CONTINUED IN

Butterfly II

COMING SOON.

DON'T FORGET TO CHECK OUT THE ETHIC SERIES.
BOOKS 1–5 ARE AVAILABLE NOW ON AMAZON.

Oddball Dsgns

ASHLEY ANTOINETTE is one of the most successful female writers of her time. The feminine half of the popular married duo Ashley and JaQuavis, she has co-written more than forty novels. Several of her titles have hit the *New York Times* bestsellers list, but she is most widely regarded for her racy series The Prada Plan. Born in Flint, Michigan, she was bred with an innate street sense that she uses as motivation in her crime-filled writings.

f /authorashleyantoinette

🐦 @Novelista

📷 @AshleyAntoinette